The Girl in Seat 24B

Jennifer Peel

SNOWY PEAKS MEDIA

ISBN 978-1-942298-26-7

Library of Congress: 2016938333

Cover design by Tom Spindle
Book design by KayLynn Flanders

www.snowypeaksmedia.com

To my daughter, Kayla,
who asked me to write a tragically beautiful story.
I hope I did it justice. Love you.

Prologue

All I wanted to do was sleep, or at least be left alone. It's nor-mally the beauty of red eye flights, and typically why I book them. There is a general consensus on these flights that there is no conversing with your fellow passengers; sure, maybe a quick acknowledgment or a simple hello, but not full-blown conversations. And if all else fails, my typically brash personality does the job nicely.

But then *she* happened, the girl sitting in 24B.

I knew I was in trouble from the moment I laid eyes on her. Not only did she come across as naturally perky, but she looked way too awake for midnight. I could spot perkiness from a mile away. It was my nemesis. As soon as I stowed away my carry-on and sat down, she introduced herself to me.

"Hi, I'm Carly Rogers."

She sounded like a cheerleader or sorority sister. I almost got up and begged the stewardess for another seat assignment. I may have, too, if I wasn't worried about appearing to act suspicious on a plane. Instead, I just looked at her outstretched hand then ignored it and her. Why did she need to know my name? We would never see each other again. All I wanted was peace and quiet for the next few hours as we traveled from New York to Atlanta, but she wasn't to be deterred.

Instead of being offended or pouting, like I expected she would do, she smiled. "Aren't polite people the absolute worst?"

I couldn't help it. I laughed and stuck out my hand. "I'm Michael Bishop. It's a pleasure to meet you, Carly."

The moment our hands touched, I felt it. I wasn't sure what it was, but it was definitely *it.* Then I noticed her. She was the most adorable creature I had ever met. She had classic beauty. Her sepia-colored, pixie-cut hair perfectly framed her heart-shaped face, but it was her eyes that really caught me. They were large and innocent, and they shined like emeralds.

"Bishop, huh? It's got a ring to it."

No one had ever called me "Bishop" before, but I found I liked it. And as the night wore on, I discovered that I more than liked her. She had just returned to the states from visiting her parents in India. Her parents were living in Mumbai where her dad worked in the American consulate. She, I discovered, was a photographer. As we talked, she pulled up her laptop and showed me picture after picture and told story after story of her adventures in India and of her family. She had documented each stop from the Taj Mahal to the orphanages where she and her mother had volunteered. To see the world through her eyes and photo lens changed mine.

She saw beauty where I saw disarray. She showed compassion where I would show annoyance. She used humor, and I used sarcasm.

The flight didn't last nearly long enough. The one time I wanted a flight delay, and we landed early. By the time the wheels touched the tarmac, I was begging her to miss her connection to Denver. She wisely said no. She didn't know me from Adam, and she was a young, beautiful woman all of twenty-three. She was right to be cautious. Instead, I gave her my number and asked her to call me if she felt so inclined. I even began spouting off references for her to check my character. I made her laugh. I really wasn't someone who made others laugh, and I had never really wanted to until that night.

She touched this hardened journalist in a way no woman had in my twenty-eight years. I walked her to her connection and, without trying to seem desperate, I asked if she planned on calling. She laughed again. I was beginning to wish there was a replay button for that sound.

"Goodbye, Bishop," she said as she walked away without answering.

I felt panicked. *I have to stop the plane*, I thought. Then, I thought, *what's wrong with me*? I was normally a very sane person, and this was beyond irrational.

But then she turned around. "Hey, Bishop. Check your phone."

I hastily dug it out of my backpack and turned it on as I watched her approach her gate to board. The seconds it took for my phone to come up seemed like eons, and yet, the time seemed to go into hyperdrive as I watched her walk further away from me. But then time stopped when her message appeared.

"Tag, you're it."

And that was it. She was it. The Girl in Seat 24B.

Chapter One

Our king-sized bed seemed too large as of late. The divide between us was growing and I wasn't sure what to do to bridge the gap. I knew something was bothering him; it had been for months, but he always denied it. However, his short temper and irritability with me and the kids said otherwise. He was closing himself off emotionally and physically. I ached to reach across the bed and touch his back, or better yet, put my arms around him and not have him pull away.

After several minutes of not being able to fall asleep, I couldn't stand it anymore. I cautiously scooted closer to him. I couldn't remember when it was that I had started feeling the need to be cautious, especially here with just the two of us. It wasn't that long ago when there wouldn't have been any space to cover; I would have already been sound asleep in his arms with his warm breath against my head. Instead, here I was, afraid to even disturb him. I slowly reached out and lightly ran my fingertips across the middle of his back. "Bishop…"

Silence. I inched closer and ran my fingers through the back of his dark, tousled hair that was just starting to turn gray.

"Bishop, please talk to me. I know you're awake."

"Carly, it's late," he barely muttered.

I slid my hand down and rubbed his neck. "When has that ever stopped us?"

I pulled my hand away as he reluctantly turned to face me. We stared at one another in the dark as we both lay on our separate pillows. I loved his face. He always had a seven o'clock shadow. I think he was what was referred to as ruggedly handsome. I inched closer again and held my breath as I gently placed my hand on his cheek. Why was I so nervous? We'd been married for ten years now and I had never been nervous around him. He didn't pull away; I took it as a good sign, so I leaned forward and lightly brushed his lips with mine. He didn't respond.

I turned and lay on my back, feeling rejected once again. The tears formed in the corner of my eyes. "Are you having an affair?"

He turned back over, away from me. "Carly, it's late," he repeated.

I sat up, stunned. I couldn't believe he was actually having an affair. I mean the signs were all there. I had gone up to his office a couple of times the past couple of weeks, and he'd either hung up quickly with whomever he'd been talking to or clicked out of the window on his laptop. I'd practically thrown myself at him for weeks, and he'd hardly touched me. There were so many things I wanted to say, but I couldn't, because it felt like a huge ball was lodged in my throat and my head hurt from the loud pounding of my heart. How could he? I loved him. He was my best friend, husband, lover, father to my son and daughter and, on occasion, co-conspirator. All I could do was cry.

He sat up. "Carly, I'm not having an affair. How could you even ask?"

"How could I not, after the way you've been behaving?"

He flipped on the lamp on his nightstand and handed me a tissue. "I wouldn't do that to you."

I turned to him. "Then what? Please just tell me what's wrong?"

"Everything," he replied angrily.

"What do you mean everything?"

"I mean everything."

The realization of that statement was like a wrecking ball, but I couldn't fall apart…yet.

"Then let's fix it."

"You can't fix this."

I reached for his hand. "You're right, but *we* can. We can do anything together."

He pulled away again. "I think we should separate."

I shook my head in utter disbelief. "I thought you said you weren't having an affair."

"I'm not, it's just…"

"It's just what?"

He looked at me as if I should already know the answer. And I guess I did, but I didn't want to admit it because he was a third of my world, and without him it wouldn't be complete. I tried my best to remain emotionless. "You don't love me anymore, do you?" I choked out.

He wouldn't even look at me. "I'll always love you, Carly. But I'm not *in* love with you anymore."

He said it so easy, like he had thought it a million times. I felt better when I thought he had cheated on me.

I didn't respond, because the lump was back and closing my airway. I think my heart stopped too, because it had just been pierced.

He turned toward me with tears of his own. "This isn't your fault, Carly. You're as close to perfect as they come."

I shook my head. "So you're saying it's you, not me?"

"Exactly."

I jumped out of bed and ran to the bathroom and turned on the sink. I thought I might puke. At the very least, I needed cool water on my face. He followed me, leaned against the door and watched me lose it.

"I'm sorry, Carly."

I stood at the sink and tried to breathe in deep. "That's all you have to say to me after all this time together? What about Ashton and Mia? Do you still love them?"

"Of course."

I thought for a moment. "Then we need to work this out. They deserve married parents. Couples go through things like this all the time. Let's go to counseling, or let's book that trip to Saint Thomas that we were going to take for our tenth anniversary."

"Carly, you're not listening to me."

"I am listening to you, Michael, but I don't believe you. I know you and you wouldn't do this to our family without at least giving us a fighting chance. We can recapture what you feel is lost. I love you."

He sat back down on the bed and put his hands in his face and rubbed. "Carly, I've already leased an apartment. I plan to move in after I return from my assignment in New York in two weeks."

I sat down on the cold, hard, Italian tile and leaned against our tub-for-two, clinging to the coolness against my skin. "You didn't even tell me you had an assignment in New York."

"Carly, it's late."

I stood up on my shaky legs. There would be no sleep after that bombshell. I walked back into our room, toward our bedroom door. I looked back at him, sitting on our four poster bed that had seen more love than most people would ever experience in their whole lifetime, and I lost it again. He looked up, and I managed to pull it together. "You'll be the one to tell Ashton and Mia why you're leaving."

I ran upstairs to their Jack and Jill rooms and, as always, I found Mia snuggled up against Ashton on his full-size bed. I stopped my shuddering as I approached my sleeping angels. I never tired of watching them sleep. I knew that when they were fully grown, I would still love to watch them sleep. I chuckled, thinking about a future vision of my fifty-seven year old self watching my adult children sleeping. I started to cry because I realized that when that time came, I would be alone. I stifled the crying and gently touched Ashton's bright blond hair. I still didn't know where he got that hair. It was so blonde even strangers in the store asked me about it. I'd even had some ask if I dyed it. Sometimes, for fun, I would say, "Yes, dyeing your seven-year-old's hair is all the rage now."

I covered up Mia. She was my mini-me, brown hair with natural red highlights and green eyes. She even had my sense of humor. I wasn't sure if I should be disturbed or proud of that. But one thing I knew was that I was treasuring this last year with her before she started kindergarten in the fall. The year was slipping too fast—we were already into March.

I backed out of Ashton's room and headed for the couch in the loft and curled up in a ball. I couldn't believe this was happening to me. My marriage was over, and I didn't even get a say. As I lay there, I tried to think of ways I could have been a better wife. I thought about what I was going to do financially. Michael had been the sole bread winner ever since the rug rats had come along. Occasionally, I still photographed families, but it was more of a hobby now than anything else. Long gone were the days where I could name my price. I had traded that in for the best job ever: mommy.

I cried harder. I loved being a wife and mother. I loved Michael. I loved him from the first night I met him on flight 416 from New York to Atlanta. He had come off as gruff at first, but all it took was one smart aleck comment and he was mine. I held on to that thought. *He was mine. He was mine. He was mine…*

Chapter Two

I MUST HAVE MANAGED A FEW WINKS. I WOKE UP AND MY HEAD HURT LIKE the dickens; and I had a crick in my neck from the awful position I had fallen asleep in. I looked up to the large wall clock, and it read five. I heard stirrings down below. Then I remembered why I was sleeping on the couch and not my bed. I willed myself not to cry; I wasn't even sure if I had tears left. I needed water.

I walked downstairs and toward our newly remodeled kitchen. That's what I got for my tenth anniversary in December instead of a romantic island vacation. I thought the gesture was sweet, now I realized he didn't want a romantic vacation with a wife he wasn't in love with anymore. The thought made me feel ill.

I entered the kitchen to find Michael fully ready in a suit and tie. His assignment must have been pretty important; he rarely had to dress formally. Michael was a journalist for an online magazine, as well as a couple of printed publications. He got to travel the globe on various assignments and report on everything from the AIDS epidemic to the Justin Bieber craze. I think he enjoyed the AIDS assignment more than the latter. No matter, he was good at what he did regardless of the subject.

He was preparing two eggs over easy and wheat toast. He had eaten it almost every morning for the last ten years. In a way, it was comforting seeing him be so predictable. He looked at me from the toaster. Maybe I should have looked in the mirror first. I'm sure I looked terrible from crying all night and reading up on midlife crises. I figured that's what this was. He was going to turn forty in the summer, and I knew that bothered him. He had all the classic signs. I needed to show him love and remember it really wasn't about me, even though it really felt like it was all about me. He was unhappy, and I was the closest punching bag.

I ran my fingers through my hair nervously. Thankfully, I had the kind of hair that looked pretty much the same day or night, even if it had been slept on. "Good morning, Bishop."

He half-smiled. It was something at least. I missed his smile. "Carly, I was up thinking last night."

"Me, too," I said quietly.

"Maybe you're right."

This is good, I thought. *And of course I'm right.*

"We'll just look at this as a trial separation, nothing permanent."

This is not good. Not good at all.

I tried my hardest not to say hurtful things and to remember this wasn't about me. I took a deep breath, because I wanted to lash out. He was killing me and he didn't even care. "I thought our relationship was permanent." We even had the pastor omit the line "until death do us part" because we knew we were forever.

"Carly, I need to do this."

I didn't even know how to respond to that, other than with fury. He needed to separate our family? So I didn't respond. I bit my tongue again. I had a feeling it would be bleeding soon. I walked to the sink and retrieved a glass and filled it with water. I took several sips. "What's your assignment?"

He looked confused by the change of subject. He could join the club, I was more than confused. I kept looking at this man in my kitchen, wondering what he had done with my husband.

"I'm covering the New York City mayoral election."

"That's a big deal."

"Yes, I finally got a decent assignment again."

He sounded relieved. I knew his job hadn't been as satisfying to him and I knew that was part of the problem. I had tried to talk to him about switching jobs, but he always said he was stuck. The pay was too good where he was at—it allowed us to live wherever we chose, and it allowed me to be at home. We chose to live in Pine Apple, Georgia, his hometown. It was tamer than he wanted, but I never lived very long in one spot growing up, and most of the time it was out of the country. I wanted something more stable for my kids, a place they could call home. I thought it was practically perfect, but I guess I was the only one.

"I'm happy for you." Then I amended, "I want you to be happy."

He came closer, which surprised me.

"I want the same for you. That's why I need to do this."

I started to cry. I tried not to, but I couldn't help it. "This may come as a surprise to you, but this makes me anything but happy."

"Carly, you deserve to be with someone that loves you the right way."

I embraced him and lay my head against his shoulder. I needed *him*. But he was stiff. "Why can't you touch me? Am I that repulsive to you?" So much for not making it about me. I had to try harder.

He did touch me, but not the way I wanted him to. He gently grabbed my arms and pulled me back to stare into my eyes. "You're beautiful, even more so now than when I met you. This is about me."

He was right, it was about him, and that was the problem: he was only thinking of himself.

I backed away and walked toward our room. "At least text me when you get there, so I know you're safe. I love you, Bishop."

Again, silence.

As I showered, I wondered if I was just naïve and a glutton for punishment. He told me he didn't love me, and I basically told him I didn't believe him. He told me again, and I told him I loved him. Have I become one of those desperate women? I had to believe, no, that wasn't my style. I have always believed you don't throw families away and if something's broke, you fix it. There was nothing in our marriage that was so damaged it couldn't be repaired—at least in my mind. In fact, I didn't think there were any damages other than his moodiness the past several months, but I thought he would eventually shake it off. I guess that was what he was doing now, but I was the part he would shake off. I started crying again.

I really needed to get that under control before the kids woke up. Since Michael was going out of town, I decided to try and keep everything normal for the next two weeks. Maybe he would get his head on straight while he was gone and forget about all this trial separation nonsense. I mean, how do you even try that on for size? And where was he getting the money to lease an apartment? I had always let him handle the finances, but maybe it was time to take a closer look. It was probably time to take a closer look at lots of things I had been taking for granted.

By the time I was out of the shower and dressed, Michael was gone. He hadn't even bothered to come in and say goodbye. Before, when he left on any trips, long or short, he would wrap me up tight and kiss me, and then let me go just to pull me back again and say, "One more for the road." He would kiss me again and whisper in my ear, "I love you, 24B."

24B. He used to call me that all the time. He even named his blog *The Girl in Seat 24B.* There for a while he had quite the following; his initial blog post about our meeting had gone viral. He was even interviewed by *The Today Show* and *Good Morning America* about it. Every week thousands of people would read his blog about our adventures in dating and finally marriage. He quit writing on that particular blog after Mia was born. His excuse was he needed to be a more serious writer. The blog was still up, but he hadn't touched it for years. Once in a while, a fan would message him and ask for an update, but he never touched the blog again.

Sometimes when I felt like reminiscing, I would read through those old posts and laugh and cry. Just thinking about them now had me tearing up. I wanted that man, the man that chased me across the country and wooed me and asked me to marry him before we even knew each other for two months. He didn't relent until I finally said yes. I can't even remember why I kept saying no. I knew he was the one, but it was crazy; I met him on a plane for goodness sake, we hardly knew each other, and my parents hadn't even had the chance to meet him. Only my older sister Melanie had; she hated him, but she hated all men, so she didn't count.

Then I thought about my parents and cried some more. They had died from the bombings in India at the U.S. consulate only a year after we were married. Michael was my rock *and* my pillow. He was a safe landing when I fell apart, and he also upheld me when I needed to be strong and stand upright. I was beginning to feel very alone. My mom was my best friend growing up because we had moved so much. I loved Melanie, but she had always had a huge chip on her shoulder. And now my best friend had hammered my rock to pieces and pulled the pillow out from under me.

I thought about calling Melanie, but I knew she would only make it worse. It would give her more reasons to hate Michael, and I was planning on making this work out. I didn't want to give her any more ammo than she already had. She hated Michael for moving me to Georgia from Colorado. No matter how many times I told her it was a joint decision, she blamed him. I asked her on several occasions to consider moving near us; she wasn't married and didn't have kids, but she wouldn't even consider it. Her reasons included hating the humidity and missing out on the snow, but yet every year she called and complained about all the snow in Colorado. I didn't know if I would ever get her. Sometimes I swore one of us was switched at birth.

If only Michael would talk to me, *really* talk to me, like he used to. He was the one I needed to work this out with, but that seemed like it wasn't an option at the moment. I just took a deep breath and styled my hair and put on my make-up. I needed to cover the dark circles my crying had created. I didn't want Ashton and Mia to think anything was wrong; they didn't deserve this burden. I went into mommy mode and made pancakes before waking them up. They were both like their daddy, they needed to eat quickly after rising or they were grumpy.

I sat on the edge of Ashton's bed and began to sing, "Once Upon a Dream."

Ashton woke up first. "Mom, I'm seven now. I'm too big for you to sing to me."

I ruffled his blonde hair and sang louder. He scrunched his cute nose at me.

Mia finally opened those pretty green eyes of hers. "I love that song, Mommy."

We had only watched Sleeping Beauty like a hundred times. I would twirl her around and sing along when that song began. I pulled them both to me and hugged them as tight as I could. It was like I was drawing strength from them. For them, I would do whatever it took to make this all right. For them, I would be strong and do everything in my power to protect them.

"Time to eat."

That was all it took to have them out of bed and zooming down the stairs. I chased them down and to the table.

"Where's Daddy?" were the first words out of Mia's mouth.

I picked her up. "Daddy had to leave early this morning for New York. Remember where New York is?"

"At the top," she said.

"You're right, it's at the top of the United States."

I had been working with them on memorizing the states and where they were. I loved globes and maps.

"Well, Daddy will be working there for a couple of weeks."

They were both disappointed. I still couldn't believe he hadn't said anything about leaving. Our kids needed their goodbyes from him. I needed them, too. Oh well. Back to mommy mode.

I served up the pancakes, and as they scarfed them down, I could barely touch mine. I felt nauseated from the previous night's events. But then I thought maybe I was catching a bug. I hadn't felt that well for the past of couple of days and I was tired. Maybe I could sneak a nap in later while Mia was at preschool.

We made lunches together before they scooted up to get dressed and brush their teeth. I came up to supervise the hair combing and to place a butterfly barrette in Mia's hair. She had been obsessed with butterflies ever since we went to the butterfly pavilion on our vacation in Colorado the previous year.

When I thought about that trip in October, it hit me: that was when Michael had begun acting out of character. Sure he'd always been a little rough around the edges, but the kids and I had seemed to soften those edges over the years. He was upset with me when I wouldn't leave the kids with my sister so he and I could get away for a couple of days in the mountains. It's not that I didn't want to be with him, but my sister was horrible with kids and it didn't feel right. He was so resentful, no matter how I tried to explain it. I even offered to do something with him as soon as we got home so his parents could be the ones to watch them. His mom hated me, but she adored her grandkids. I've always felt comfortable with Michael's parents watching our kids. Michael accused me of loving the kids more than him. It was true, I loved them differently, but not more. They were completely different types of relationships. I'd always tried to put Michael first.

From then on, it was like he looked for any situation where the kids came first, he even seemed to twist scenes. He had also become more critical of my parenting style. He thought I should be tougher. I disagreed; it wasn't me, and I knew that's not what Ashton and Mia needed. I even found myself asking Michael to be gentler with his words when it came to them. He had become short and impatient. Ashton particularly had felt it and he had even asked me why Daddy didn't love him as much anymore. That broke my heart. I told him his Daddy loved him just as much, but kids know when things aren't right.

Even this morning I noticed Ashton looking pensive when I told him his daddy was on a trip. It worried me, especially since Ashton was like his daddy and had a tendency to bottle feelings. Not Mia, she was like me. She put it all out there. I made a mental note to keep an eye on Ashton's behavior and to also remind Michael that this wasn't only about him.

Chapter Three

WITH THE KIDS BOTH AT SCHOOL, I BEGAN TAKING A CLOSER LOOK. I HEADED up to Michael's office. I had wanted that room to be a nursery, but Michael was happy with a boy and girl. "We have the best of both worlds," he would always say. Me, I always felt like we were missing someone, that not everyone had joined the party. I know it sounds weird, but I could never shake the feeling, and I had been trying to change Michael's mind for years, to no avail. He used to tease me we could practice all we want. At this point, I could do with some practicing, or even a warm up, but even that didn't seem to be in the cards for him.

Never mind.

I looked around his office at all of his awards and pictures of us and the kids. They were such happy memories from our honeymoon in Tahiti to the day we brought Ashton and Mia home from the hospital. He even had his ticket framed from flight 416. My heart was telling me he still loved me, he only needed to remember.

But then I started looking through his filing cabinet; I found a bank statement for an account that only belonged to him, and it had several thousand dollars in it. I also found several brochures for apartments in the area.

He definitely wasn't acting like a man in love. He wasn't acting like *my* man.

We didn't we have any secrets, or so I thought. We had decided at the beginning that we would be open and honest even if it was painful, because at least then it would be out in the open and we could deal with it. In discovering he had a secret bank account, I found I had a lot to deal with. I had no idea how long he'd had that account. The only draw I could see on it for the last couple of months was to what I assumed was his apartment. It looked like he had leased at Magnolia Heights. They were new apartments that had recently been built and were a couple of miles from our home. The deposit was for a thousand dollars.

I felt anger welling up inside me. I had to employ all my determination not to pick up the phone and ask him what this was all about. Or at least leave him a scathing message. Secret accounts and secret apartments and now secret trips? It made me wonder if he really was telling the truth about not having an affair. I took a deep breath and told myself to remain calm. No sense in making up more problems until I actually knew they existed.

It still didn't stop me from vomiting. What little I had eaten all came up. At least I felt better, maybe it was a short passing bug. I hoped the kids didn't get it. I lay on my made bed and decided to take a short nap before I had to pick up Mia. I was asleep before I even thought about it. When I woke up, I still felt crappy, but it didn't matter, moms don't have time to be sick, especially ones that had rugs pulled out from under them. I needed to come up with an offensive plan and stop playing defense.

On my drive over to the preschool, I thought about what my next steps should be. I thought if I started up my photography business again, at least part-time, maybe that would take some pressure off of Michael and he could look for employment that made him happier, even if it wasn't as lucrative. And we always had the trust fund my parents left me as a cushion, if needed. We were saving it as our nest egg, but maybe we could use some of it now if it would help. I put a pin in that thought and focused more on the photography. I mean, Mia would be in school full-time starting in August.

As I waited in the car line to pick up Mia, I received a text from Michael. "I just landed."

I sighed. Where was the "Love, Bishop" or the "I miss you?"

"Thanks for letting me know. Please call me later when you get a chance," I texted back.

"It's going to be a late night."

I was getting beyond frustrated. "Mia and Ashton want to talk to their daddy."

"I'll see what I can do."

Thankfully, I was wearing sunglasses as the tears formed again. I wasn't even worth calling now. But I gave Mia a big smile when she got in the car. Hearing her say, "Mommy," made me feel better.

We got home, and I made Mia lunch and barely kept myself from vomiting again. I guess it wasn't going to be a quick, passing bug. I let Mia eat picnic-style on my bedroom floor while I pulled out my laptop and began researching how to create websites and how much photographers with my skill set were charging these days. I also researched how to use social media to advertise. In between, I threw up again. At least I felt better for a little while after.

After school was always busy; we had ballet, soccer practice, and, of course, dinner, which I had no desire to make. The thought of food was making me ill, so I did the daddy thing. After soccer and ballet were done, we stopped at the kids' favorite fast food place that I abhorred. But as long as I didn't have to eat it or see it, I was okay. Or at least I thought I was. As the smell permeated my 4Runner, I quickly rolled down the windows. We made it home just in time for me to throw up again.

I was so thankful when bed time rolled around. I needed to rest. I knew I would feel right as rain in the morning if I could just sleep. The only damper was that Michael never called and Ashton and Mia were disappointed. I even read extra to them to try and compensate, though it cost me physically. Normally I would clean up after I put the kids to bed and maybe read a good book, but all I wanted to do was lie down, so I did just that.

Around midnight I was awakened by my phone vibrating. It took all my energy to roll over and pick it up. It was a text from Michael.

"Sorry, I just got to my hotel room. I'll call in the morning."

I didn't have the emotional or physical energy to respond. I fell right back asleep and slept straight through until my alarm went off at six. It was the worst sound I had ever heard. I wanted to cry, but I knew it wouldn't do any good. I got up and started the day. During breakfast, which was cold cereal because it was odorless, Michael called.

He talked to Ashton first. "Dad, you should have seen the goal I scored last night," I heard Ashton say. He also mentioned the trip he was taking to the Art Museum later that morning.

Mia was next and she talked a million miles a minute. "Slow down," I could hear Michael say on the other end. I had to laugh a little at her. She tried, but it wasn't in her. She was too excited. "And Mommy keeps throwing up. Okay, love you, Daddy."

She handed me the phone. "Daddy wants to talk to you."

I was surprised. "Hey, Bishop."

"Are you okay? Mia says you keep throwing up."

"I'm fine, it's just a bug."

"Maybe you should go to the doctor."

"Really, I'm fine."

"Which means you're not."

I sighed. I wanted to say, *of course I'm not fine. My life is crumbling around me.*

"I have some ideas I want to discuss with you…" I tried to respond.

"I've got to go, Carly," he cut me off.

"Of course you do. Bye, Michael."

I hung up. I don't even know if he responded. I was too tired to care. And I was living off of Gatorade. It was the only thing I could keep down. I lived like that the rest of the week and through the weekend.

By Monday I was exhausted and worried. I called my doctor. Thankfully, she could get me in while both kiddos were at school. I guess it helped that we were friends. Dr. Emma White and I had met during unending soccer practices for our sons. Her husband, Jace, coached Ashton's team and had since he was four years old. On occasion, we had a girl's night out or our families barbecued together. It was perfect; they had a seven-year-old son and a four-year-old daughter, just like us.

I was lying on the table when she came back to my examination room. I didn't have the strength to keep sitting up.

She took one look at me. "Professionally speaking, you look like crap."

I managed a weak smile.

She helped me up. "How long has this been going on? You look like you've lost ten pounds, and you were thin to begin with."

"Around five to six days."

"You should have come in earlier."

"I thought it would pass."

She began to examine me from head to toe while she asked me a series of questions. It was all normal stuff, but then she asked, "When was the date of your last period?" I thought back and I was having a hard time remembering. I'd had so many other things on my mind.

She smiled. "I'm going to run a pregnancy test."

"No, no, no, no. I can't be pregnant." I started crying.

She set down her clipboard and took my hand. "This isn't like you, what's going on?"

I started crying harder. I had to talk to somebody, and she was not only bound by patient-doctor privacy laws, but she was my friend. And I needed a friend, so I told her what was going on.

She stared at me dumbfounded. "I have to say I'm surprised. You and Michael were like the perfect couple in my mind. I have always wished Jace adored me like Michael adores you."

"Well, he doesn't adore me anymore. He's been gone almost a week and I've barely talked to him twice."

"Don't worry," she said. "I'm sure he'll come to his senses. I've seen the way he looks at you." She patted my hand. "Honey, I need to run a pregnancy test."

Chapter Four

All the way home I kept touching my abdomen. I couldn't believe I was pregnant, but the tests were 99.9% accurate. It wasn't that I didn't want another baby; I'd wanted one for years, but not like this. Not when I was possibly on the verge of being a single mother. I knew this wasn't going to make Michael happy. He hadn't wanted another baby when he did love me, how was he going to feel now that he wanted to leave me? I decided I wasn't going to tell him. I knew eventually I would have to, but I could wait. Wait and see if he could get his head on straight and come back to me, to our family.

I knew I didn't have long. I was already seven weeks along and had maybe five to eight weeks before I started showing—if I was lucky. I swore Emma to secrecy, but she, too, reminded me I didn't have long. She ordered me to keep my stress under control and at least try to get some nutrients in me. She prescribed some anti-nausea medication and prenatal vitamins. I was going to have to find a safe, hidden place for those.

After I put the kids to bed and was by myself, lying on my bed, I kept touching my bare abdomen. "I want you to know that no matter what, I see this as a blessing, even if I have to do this alone, but I promise you I will do my best to make sure that doesn't happen," I said aloud to my unborn baby. I already felt such love for this child. It's amazing how your heart can grow. I remember thinking I could never love a baby more than Ashton and then Mia came along and that loved swelled. I could feel that swelling now again.

I pulled out my calendar and circled the seventh of November. It was easy to calculate a due date. I knew the exact date of conception; it wasn't like the other times before when it could have been almost any day. What I would give to have those days back, and it wasn't about the sex—I missed the connection and the closeness our intimacy brought. I also felt bad that this baby was practically conceived out of coercion. Okay, maybe coercion was the wrong word, but it was definitely different than the other times when we were trying, back when I felt like Michael and I were doing this together.

I started crying again, but I tried to calm myself. I invoked my yoga breathing techniques, and I could feel my heart rate slow. Then Michael called.

"Carly, I know it's late, but I wanted to check on you. Did you go to the doctor?"

I was surprised by his concern. "Yes."

"And…"

I had to tell the truth but not lie at the same time, if that made sense. "She prescribed me some medicine and told me this would take some time to work out, but I should be fine."

"I hope the kids don't get it."

I almost laughed. "I'm pretty sure they won't. So how's the election coverage going?"

"I think I would rather run my fingernails against a chalkboard than listen to one more campaign speech."

"That sounds about right. If it makes you feel any better, we all miss you." He didn't respond right away, so I continued speaking. "I've decided to start up my photography business again. I've been working on my website design. I think it's coming along really well."

"I was still planning on supporting you regardless, Carly. You don't need to work."

"I thought maybe this would help. Maybe it would allow you to look for something else. Something that makes you happy, like finishing your novel or teaching?"

"Carly, I can provide for my family."

"Bishop, this isn't an indictment against you. I've always told you what a wonderful provider you are and how much I appreciate the hard work you do. But the thing is, what happens when you decide you're tired of doing that, too, just like you're tired of me?"

"I wouldn't do that to you." I could hear the steel in his voice. I'd hit a nerve.

"You said you'd never leave me, either. Goodnight, Michael." I hung up on him again. Maybe it wasn't the best thing to do, but I was tired and hurt and pregnant and alone.

The medication helped significantly; at least I was able to keep most of my food down. Even though I could still only manage half of what I should be eating, it was better than it had been. And I had a little more energy. I even ventured to take my rug rats to the aquarium on Saturday. Michael was returning on Tuesday, so I wanted to give them a good weekend. I knew what was awaiting us all next week. He hadn't given any indication he had changed his mind, and I'll admit, I figured out how to log into his secret account. I saw new debits for furniture and cable. I still couldn't believe it was happening.

Those debits made me more determined to get my own business back up and running. I also rededicated myself to not lashing out or reacting poorly when he was apathetic or unresponsive or just plain mean. I reminded myself that this was about him and not me. This was his choice, not mine, and I could choose to be happy no matter my circumstances, especially now that I had three little ones that were counting on me.

Speaking of my third little one, I had a follow up appointment on Monday where Emma did an ultrasound. I loved seeing that little peanut move around inside of me, and hearing the heartbeat was like music to my ears. It made me forget, for a moment, that the timing was horrible and that my husband didn't love me. All I could think about was the love I felt for my unborn baby.

Before I left her office, I had an idea. "Would you be willing to let me place some brochures for newborn and family photos in your waiting area?" I asked her.

"Absolutely, I'll even be your first customer," she responded enthusiastically.

I left feeling better than I had in two weeks.

That was good, too, because I needed it. Michael dropped by on Tuesday evening with no luggage in hand, and he parked in the driveway instead of the garage. I knew what that meant, and I had to hold back the tears as Ashton and Mia rushed to their daddy as he walked through the front door, not the garage entrance. I watched him as he knelt and the kids clung to him. He looked up at me with guilt in his eyes. I wiped the corners of my eyes and turned away for a moment. But I reminded myself I needed to be brave for Ashton and Mia and my little peanut.

I was doing really well with that for all about a minute.

"Aren't you going to kiss Mommy, too?" Mia asked.

"Mia and Ashton, I want to tell you something," Michael said.

He led them to our living room couch and sat them down. He took the coffee table, and he held on to their tiny hands. He reached into his pocket. "I almost forgot, I brought you something back from New York."

I saw the excitement in their eyes, and I wanted to smack him. No matter what he bought them, it wasn't going to make up for what he was about to do to our family. I wanted to look away, but I knew I couldn't. I had to be there for my children because they were going to need me more than ever. I stood at the fireplace and prayed silently that I would know what to do to help them. I prayed for a way that this would not really happen. I would be up for a miracle right about now.

Michael pulled out two gold coins. I wanted to smack my head. He could have at least gotten Mia a doll and Ashton some type of sports memorabilia or Legos. They looked at the coins like, *so what.* It meant nothing to them. Michael looked at me, and I looked at him like, *you're on your own buddy.* What had happened to him? This was not my Michael. I could guarantee this was something he had gotten at the airport because he hardly thought two seconds about us while he was gone. My Michael would have made a special trip to make sure he brought back something meaningful and something his kids would love. Not gold coins.

He placed the coins on the table and took their hands again. By this time, the kids looked confused. They were ready to tell him more about the aquarium and field trips and ballet recitals, but Michael plowed through with his stupid speech. "Ashton and Mia, I'm not going to live at home for a while. But I'll be close by and my new apartment has a pool that you can come over and use. I need to figure some things out, but just know I love you." It sounded so pathetic and he couldn't even look at them when he spoke.

I wasn't sure how much Mia got; she looked at me and my tears and she started crying too, but it was Ashton that really concerned me. His sweet little face was red and his baby blues were as wide as I had ever seen them.

He stared coldly at his father and, without warning, he jumped and ran to me. "I hate you," he yelled at his father. He had never used those words.

I don't think hate had ever been spoken in our house before, but I knew how he felt. I felt hate, too.

He clung to me, and I clung back. Mia joined us, and we held on to each other for dear life. I looked up at Michael. He had tears in his eyes, but I could tell the scene before him wasn't going to change his mind. Like a coward, he left me there with his crying children.

"I'm sorry. I'll call later," was all he could say to us.

He left me to pick up the pieces of their shattered little hearts, so I moved us to the couch and sat them both on my lap, which was getting more difficult as they aged. In a few months I knew it would be impossible as my lap space would be shrinking. At least for tonight we managed.

I wiped their tears and told them I loved them at least a million times. "Your daddy's going through a hard time right now and sometimes when people are hurting or confused they do things they shouldn't do, but it doesn't mean we don't love them. In fact, we should show them more love because they need it more."

"I can make Daddy a card," Mia offered.

I kissed her head. "I think he would like that, my sweet girl."

I looked at Ashton who was still crying. My heart broke. I stroked his hair. "Talk to me, little man."

"Are you going to get divorced?"

I was surprised Ashton even knew what that was.

I pulled them both to me again. "I sure hope not."

We sat there together for several minutes, crying and wallowing in our grief. After which we decided we were all hungry; well, at least the kids were. I was still having issues with food, but I at least pretended. We decided to order in pizza and make it a family game night, minus a big chunk of our family. It was subdued, but there were a few laughs here and there. As I tucked them in and they said their prayers, they each prayed their daddy would come home. I silently prayed that, too. I tucked Mia in first, and then Ashton.

"Ashton, you can come and talk to me anytime," I said as I stroked that beautiful hair of his. "And it's okay to feel the way you're feeling. I know you feel bad about what you said to your daddy, but I know, and he knows, that you only said it because you love him so much." Tears ran down his smooth cheeks and it caused my eyes to well up. "Remember that love is the most powerful force on earth and it can change people." It was a lot to lay on a seven-year-old, but I think he partially got it. I kissed his sweet head and tucked him in.

After the house was sparkling, I finally crawled into bed exhausted. It was that moment that Michael chose to call.

"Carly?"

"Who else?"

"How are the kids?"

"They're hurting, and they miss you."

"Carly, I know that you don't agree with the way I'm going about this, but I have to do this."

"You're right, I don't agree with this. In fact, I know what you're doing is wrong and I know, deep down, you know that too. I'm not sure what's going on with you, but for the sake of everyone, I suggest you figure it out quick. There's more at stake here than you know."

"What does that mean?"

"Exactly what I said."

"Can I come by tomorrow morning and pick up some of my things?"

"Michael, this is still your home, you don't have to ask to come home." The dumb tears came again.

"Carly…"

"You can come. I won't be here, anyway."

"Where will you be?"

"I'm meeting with my web designer after I drop Mia and Ashton off at school."

"I thought I told you I would take care of you financially."

"You did, but I have a hard time believing that right now."

"Carly, I've got it covered."

"You don't get it, do you? It's not your money that I want or even need."

"Then what do you want?" he shouted angrily.

"The only thing I ever wanted for the past eleven plus years of my life. You," I responded quietly and lovingly.

"I need to go."

"You can't keep running away from this or me, Bishop."

"Goodnight, Carly."

Yeah, goodnight. I wasn't sure what those were anymore. I rubbed my little secret and whispered, "Don't judge your daddy by tonight. Honestly, he wasn't such an idiot when I married him."

Chapter Five

THE NEXT COUPLE OF WEEKS PROVED TO BE THE MOST DIFFICULT OF MY LIFE as the kids and I adjusted to this new reality. Sadly, Michael didn't seem that affected by it; if anything, he seemed happier when we saw him, which wasn't often at all. He said he was taking more out-of-town assignments and that we shouldn't count on him being around much. I tried to include him in all of our family activities, but each invitation was declined with some excuse or another.

I was mourning his absence. He had cleared out all of his drawers, and his office was mostly empty, except he left the pictures. It was like a slap across the face, like he wanted to forget us. The kids were confused and sad. I would say Ashton was even angry, especially after Michael missed both of his soccer games. I tried to talk to Michael and tell him what he was doing to our children, but he wasn't listening. His excuse was he was supporting us financially, which required him to work hard. I wanted to say, *you don't know what hard work is. Try being a single pregnant mother who pukes on a daily basis and has to pee every thirty minutes, but yet still has to run a household and take care of two little ones who are going through emotional trauma.* And to top it off, I was working again. Instead, I tried to be loving and tell him we missed him and he could work less if he needed to. He didn't listen.

Finally, after two weeks, he came and picked up the kids for the evening. I was grateful for the break. When he walked in, he looked at me, like *really* looked at me. I don't think he had done that in weeks.

"You don't look well," he said as he stood in our entryway, waiting for the kids to get their shoes on.

"Thanks, Bishop."

"I didn't mean it that way. Is everything okay? You look like you've lost a lot of weight."

I ran my fingers through my hair. I knew I wouldn't be able to keep my secret much longer. I was already over ten weeks along, but I didn't want him to come back because of guilt. I wanted him to come back because he loved me and wanted me.

"I've been under a lot of stress lately." It was true. I had never been this stressed out, and stress has always had a tendency whether good or bad to make me lose my appetite.

"Well, try and relax and maybe eat something."

I rolled my eyes. "Wow, why didn't I think of that?"

He really was turning into an idiot, or maybe a selfish ignoramus. There was no acknowledgment from him that he had anything to do with the state of disarray in my life. I shook my head at him and then turned toward my babies and helped Mia with her shoes.

"Mommy, please come with us?" she pleaded.

Ashton asked, too. I could tell it was making my husband uncomfortable.

"Mommy can't come. I have lots of work to do tonight, but you guys go and have fun with your daddy."

I stood up and Michael motioned for me to come closer to him. I thought it was weird, but part of me was happy. I wanted nothing more than to be close to him.

"What do you mean work?" he whispered so the kids couldn't hear.

"I told you, I'm starting up my photography business again. I've already had two shoots, and I need to do some editing."

"I told you that you didn't need to do that."

"Are you ready to come home Michael?"

His blue eyes looked guilty once again. He didn't answer.

"Then I need to do this."

"Maybe if you weren't working, you wouldn't be so stressed out."

I sighed. "Michael, if you think that's what's stressing me out, you don't know me at all."

"Carly…"

The kids were ready, so they both came up and hugged me tight and said how much they would miss me. I think it bothered Michael, but what could he expect? He'd been absent for almost a month. I sent them off and tried to hold back the tears. I didn't want this to become our lives.

"Don't keep them out too late," I called. "It's a school night."

Michael looked up at me from the bottom step of our stone porch. "I got this, Carly."

"Okay." I smiled.

I walked back in and rubbed my abdomen. I did that a lot lately. I drew comfort from it. Then I puked. It was lovely. Once I got my nightly ritual of losing my lunch over with, I walked up to the loft and put on some classic rock and went to work. I started first with Dr. White's family. We'd done a photo shoot at the old railroad station and the pictures turned out completely adorable, if I did say so myself. I had pangs of jealousy as I edited the pictures of the happy family, especially the shots of only Emma and Jace. I so wanted that again.

Halfway through editing my senior photo shoot, my rug rats returned with their daddy in tow. I was surprised he walked in. I half-expected him to drop them off at the curb and have them ring the doorbell. The kids called out, "Mommy," and I yelled out that I was upstairs. I immediately heard tiny footsteps running up the stairs toward me. I loved that sound.

They both looked happy as they flew into my arms. I hugged and kissed them until they giggled. I looked up to find Michael staring at us. I hadn't heard him come up.

"Daddy's going to tuck us in tonight," Mia explained.

I smiled at Michael, and for a moment I saw something of the man I loved in his eyes.

"Then I guess you better get your jammies on and brush your teeth."

They both quickly ran to their rooms. Michael sat down on the chair near the couch where I was sitting.

"Did you have a good time?" I asked.

"Yeah, I took them to the new indoor miniature golf course."

"That sounds like fun."

He leaned forward. "Carly, I want to talk to you after I put the kids to bed."

"Okay. I'll be here."

He got up and walked to Ashton's room. I watched him go. He sounded solemn when he asked to speak to me. I wasn't sure what that meant, but

I listened as he tucked the kids in and read to them. I was called in to give kisses and hugs and sing to them. Michael stood by and watched. He used to kneel down next to me, and oh, how I wished he would. I looked up at him, and he was looking at me like he was remembering something. I smiled at him and he even smiled back, but it was like he realized what he was doing and he quickly turned. I couldn't figure him out. What was going on in his head?

Once we had them tucked in, we quietly exited. I went to sit back on the couch in the loft, but Michael had other plans.

"Let's go downstairs and talk."

I grabbed my laptop so I didn't have to come back up for it. The more energy I could conserve, the better. This baby seemed to zap the energy out of me more than the first two did. I'm sure the emotional turmoil didn't help one bit. Michael sat on the living room couch and I sat next to him and placed my laptop on the coffee table.

He turned the laptop toward him to see what I was working on. "I forgot how talented you were."

"Thanks, I think."

He half-smiled in response. He pointed at my logo. "Studio 24B?"

"I thought it had a nice ring to it."

He turned toward me with confusion in his eyes. "You don't have to work. I promise I'll take care of you and the kids."

"Michael, I realized this past month how many things I took for granted, thinking they would always be there, and how blind I've been about the things you've kept from me. I want to trust what you say, but I can't right now."

"What do you mean, things I've kept from you?" he asked defensively.

"Well, for starters, you leased an apartment and took assignments without consulting with me. And I found your secret bank account with thousands of dollars in it. How long have you had that?"

He looked stunned. "How did you find out about that?"

"You didn't answer my question."

"Well, what about you?" he fired back. He still didn't answer my question.

"What you mean?"

"The kids told me how you're still throwing up every day and you look like you're about done for."

I started crying. "You have no idea what I've been through this past month. Do you know how hard it is to take care of two suffering kids all by yourself, all while suffering yourself, and then keeping up with the house and all the kids' activities and starting up a business? I'm doing the best I can by myself, Michael!"

"Then don't work."

"That's all you have to say to me? Don't work?"

"What do you want me to say to you?"

I picked up his hand and held it. At least he didn't pull away.

"I want you to tell me why you're really doing this and what's really going on. I want you to tell me that you're coming home where you belong, so we can work this out together."

He looked away from me.

"Please look at me. I deserve that, at least."

He slowly turned back to me. I reached up and placed my hand on his cheek. "Bishop, I love you. I love our life together." I moved my hand down to his chest over his heart. "And somewhere in there, I know you do, too, but for some reason you're fighting it."

"It's late, I've got to go."

I sighed and dropped my hand. "Okay, go. But know, someday I'll quit trying."

His eyes widened for a moment as he stood up. "You should go back to the doctor about the vomiting."

I sighed. He wasn't getting it.

"I already have an appointment for next week." It wasn't about the vomiting, per se. It was my monthly exam, but he didn't need to know that yet.

"Oh, well…good. Goodnight, Carly."

"Don't let the door hit you on the way out, Bishop."

Chapter Six

So the good news was that I was out of my first trimester and I wasn't vomiting every day. The bad news was, okay it wasn't really bad news, but it meant my secret wasn't going to be a secret much longer. I looked down in the shower and noticed a small bump. I could swear it wasn't there the day before, but it was definitely there now.

The other bad news was that Michael was still living alone and doing his best to avoid us. We even tried dropping by his favorite cookies one night only to be disappointed by his lack of hospitality. He ignored Mother's Day, which was beyond hurtful. My kiddos did their best to make sure I knew I was loved, but it wasn't the same without Michael. Every year since we had Ashton, he would make me breakfast in bed, add a rose bush to my rose garden, and he always got me some sort of gift certificate to a spa or for a shopping spree. This year I didn't even get a phone call.

I kept wondering why I was even trying. Then I rubbed my baby bump and looked at my son and daughter, and even into my own heart, and I reminded myself why. I wasn't sure how long I could keep it up.

Some other good news, my business was taking off like wildfire. I even had to turn down some shoots. It was annoying to Michael, though I couldn't understand why. He'd never had a problem with me working before—he wasn't a male chauvinist pig. Okay, he was kind of a pig now, but at least not the chauvinist kind.

Mia was doing okay. She was resilient, but Ashton was more quiet than usual. He wondered if his dad didn't love him, or if he was mad at him because he'd said he hated him. I tried to assure him it had nothing to do with him. I also had to assure myself it had nothing to do with me, but that was becoming increasingly more difficult to believe.

I also worried about how to tell Michael I was pregnant. I had lost all hope he was coming home anytime soon, if at all.

I didn't have to worry about it long, because the decision was taken out of my hands. School ended right before Memorial Day weekend. Michael had missed the end-of-school awards and field day due to an out of town assignment in Florida, or so he said. I was feeling better, so I decided we were going to celebrate the end of school and the awards Ashton had won. He had read the most books in the first grade and he was Star Student. Mia learned how to tie her shoes and she graduated from preschool. I was so proud of them, and I was especially thankful for the shoe tying accomplishment; I had a feeling bending over was going to be difficult in the near future. We settled on going to Lego Land in Atlanta on that Friday since it was only a half day of school.

I had been working late every night that week, editing after the kids went to bed. I was having a hard time sleeping by myself, anyway. I was tired, but not overly so, at least that's what I thought. We had a terrific time at Lego Land, and we walked out of there with more Legos than was necessary, but I'd had a hard time telling them no even before this fiasco. The kids were as happy as they had been in the last couple of months when I tucked them in that night. We talked about all the fun things we would do this summer. I hoped Michael would be a participant.

I was happy to see them happy, but very tired. I skipped editing and went straight to bed, but it was anything but restful. I was up to use the bathroom more than usual and my back hurt. I figured I'd likely just overdone it, like I had a tendency to do, especially lately. Single parenting really stinks.

I woke up the next morning feeling like I had been hit by a train, and I was back to vomiting. I called Michael, but he didn't pick up. I left him a message and asked if there was any way he could take the kids for the day. I had never done that before, but I had never felt so awful in all my life. He never called back. Poor Mia and Ashton did their best to take care of me. I was grateful Ashton knew how to make cereal and sandwiches. I wasn't sure I wanted to see what the kitchen looked like, but I didn't really care.

Late that afternoon I called Dr. White's office, but she wasn't on call.

Her after-hours service just directed me to the emergency room. That was going to be difficult with two little ones, and I wasn't even sure I was safe enough to drive. I tried to push liquids and hoped it would pass. I called Michael again, but still no response. I was really starting to hate him. By eight that night, I was more than worried. There was blood in my urine, and I knew I had no choice. I had to seek medical attention.

In my desperation, I called my in-laws. I probably should have called them earlier, but my mother-in-law, Danielle, really didn't like me. I'm not sure what I ever did to her, but I wasn't high on her list. I'm sure she was happy to see that Michael and I had separated. She had wanted him to marry his on-and-off girlfriend, Lyla June. What kind of name was that anyway? I prayed Jack would answer; he actually liked me, but he could only show it when his wife wasn't around. Finally, something went my way when Jack answered.

"Hi, Jack," I could barely get out. "Do you think you could drive me to the hospital while Danielle watches the kids? I'm not feeling all that well."

"Yes," he responded with no hesitation or even a question why.

I turned to my sweet kiddos. "Mimi and Papa are on their way."

I could see the relief in their eyes that help was on the way. I knew I was relieved, even though Danielle was not my biggest fan.

Mia reached up and touched my cheek softly. "It will be okay, Mommy."

Poor Ashton looked pensive. He had been asking me all day what he could bring me. I sure did love my kids.

My in-laws lived about twenty minutes from us, and within the half hour, they were there. I could barely make it to the door when they knocked. I had to keep stopping on the way there. By the time I made it to the door, Danielle looked quite put out.

"It took you long en…" she began to say. Then she looked at me.

Jack rushed to my side and helped hold me up.

The kids came running out and Danielle turned her attention to them.

"The kids can sleep on my bed," I managed to tell Danielle. She didn't say anything back, which was a nice gesture on her part. She never had anything nice to say to me. "Thank you. I'm sorry it's so late."

Danielle pretty much ignored me, but Jack waved off my apology. "Don't even think about it," he said. "Can you walk to the truck? You look like we should call an ambulance."

I panicked. "No, I don't want the kids to worry. I can manage to the truck."

I had Ashton bring me my purse, and he and Mia both hugged me goodbye. They looked so worried.

"I'll be okay." I tried to smile at them both. It didn't help.

They both started to cry and I did, too. Thankfully, Danielle came and scooped them up and reiterated I would be fine. I was more than grateful to her at the moment. I leaned on Jack all the way to his pickup truck. He helped me in and hurried to the driver side. He drove quickly toward Pine Apple Hospital.

He kept looking over to me. "Honey, did you call Michael?"

"I tried. He's not one to answer my calls anymore," I practically cried.

He shook his head in disgust.

As we neared the hospital, I knew I was going to have to reveal my secret. "Could you please go to the Women and Children's entrance?"

"This is an emergency, let's go there."

"Jack, I promise they'll send me there. I'm pregnant." There was no other way to say it.

"Well, okay. I wasn't expecting that."

I tried to laugh. "Yeah, me neither."

"Does Michael know?"

"No."

"Honey, what's going on between you two?"

I leaned my head against the window. "Can we talk about that later?"

"Sure, honey," he said as we pulled into the entrance. He pulled up curbside and went in. Moments later an attendant brought out a wheelchair.

I hated wheelchairs, but I practically kissed this one. There was no way I could walk in. Jack parked the truck and met me at patient registration. His presence was a comfort to me. I had always really liked Michael's dad. I always felt like we would have been good friends if Danielle liked me. Tonight his concern was more than appreciated. If I felt better I would have smiled at his behavior. I don't know how many times he asked the registration attendant if they could just take me back, but I could tell she was getting annoyed. I didn't even take offense when he kept pointing out to her how horrible I looked. I did look horrible.

It was to no avail. They refused to take me back until every "T" was crossed and every "I" was dotted on the endless paperwork the attendant had given me. Finally when the time came the nurse told Jack they would come get him when I was in a room. Jack kissed my head before they wheeled me off. It was a very sweet gesture, and one I welcomed. I needed some affection.

The nurse that showed me back took my stats and vitals, and asked about my symptoms. She also asked me how far along I was. I was already fifteen-and-a-half weeks. The weight loss and loose clothing helped me hide it, but now the secret was out. I was afraid to tell Michael, but I guess I had no choice now. I would have to worry about it later. Right now I was worried about what was going on with my body. I was shivering and felt like I might pass out. The thermometer that had been placed under my tongue read one hundred and two. I could tell that concerned my nurse.

She set the thermometer down and handed me a plastic cup. "Do you think you can manage to give us a urine sample?" she asked.

"I'll try." It took everything I had in me to make it to the restroom. I prayed nothing was wrong with the baby.

I barely managed the task. My nurse's look of concern returned when she noticed the red tinge. Apparently, it was enough that I was taken straight back to a room and admitted. Once they had me in a lovely hospital gown and hooked up to an I.V., they called my father-in-law back to be with me. He came right to my side and held my hand. He had never done that before. It made me miss my own father, and of course Jack's son. It reminded me how utterly alone I had been feeling.

I started to cry. I did that a lot lately.

My father-in-law swept away my tears. "Now, now. There's no need for those. It's all going to be okay."

"Jack, thanks for being here with me."

He squeezed my hand tighter. "Don't mention it, my dear."

Jack and Michael looked very similar, but Jack looked kinder. I wondered if that came with age. Jack was sixty-seven and thinking about retiring. He was an aerospace engineer, and for the last couple of years, he'd talked about retiring but never pulled the trigger. I wondered if this was the year.

Several nurses came in and out. I was hooked up to all sorts of machines, including a fetal monitor. Hearing my baby's heartbeat made me feel better. It was strong at one hundred and fifty beats per minute. Music to my ears.

I looked at Jack and he smiled. "Is that my grandbaby's heartbeat?"

I nodded my head yes and smiled.

"You know, honey, you're going to have to tell my son."

I closed my eyes and sighed. I didn't want to think about it. "I know, but he's making that very difficult."

"What's going on? He won't say, and he keeps avoiding us."

I slowly opened my eyes. "Jack, I wish I knew. He told me one day that he didn't love me anymore and he rented an apartment and left, just like that. He rarely sees me or the kids and he won't talk to me, either."

Jack shook his head, dumbfounded. He found me a tissue and handed it to me. "I don't believe that he doesn't love you."

"It's true. If he loved me, he would be here and not you." I squeezed his hand. "Not that I'm not happy you're here."

He laughed, but his demeanor was anything but lighthearted. "I don't think I ever told you this, but when Mike came home after meeting you, there was this excitement in him I had never seen. And then the first time we met you I saw how enamored he was with you. He was never the same after that. I thought he would be an eternal bachelor, but you changed him for the better. And I've frequently seen that enamored look he has when it comes to you."

"Well, that's long gone. He won't even look at me now."

"I can't believe it," he kept saying.

"I couldn't at first either, but believe me it's true."

We had to put our conversation on hold. The attending physician finally came in. "Mrs. Bishop, I'm Dr. Cameron Shay." I wondered how long I would have that title. I introduced my father-in-law.

Dr. Shay looked over the nurses notes and what I assumed were my lab results. "You have a kidney infection and you're dehydrated," he informed me. "We'll need to keep you overnight, maybe longer to make sure the infection doesn't cause preterm labor."

My eyes widened at that news.

I'm sure he could see my concern. "Don't worry, we'll monitor you closely and we'll begin administering antibiotics intravenously as well as something to reduce your fever. All safe for your baby, of course."

He must have read my mind. That was going to be my first question.

Once the doc left, I turned to Jack. "Do you guys mind keeping the kids overnight?"

"Not at all. Why don't we keep them for the holiday weekend? You look like you could use a break."

"You have no idea," I said through tears.

He kissed my forehead. "Get some rest, my dear. I'll be back in the morning to check on you."

"Thank you, Jack. Please tell my kiddos I love them and that I'm okay."

"Will do."

"Oh, and Jack. Please don't say anything about the baby."

He turned and smiled from the door. "I'll let you do the honors."

"Thanks."

I quickly drifted off to sleep, which was a feat in the hospital, but my body was done for. I was woken up a couple times during the night. I kept expecting to see Michael on the chair next to me. I had never been in the hospital except to have Ashton and Mia, and each time he never left my side. I couldn't understand what had changed. I wanted him to be enamored with me again.

I woke up Sunday morning and called him. No answer. I didn't even bother with a message this time. But I was concerned that maybe something had happened to him. Jack called me that morning and I asked him if he would swing by my house and indulge my vanity. I wanted my own pajamas and my makeup bag. I also asked him to swing by Michael's.

He laughed. "That is a dangerous proposition. I might just beat the hell out of him."

I almost had enough energy to manage a laugh. "Be my guest," I encouraged him. I couldn't let him go without asking him about my babies.

"We're spoiling them rotten," he reported.

That did my heart good.

My fever was down to low grade status and the baby was doing well. I still didn't feel well, but I was leaps and bounds better than the night before. What people ever did without antibiotics and pain relievers, I would never know. Oh, yeah, they had short life spans. I was thankful to be living in this day and age.

Jack showed up mid-morning with my requests, a bouquet of daisies, and handmade cards from my wonderful kiddos. He also reported that no one answered at Michael's apartment. That bit of news concerned me.

"Don't worry about him. You worry about yourself and getting better." I could tell he was angry at his son. Not only was Michael not at home, but he didn't answer Jack's calls, either. It sounded like Jack didn't leave a very kind message for his son. Normally, I would disagree with that approach, but I was beyond the "show more love" phase.

We spent a lovely morning talking. He told me several stories of his childhood and rowdy teenage years. I had no idea what a troublemaker he used to be. He divulged stories about breaking into his school and hot-wiring cars.

"How did you and Danielle meet?" I asked him. She seemed too straight-laced for him.

His eyes twinkled. "We met at Georgia Tech. We had chemistry together." He winked.

I smiled in return.

A wicked grin spread across his face as he remembered. "In an attempt to impress her, I made an idiot of myself and I accidentally started a fire in lab. There wasn't any serious damage to the lab or my chances with her. She eventually gave in and went out with me. But marrying me was another story. I asked her a handful of times, only for her to refuse me."

"Like me and Bishop."

"How many times did he ask you?"

"At least a dozen." I smiled at the memory.

"Smartest thing he ever did," Jack replied.

"Maybe," I said quietly.

"Honey, I don't know what's going on in that thick head of his, but he'd be the biggest fool if he lets you go. You're the best thing that ever happened to him. I was worried he would never settle down and think about anybody but himself. I worried that we had spoiled him as the only child, but something in him changed when he met you."

"Apparently, I don't have staying power."

"That's bull, dear. This is his problem, not yours."

"Yeah, that's what I keep trying to tell myself, but it gets harder and harder to believe it."

"Well, believe it."

"Thanks, Jack. Can I ask you a question?"

"Shoot."

"Why doesn't Danielle like me?"

He shifted uncomfortably in his chair and pulled on his collar. "Well, my dear, when you entered the picture, you became Mike's whole world. It didn't leave much room for his momma. And Mike was her world."

"I'm sorry."

"Don't be, that's the way it should be."

"I never tried to keep Michael from her."

"I know that, dear. And, deep down, Danielle knows it, too."

He patted my hand and grinned mischievously. "You know, it might help if this baby is a girl, if you name her Danielle."

I contemplated the request for a moment. "I'll think about it. I hope she wasn't upset we named Mia after my mother. I only wanted to honor her memory, since Mia would never get to know her."

"Well, it's a touchy subject, she was hoping for at least a middle name."

That made me feel terrible. "Oh. Well, we thought not giving Mia a middle name meant she could keep Bishop as her middle name."

"That makes sense. You may want to throw that into a conversation sometime around my wife."

I winked at his smiling face. "I'll work on it."

I grabbed his hand. "Jack, just so you know, no matter what happens between me and Michael, I'll always want you both to be part of my children's and my life."

He squeezed back. "I wouldn't expect any less of you, but don't give up on my son just yet," he practically begged.

"It's not me that has given up."

He looked at me thoughtfully for a moment and then, like a true man, he turned on the Braves game. We spent the afternoon watching baseball, talking about my childhood, and my travels overseas with my parents. He left around dinner time with a promise to return in the morning. He didn't leave, though, without ordering me to get some rest.

There wasn't much else to do but rest. The doctor said I couldn't leave until my fever was completely gone, so I was stuck for at least one more night. At least they let me shower and get changed into my own pajamas. I knew I was in the hospital, but makeup does a girl good. I kept looking in the mirror at my pale complexion, thinking, *I need some sun and to gain some weight back.*

Once I was back in bed, the kids called and told me all about their day with Mimi. It sounded like they had a great time picking strawberries and swimming in their pool and playing with their golden retriever, Beau. It was like kid heaven over there. I asked to talk to Danielle. She wasn't very talkative, but I wanted to express my thanks. I also wanted to try and repair our relationship, and this was the first step.

When I got off the phone, I realized the kids didn't even ask about their daddy. I hated that they were getting used to him not being around or unavailable to them and me. I hoped whatever he was doing was worth what he was missing out on, but I knew it wasn't. Nothing compared to Ashton, Mia, and my little peanut, who was now the size of a bell pepper.

It was weird to spend a whole evening alone, but it was nice to worry about me for a change. Not that I didn't love worrying about my kiddos, it's just that I'd been worrying so much lately, it was nice to relax, watch a movie on T.V., and rest. I would have rather done it on the beach or in a spa, but I guess the hospital would have to do. I hoped I could go home the next day.

I slept on and off as the nurses kept coming in and checking vitals and the baby monitor. Everything was looking good, but I hated being prodded during the night. My body was craving sleep, and I woke up at seven a.m. only to fall right back asleep. I wasn't sure how long I had slept, but as I was coming out of sleep mode, I heard two voices in hushed tones, although I could tell it was a heated discussion. I finally recognized the voices. It was Michael and his dad. My heart leapt a little at hearing Michael, not because I was happy to have him there, but because I was nervous. I had enough presence of mind to keep my eyes closed. The conversation was quite interesting.

"Son, I never thought I would say this to you, even after all of the stupid stuff you did in high school and college, but I'm disappointed and ashamed of you. I didn't raise you to be this kind of man. I can't believe what you have put your wife through these past few months. Nothing is worth losing Carly and your kids."

"What about my happiness?"

"Your happiness? Is that what this is all about? Why don't you think about Carly's and Ashton's and Mia's happiness? That's where you will find your happiness. And if you can't find happiness with them, then you don't know what true happiness is."

There was a long, silent pause. If only it could have lasted. Unfortunately, Michael was observant.

"Is that a fetal monitor?" I heard him ask.

I guess it was time to wake up and face the music.

"I've got it from here," I said as I sat up.

Jack came immediately to my side and helped me sit up. He even fluffed my pillows.

I delayed looking at my husband as long as possible. "Thanks, Jack. How are the kids?"

"They miss you, but Danielle is taking them to the parade and letting them decorate the wagon."

"I'm sure they'll love that. Thank you again for everything. I don't know what I would've done without you this weekend."

He kissed my forehead. "Anytime, my dear." He looked between me and my husband, who I noticed looked more like Grizzly Adams and smelled of campfire. "I'll leave you two alone now."

I looked over to Jack. "Do you have to?"

He smiled at me, but scowled at his son. "Can I trust you to take care of her?"

"I've got it," he replied with steel in his voice. He was not happy with his dad.

"Make sure you do," his dad said as he walked out.

Michael approached my bedside.

"Hi," I said.

"Hi. Do you have something you want to tell me?" he asked.

"Do you have something you want to say to me? Like why you didn't answer my calls or maybe ask me how I am and am I going to be okay?"

He sat down on the chair next to my bed and stared at the fetal monitor, before he looked back at me. I wasn't budging.

"I'm sorry I didn't answer your calls, I was camping with a couple of buddies and the reception was terrible."

"How nice for you to just be able to take off whenever you want to."

He didn't respond to my jibe. "Are you okay?"

"Could you say that with any less emotion?"

"What do you want me to say? Okay, I'm sorry. I'm tired. I drove through the night so I could get here after I got yours and my dad's messages. I had no idea you were so sick." He looked at the monitor again. "Why didn't you tell me?"

The never-ending supply of tears started up again. I took a deep breath and placed my hand on my ever growing midsection. "I wanted to, but between you telling me you didn't love me anymore and moving out and then cutting me out of your life, there never seemed to be a good time."

He stood up and started pacing and running his fingers through his hair. "How far along are you?"

"Almost sixteen weeks. The baby's due November 7."

"How did this happen?"

"Well when the egg and spe…"

He stopped and looked at me. I could tell he was annoyed. "I don't need a biology lesson. I thought you were on the pill, and I don't remember you know…"

"Yeah, I know. Let me refresh your memory since apparently it meant nothing to you."

"Carly, please quit taking everything in the worst possible way."

"Fine. Valentine's Day morning in the shower. Does that ring a bell?"

I thought about that morning. I was tired of being ignored, so I took matters into my own hands. After that morning, I thought things would get better. I could feel that he wanted me, but it was short lived.

He sat down and surprised the heck out of me and took my hand in his. He hadn't done that in months. "I remember, Carly." His eyes softened a bit. I recognized a little tenderness in them.

Tears were still trickling out of mine. "I didn't mean for this to happen. I forgot about taking the pill because you hadn't touched me in months. But regardless, I want this baby."

He looked toward the monitor and watched our baby's heartbeat. "Is the baby doing okay through all of this?"

"Yes."

He turned back toward me. "Are you doing okay? My dad said something about a kidney infection?"

"I'm better."

"Well, I guess this changes things."

"What do you mean?"

He didn't answer because Dr. White, who was finally back in town, walked in. I had a feeling he wasn't going to answer anyway.

She walked in and looked between the two of us. Her glance at me asked, *how do I proceed?*

"He knows," I said.

"Well, good," she said. But I noticed the dirty look she threw him. She was my friend too, after all, and the only person that I had talked to about my ugly situation. I think he was surprised by the cold reception.

She approached the bed and asked Michael to move out of the way so she could examine me. I hated letting go of his hand. It had felt so nice. After her thorough examination, she slyly grinned at me. "I don't think I've ever said this to a patient, but drink a milkshake or two and maybe eat a cheeseburger. You've got to get some weight on you."

"I've been trying."

"Well, try harder." She winked at me. "I want to do an ultrasound to make sure everything looks okay. Okay?"

I nodded my head yes. I was eager to see my baby.

A tech rolled in a cart with an ultrasound machine while Dr. White doused my stomach with cold blue gel.

I looked over to Michael who was still leaning against the wall after his earlier dismissal. "Do you want to see?" I asked, with hope.

He joined me at my bedside. He looked unsure. I wanted him to look happy and excited, but I guess that was too much to ask for. I decided to just pay attention to the monitor. And there was a baby, a very active baby. The tears streamed down my face.

"Your baby looks perfect." Dr. White smiled at us. " So... it's a little early to tell, but I have a good guess on the sex if you want to know."

Well, that was a surprise. I instantly said yes and Michael immediately said no. I looked over to him.

"I thought we decided if we ever had a third child, we would keep it a surprise since we already had one of each."

I couldn't believe he remembered that. "Okay." I looked over to Emma. "I guess we'll wait," even though I really wanted to know.

"If you change your mind, we'll still do the ultrasound at twenty weeks."

"Great."

She gave me more good news, pronouncing everything looked good and my fever was gone, so they were going to discharge me. The news made me beyond happy. I was more than ready to go home. She instructed me to take it easy and to drink more. She prescribed me oral antibiotics and some iron because I was anemic. That made sense—I had been so exhausted. Once she left, I looked at Michael who had a deer-in-the-headlights look.

"Are you at least a little happy about this?"

He kept running his fingers through his dark mop. "It's a lot to take in."

"Yeah, I guess so. Could you please hand me my phone in my purse?"

"Sure, why?" He reached into my bag on the little couch.

"I need to call your dad to come and get me and to bring the kids."

He put my phone back in my bag. "Carly, I was planning on taking you home. I know how to get there and everything."

I loved hearing him tease. He hadn't done it in it so long.

"I was beginning to think you had forgotten."

Chapter Seven

I THOUGHT THAT MEMORIAL DAY PERHAPS WAS THE TURN IN THE ROAD, that Michael would come to his senses and come home. He almost acted like my husband when he stopped on the way home from the hospital and bought me the biggest chocolate milkshake I'd ever seen. I couldn't even finish half of it. He ended up finishing the rest. He even stayed with me at the house and waited until the kids got home so he could see them. We didn't talk about anything important, he was still closing himself off, but at least we talked. The only thing of substance we discussed was a moot point in my mind. He couldn't seem to get over the fact that I was working again. He reasoned that was the root of all my ills and asked me to quit.

Ashton and Mia were happy to see their daddy, but it was me they ran to and stayed near. It made me sad. I loved them being next to me, but I could tell they were treating him differently. He could tell, too, and I could tell it confused him. It was like this was what he wanted, but then he didn't want it. With Michael still there, I decided I should tell the kids about the baby. I had pictures from the ultrasound to show them. They were very excited. Ashton was, of course, hoping for a brother, and Mia wanted a sister.

Jack and Danielle had come in with the kids, and they were both happy about the news. Even Danielle gave me a little smile. She had never done that before. She suggested we should all have dinner together since we were all there. Michael declined and offered up some lame excuse. I thought his dad was going to smack him.

Before Michael left, he walked over to the couch where I was laying and knelt beside me. "I have to fly to D.C. in the morning, but I'll call and check on you. Please try and stay down."

I looked over at our very active seven-year-old and almost five-year-old. "Easier said than done."

"Don't worry, I'll come and help with the kids," his mom offered.

Michael stood up and kissed his mom's cheek. "Thank you."

His dad shook his head at him in disgust.

Michael bent down and kissed my forehead. "Bye, Carly."

"Bye, Bishop."

He picked Mia up, hugged, and kissed her goodbye. Ashton was next.

"Bye, Dad," Ashton said sadly. He snuggled in next to me on the couch.

I pulled him closer and looked up at my husband. "Please stay," I mouthed.

He looked torn, which I thought was a good sign. It was like everyone stood still as he contemplated the request. Our eyes were locked. But just like that, he turned and left.

I sighed and pulled my son closer to me and kissed his sweet head. "Why don't you get that new Lego set and we'll build it on the coffee table?"

My father-in-law offered to help with the Legos while Mimi and Mia got dinner. We all agreed on the plan. I loved the support and backup. I only wished my husband would jump on board. I was at my wits' end and ready to give up. I was beginning to think that maybe I should file for divorce. I was tired of living in limbo and being rejected over and over again. A girl could only take so much.

As I lay in bed that night, I thought a lot about divorce. I even pulled out my tablet and started researching the laws in Georgia. Online, it made it sound so easy, too easy in fact. If it was a no contest or no fault divorce, we could be divorced in as little as a month, but since there were children and property involved, it probably wouldn't be that simple. My heart ached to think about it, but I would be delusional to think this was heading anywhere else. At least this way we could move on, and maybe it would be better for the kids, too. I just didn't know.

I knew I should have been resting, but thoughts like those had a tendency to keep me up. At least school was over, and Danielle was coming back to help. Michael called on his way to the airport, around seven a.m. I had been up for hours by that time, laying in bed mulling things over. I decided it was time to broach the subject.

"How are you this morning?" he asked.

"I'm better, but I've been thinking." I took a deep breath and mustered up my courage and I tried to hide the fact I was crying. "Michael, I heard what you said to your dad yesterday. I know you're unhappy and I don't know what I've done, but I know you're not coming back, so I think it's time I face reality and we file for divorce."

All I heard were faint mutterings of cursing and tires squealing.

I sat right up in bed and panicked. "Michael, are you okay?"

"Yes!" he yelled. "I needed to pull over. You could have picked a better time to bring this up."

"Oh, I'm sorry. I didn't ever think I would have to."

He paused. "Carly, I'm sorry, you just caught me off guard."

"Yeah, well, this whole situation has caught me off guard, Michael, but I'm tired of living like this."

"Carly, we're having a baby. Can we get through that before we discuss this?"

"What difference will it make?"

"Carly, please. I'm trying to work through this. I just need some more time."

"More time for what? Partying with your friends and ignoring your wife and kids? Or maybe let's go back to my original assumption. You're having an affair."

"Dammit, Carly. I'm not having an affair. You don't know what I'm going through."

"Don't swear at me, Michael Bishop. And you're right, I don't know what you're going through because you won't talk to me!" The tears were coming on full force. There was no stopping them. I sniffled into the phone.

"Carly, please don't cry. It's not good for you or the baby. Please try and relax and get better. When I get home from this trip, I'll come and get the kids for the weekend. Let's just put a pin in the divorce talk until at least after the baby's born."

He loved to say, let's put a pin in it. I wanted to say, I know where we could put a pin, but instead I relented. "Okay, I'll drop it for now."

I could hear a sigh of relief on his end.

"But Bishop, I can't take much more of this."

"I know, Carly. I'll call you later."

I was more than awake by the time the call was over, so I got up and jumped in the shower. I wasn't sure how to feel after that conversation. On one hand, it was hopeful, but on the other hand, it was depressing. He didn't take divorce off the table, and my fear that he would only stay because of the baby felt like a real possibility. I wanted us to be a family, but not out of guilt, but because he wanted us and because he really loved me. I didn't want the kind of marriage we had had the past seven or eight months.

It felt good to be up and out of bed, but it wore me out just walking up the stairs. I used to run 5K's in my sleep, now I got winded walking up the stairs to wake up my kids. Per the usual, they were in Ashton's bed. I wondered when he would tire of her invading his space. I hoped not too soon. They looked adorable together. I went and grabbed my camera so I could capture the moment. Sometimes, I wished they could stay small.

As I took a few shots, I got an idea for the nursery. Yep, I decided I was getting my nursery. Even if Bishop decided to move back home, or if I let him move back home at this point, he would have to figure out a different space for an office. As far as I was concerned, that bedroom was mine to do with as I pleased now. Finders keepers, right?

I snapped one more picture, for the heck of it, before I woke them up. Today's musical renderings came from Mary Poppins, *Supercalifragilisticexpialidocious*. Try spelling that. Per usual, as of late, Mia was happy with the singing and Ashton pretended he didn't like it. I could seriously eat them up. Before we went down together, I took the time to talk to them about the baby some more. We didn't get a good chance yesterday. I wanted to know if they had any questions. The first one was where babies came from. Maybe I should have thought about that beforehand. Ashton was only a toddler when I was pregnant with Mia, so we never had this discussion. I went the honest route, without giving out too much information—that could come later when they were older, I thought. They looked a little confused, but thankfully we didn't have any follow-up questions.

I let them touch my midsection. "You know, pretty soon you'll be able to feel the baby."

Their eyes lit up in wonderment at the prospect. I had felt some movement, but nothing externally yet. We breakfasted together. It was only cereal again, but hey, it was life-sustaining. My mother-in-law came around ten. I could tell she was uneasy about it, and I was, too. We had never spent a day together without our husbands involved.

"Hi, Danielle," I said as brightly as I could when I opened my front door for her. "Thanks again for coming."

"You're looking better," she said stiffly.

"Not one hundred percent yet, but definitely better."

The kids were already playing in the backyard, so we walked back there together. As soon as the kids saw Mimi, they ran to her. No matter what kind of mother-in-law she had been, she was an excellent grandma, and I had always appreciated that. Deep down, I knew not even my own mother would have been as good and as attentive as Danielle had been. My parents were great, but they lived a very different lifestyle. They enjoyed the high life and world traveling, where Danielle and Jack enjoyed the simple pleasures. They had no problem getting down and dirty with the kids. My mom would have been good with them when they were older, when she could bore them with art museums and symphonies. All things I learned to appreciate as I grew up.

Danielle and I each took a seat on my deck as the kiddos went back to playing on the jungle gym that Michael had built when Ashton was four. It was a labor of love. *Where was that man?* I kept wondering. We sat silently for several minutes. I kept trying to think of things to say, but I came up short. It was sad, I had been part of this woman's family for over ten years, and I was still uncomfortable around her. I finally settled on what I hoped was a safe topic.

"So, do you think Jack will retire this year?"

She rolled her eyes. "Your guess is as good as mine."

Okay, so I picked a touchy subject. *Way to go*, I thought. More silence ensued.

Purposefully, she turned my way after several minutes. "Speaking of work, when do you plan on giving up your new job?"

I wasn't expecting the question or the malice that accompanied it. I sighed. I didn't need this from her, too. "I don't plan to for the time being," I said kindly, but with authority.

Her eyes widened, and she made a tsking sound.

"Why does that bother you?"

"It makes my son unhappy and you have children to think about."

"You're right, I do have children to think about, and that's why I'm working. And believe me, I try to spend as little time as possible away from them."

I stared directly into her eyes. "I didn't choose this, Danielle. I wouldn't have chosen this."

"But, maybe if you quit, he would come back."

"You and I both know that's not true."

She turned from me, crossed her arms, and watched her grandchildren. This wasn't going as I had hoped. I wished Jack didn't have to work. Better yet, I wished my husband was home, and then I wouldn't have to have these conversations and defend myself. I tried something else.

"I had an idea for the nursery today. Would you be willing to let me copy some of Michael's baby pictures?"

"Where are you putting the nursery?" She turned to me with shrewd eyes. She and Michael had the same blue eye color. But her eyes reminded me of a hawk. Like she was going to swoop in and grab me with her claws.

I sighed. "In Michael's old office."

She went in for the kill.

I braced myself by holding onto my lounge chair.

"So you're going to push him out of your life?"

I closed my eyes for a moment and breathed in deep. I didn't need this this morning, especially from her. But I composed myself and reminded myself I wanted to repair this relationship, not damage it further. I opened my eyes to see her glaring at me. "Danielle, I've done everything I can think of to get Michael to come home. I didn't ask him to leave. I begged him not to go. He's rejected me to the point of humiliation, but yet I still keep trying. But I'm not going to waste my life away waiting for him. That wouldn't be good for me or the kids. Michael knows he's welcome, at least for now, to come home anytime he wants."

Her eyes narrowed some more. "What do you mean, at least for now?"

"This can't go on forever."

She turned away in a little of a huff. I reached over and touched her arm. She still didn't look my way.

"Danielle, I'm sorry for whatever it is I've done to make you not like me. I was hoping we could get past that because I have a feeling I'm going to be needing a mother soon, or at the very least, a friend."

She slowly turned my way. If I wasn't mistaken, her eyes looked a little misty.

"I'll bring the pictures over tomorrow."

I squeezed her arm quickly and smiled. "Thank you."

Chapter Eight

As I started feeling more like myself, or at least more like a normal pregnant lady, I began to make plans and map out our summer. I was determined it was going to be fabulous, with or without Michael. My first order of business was to make reservations for a condo at the beach. In addition, I bought passes to the waterpark and a couple of museums in the Atlanta area. I made a calendar and emailed it to Michael. I simply told him he was invited to join us for each excursion, including our week in Florida at the Gulf Coast, which was coming up in two weeks. I even included my scheduled doctor's appointments. The next one up was the ultrasound in a little less than four weeks.

I also began sketching out my plans for the nursery and shopping for baby furniture. I found this lovely baby boutique and became fast friends with the owner, Laura Hansen. After a few visits, we started talking about what I did, and I showed her some of my work.

"I'm impressed," she remarked as she perused my website.

She was so impressed she asked for a quote to update her posters and website pictures. She even allowed me to place my brochures on her counter. I was already full through summer with scheduled sessions, but it didn't hurt to advertise more. Currently, I was only taking two sessions a week, unless it was a wedding, then that was my only outing for the week. Thankfully, I only had two of those on the schedule. They were grueling.

Michael eventually responded to my email by calling me. "I'll be traveling a lot on assignment, so I'm not sure what I can do." It was the same tired old excuse he had been giving me for months.

"That's fine with me," I replied. "It's no big deal. I just wanted you to know you were invited." I tried to play it all off like it didn't bother me one iota.

Oddly enough, he called a few hours later and changed his tune. "I'll try to make it to the beach for a couple of days and I'll for sure be there for the ultrasound."

I smiled to myself. "Okay," I responded to him casually.

He was still absent a lot, but I tried my best not to let it get to me. Like I said, I was determined to make this a fabulous summer. We picnicked in the park and fed the ducks, swam at Mimi and Papa's, and went to the water park. I also braved sleeping in a tent with the kids in the backyard. That was definitely not happening again with a pregnant body. Michael would call and talk to the kids each night while he was out of town, and they would tell him of our adventures. Each call ended with him and me. The regret was apparent in his voice each time he vocalized that it sounded like we were all having a great time. And we were, but there was something missing, even though I decided since he wasn't making an effort to be involved, I wasn't going to beg anymore.

Father's Day rolled around, and I asked him if he wanted the kids for the weekend. He declined, saying he would be getting back late into town from his assignment in Boston. While that irked me, I decided I should be the better person and acknowledge the day, even though he had completely ignored Mother's Day. More than anything, I didn't want this to make me spiteful and hateful, although at times I so wanted to be. When someone you love so much constantly hurts and disappoints you, it's hard not to be that way, but I swallowed my hurt and pride and helped the kids pick out gifts for their dad. I even did a photo shoot of them and put together a photo book with the pictures for him.

My in-laws invited us over for church and lunch that day, and I gladly accepted. I knew Michael was extended the same invite, but I didn't know if he would come. Regardless, I got up and made his favorite that morning, cinnamon rolls. While I was kneading the dough, I questioned my sanity and why I was going through the trouble, but then the baby moved and I was reminded what was at stake here.

We dressed up in our Sunday finest, which meant I had to break down and buy some maternity clothes. For the occasion, I bought a lovely royal blue dress that showed off my now tan legs quite nicely. It was form fitting, and it showed off the baby bump. I didn't think I felt this comfortable with my body the last two pregnancies, but I guess there were advantages to being older and feeling more comfortable in your skin. It didn't hurt that I was finally feeling well and my face had color back in it.

The kids and I gathered up all the gifts. I wrapped a pan of cinnamon rolls up, and we headed out the door. We were going to stop by Michael's apartment on the way to his parents' place. It seemed so surreal. I kept thinking it was only a short year ago when Michael was home and Sunday mornings had meant lazily lying together in bed with him begging me not to get up. I almost started to tear up, but I stopped myself. I was so tired of crying over him.

I wasn't sure how our reception was going to be, so I tried to brace myself as we knocked on his door. I prayed he would see how excited the kids were to give him their gifts and that he would at least pretend. *Maybe I should have called*, I thought. But I was afraid he would say not to bother. It took a minute for him to answer. By the looks of it, we had woken him up. He was in his boxer shorts and t-shirt, and he looked tired and haggard. His seven o'clock shadow was more like a full grown beard. We hadn't seen him in a couple of weeks, so I was surprised. He seemed embarrassed and uncomfortable when he looked at me. I honestly barely recognized him. I smiled and looked down at the kids. Mia was bursting with excitement and Ashton was hesitant. Thankfully, he invited us in and responded well to the kids. He sat on his new leather couch, where the kids joined him, one on each side. I walked back and put the cinnamon rolls on his kitchen counter.

It was a small apartment, and it was made smaller by his desk and chair and a ginormous flat screen TV. I kept looking around thinking, *is this what he really wanted, a bachelor pad?* The space was cold and uninviting. No wonder the kids didn't really like coming here, not like they ever really got the chance to.

I walked back into the front room and stood as I watched Michael open his gifts. Mia got him tennis balls and a tie. Ashton got him a new tennis racquet. He loved to play tennis, and his apartment had tennis courts. He liked both gifts and hugged and kissed the kids. I was relieved. Ashton gave him the photo book I created of the two of them. He opened it and flipped through the pages. He looked up at me, but didn't say anything. His stare was a little unnerving.

"We better go; we're going to be late," I said as a way to divert his attention. I pointed to the kitchen. "I left a pan of cinnamon rolls for you."

"Thanks," he said quietly.

Mia hugged her daddy's neck tightly. "I love you," she expressed easily.

Ashton looked unsure. Once Mia released Michael from her death grip, Michael looked at his son and wrapped him up tight. My eyes began to water.

"I love you, Dad," Ashton whispered ever so quietly. I barely heard the three little words.

"How about I teach you to play tennis?" Michael asked our son. Ashton's eyes lit up and he nodded his head yes. I hoped Michael meant it.

I began to walk to the door, and the kids followed. Michael came, too. I opened the door and let some light in. His apartment was so dark. The kids waved goodbye as we walked out. Michael grabbed my hand and pulled me to him. I was stunned, to say the least.

"Carly..." He stared at me for a moment again. I thought he was going to reach up with his other hand and touch my cheek, but he stopped short.

I held my breath in anticipation. I was almost eye level with him in my heels. His blue eyes looked troubled and confused. I wanted to reach up and touch his face, but I restrained myself. I couldn't deal with rejection this morning.

"Thank you," he said.

"You're welcome, Bishop."

I turned to walk away. He pulled back.

"Carly, I'm sorry about Mother's Day. I really screwed up."

I willed myself not to cry. I smiled. "You've been doing that a lot lately."

"Yeah, I know." He let go of my hand.

"See you later, Bishop."

"You look beautiful, by the way," he tentatively called out as I walked away.

I turned back and smiled for a second, then I took my little ones by the hand and kept on walking. My heart was racing. I wanted to go back and demand him to take me up in his arms and stop with all this nonsense, but I didn't. I figured his legs worked just as well as mine and he would come after me if he really wanted to. But he didn't.

As we spent the day with his parents, I could tell we all kept waiting for him to show up, but he never did. I think his mom was finally starting to get that this was his deal and not mine. Jack was now open with his feelings for me. It was like he could finally come out of the closet and admit that he had liked, and maybe even loved, me all along. I also made him a photo book of the kids, like Michael's, and the kids got him lots of items that were inscribed with "World's Greatest Grandpa." He loved them all. We had such a good day, we even stayed for dinner.

I helped Danielle prepare dinner while Papa rode the grandkids around on his riding lawnmower. At first, it was only polite conversation, nothing heavy or meaningful, but eventually she began to ask me about me. She was interested to know about my parents, and how I dealt with the tragedy of the bombing that took their lives. She asked about my sister, whom she had only met at our wedding. We, of course, talked about the baby and her son. She was more than concerned.

"Do you think drugs or alcohol are to blame?" she asked worriedly.

"I don't think so."

"Maybe he's depressed and he needs to see a doctor or counselor," she suggested.

That kind of made sense in my mind. I shrugged my shoulders. "Maybe."

"Do you think it's someone else?" she asked delicately.

"I asked and he adamantly denied it."

"Do you believe him?" she asked hesitantly.

I stood at the stove, stirring the gravy. "I want to believe him. I guess if I didn't, I would have already filed for divorce."

She stopped slicing the ham for a moment. "*Are* you going to file for divorce?"

I shrugged my shoulders. "We said we wouldn't talk about it until after the baby was born, but I don't know how much longer I can hold on."

"Don't give up just yet," she pleaded.

"I thought perhaps you would be happy if we got divorced," I responded cautiously.

She set down the knife she was using. I thought maybe I shouldn't have said that to her with a knife in her hand. But she approached me, knifeless. I wasn't sure what to do. She looked unsure, too. It was like awkwardness squared. She took the gravy off the stove and took my hands in hers. She was a tiny little thing, a few inches shorter than me. She had to look up at me.

"Carly, I'm sorry. I should have said that a long time ago. I've watched you these past few months, and I'm in awe of you."

The tears came, but this time they were happy tears.

"If I were you, I would have walked away by now, but I hope you don't. My son needs you."

"I just want him to want me."

She freaked me out a bit and hugged me. I was hesitant at first to respond, but I thought, *What the heck*. She was my mother-in-law, after all, and she really did seem to mean well. And I was serious when I said I could use a mother. As we were embracing, the rug rat brigade came in, with Papa following. My father-in-law took in the scene before him and smiled. Danielle and I moved apart and went back to preparing dinner like nothing happened. But, inwardly, I was smiling. If anything good had come out of this sad mess, this was it.

Michael never showed up at his parent's house, but when I got home, there was a surprise for me on the kitchen counter. There sat a very large bouquet of peach roses in a vase. I carefully picked up the card that was attached and opened it.

Dear Carly,

Thank you for being the mother of my children.

When life settles down, I promise to plant a peach rose bush in your garden.

Love,

Bishop

It wasn't as heartwarming as his cards had been in the past, but I wasn't going to complain at this point. I held his words to my heart and breathed in the smell of the roses deeply. I could hold on a little bit longer, right?

Once I got the kids settled into bed, I called Michael to thank him for the roses. He was at the airport waiting to fly to Chicago. He had never traveled this much. I think it was wearing on him, he sounded tired.

"Are you okay?"

"Yes. This is just life," he responded gruffly.

"Are you still meeting us at the beach this weekend?" I asked cautiously.

"I'm going to try, Carly. I really don't like you driving down there with the kids all by yourself."

"Then take the week off and come with us."

"I can't right now."

"Can't or won't?"

"Carly, my work schedule is insane right now. I don't have a choice."

I sighed.

"If I want to stay relevant and stay on top, this is the price that has to be paid."

"Michael, there are other options."

"Like what?"

"Well, my business is doing really well. I could take on more clients or we could start using my trust fund until you found something else."

"Those aren't options in my mind."

"Why?"

"Carly, I can provide for my family."

"Of course you can, no one is discounting that. But, Michael, at what expense? We need *you* more than we need your paycheck."

He was silent for a moment. I could picture him pinching the bridge of his nose or rubbing his cheek.

"Carly, I don't want to keep having this discussion with you. This is the way it has to be."

I went to interrupt because that was dumb. It wasn't the way it had to be, but he plowed on, not letting me get in a word edgewise.

"I'll search the best routes for you and the kids to drive down and email them to you. Make sure you take the Triple A card and I'll try and meet you there Friday night."

I sighed inwardly. He was being a stubborn fool. With him, it was like one step forward and ten steps back.

"Bishop, in case I haven't said it, or expressed it lately, thanks for providing for our family. And…I really do love you." I couldn't help but say it. I knew it wouldn't be returned, but for some reason I couldn't understand, I still loved him and wanted him.

"I'll call you tomorrow. Goodnight, Carly."

I was becoming a masochist I thought, as I hung up with him. I lay down on the bed and placed my hand on the baby growing inside of me. I felt a slight movement on the outside. I smiled, but just as quickly, I was saddened because I had no one to share it with.

"What do you think I should do, little one?" I said out loud.

No response.

"I don't know what to do, either."

So I went to bed and prayed tomorrow would be better and that my husband would get his head out of his butt. Okay, maybe I said it a little nicer, but in essence that's what needed to happen.

I spent the next two days packing for our trip. We were leaving Wednesday and I couldn't wait to hit the sand and water. Michael sent me a myriad of emails and texts reminding me of things I should bring and what the best and safest routes were. My favorite was the sunscreen reminder.

"It's almost as if you care about me," I texted.

"I do care about you," he texted back.

"Just checking the emergency broadcast system," I replied.

"Keep you and the kids safe."

"I always do."

And I did keep us safe all the way there, even among the myriads of bathroom stops for me and the kids and the constant nagging question, "When are we going to be there?" and a clean-up in the back seat. Mia got car sick. By the time we got to the condo, we were all more than ready to be out of the car. I had to hold them back, though, from running to the beach. I told them we had to unpack first and, of course, put sunscreen on. Oh, and I promised Michael I would let him know we made it there safely.

"Made it here with the sunscreen. Might have left a child at a rest stop, but other than that, it was uneventful." I texted.

"I'm glad to hear you made it there safely. Thanks for the laugh. I needed it."

"Anytime. Everything okay?"

"Yep."

"Alright. See you Friday."

I hoped and prayed he would actually make it. His track record stunk lately. But regardless, this was just what the doctor ordered. As soon as my bare feet hit the sand and I took in the sea air, I immediately felt my spirits lift. The kids and I spent the first afternoon building a sand castle and making new friends. There were plenty of kids to play with. One of the dads even chatted me up. I think he said his name was Tim Kearns. He was staying a couple of doors down from us. He had twins that were ten, a boy and a girl. The girl was very nice to Mia and helped her collect shells and clams. The boy played Frisbee with Ashton.

All in all, it was a lovely afternoon. I only wished it was my husband I was talking to and not a stranger. The guy was nice and all, but I missed my husband. I had never vacationed without him since we had been married. It seemed dumb, seeing as I used to travel the world by myself, but once we were married, I could never dream of doing that without him, but here I was. I had to remind myself to be happy and that this may be my future reality that I would have to deal with.

After a few hours, I was ready to go in. My back was a little sore, and I stretched as I got up. I guess it showed off my bump in my short sun dress.

"Oh, you're pregnant," my new-found friend remarked. He immediately acted embarrassed. "I'm sorry. I shouldn't have said that, but please tell me you're really pregnant."

I laughed at his reaction. "You're in luck. I'm about five months pregnant."

I called Ashton and Mia to me.

"I really am sorry, my wife told me to never ask a woman if she's pregnant."

I looked down at his red face. "That's very good advice. Is your wife here with you?"

His shoulders dropped while he looked over to his children. "My wife passed away last year," he said quietly.

"Oh. I'm so sorry."

"This is our first vacation without her."

"I'm sure it's difficult for you."

I could feel for him. I mean, my husband hadn't died, even though it kind of felt like it, but, I could understand being alone in a situation where you were used to being with your partner.

He looked back toward me. "It's been a rough eight months, but we're managing."

My kids joined me, and his children joined him.

"Well, I'm sure we'll see you around," I said.

I didn't want to talk about death around the kiddos. We gathered our chairs, towels, and little cooler and headed back to our condo on the beach. Tim offered to carry the chairs, but I told him I had it covered. We all waved goodbye.

As we walked toward our cute little bright green condo, I decided we were ordering in food. I was tired from the drive and the sun. The kids must have been tired, too, because after I fed and bathed them, they both crashed. The condo had two bedrooms, and I put them in a room together. I wasn't sure what the sleeping arrangements would be when Michael got there. I knew what I wanted them to be; we hadn't shared a bed in three months. I sighed.

I took advantage of the quiet time and went out onto the deck, soaked in the gorgeous view, and reveled in the sound of the ocean crashing against the shore. I also pulled out my tablet and caught up on my reading. I had been trying to make sure I read all of Michael's pieces. He had been reporting on everything from political candidates and policy to medical research and breakthroughs. They were all well-written and executed, but I noticed how edgy he was becoming. He had been that way when we first met, but he had toned it down. Now he was edgier than ever, and I wasn't sure what to think about it.

As I was pondering, he called. As per his usual, he asked first to talk to the kids.

"They're asleep. Do you want to call back in the morning?" I asked.

"Sure, but first tell me how you're doing."

Uh, I thought. *Real concern?*

"I'm on the beach watching the sunset, so I'm good. How are you?"

"Not as good as you."

"Well, there's an empty seat with your name on it next to me."

"I'm going to try, Carly."

Before I could reply, our new friends walked by. "You and the kids should come out and crab hunt with us," Tim yelled out to me.

"Can you hold on, Bishop?"

I yelled back that the kids were already in bed, but to enjoy.

"Who are you talking to?"

"Oh, we met some of our neighbors today on the beach. He was just inviting us to go crab hunting with his kids."

"Did you say he?"

"Yeah. It's really sad, his wife died of cancer last year and he's here with his ten-year-old twins. I think he said they're from Wisconsin. His son and daughter were really great with Ashton and Mia today."

"So you hung out with him all day?"

"No. Why do you sound so accusatory?"

"Does he know you're married?"

I started laughing. "Bishop, I'm five months pregnant with two children in tow. No one is looking at me on the beach, or anywhere else for that matter."

"Carly, you're so naïve about how attractive you are and about men."

I was still laughing at him.

"And it's not safe for a woman who's alone to be talking to strange men. I knew this trip wasn't a good idea."

I stopped laughing. "Fine. You know what, if it will make you feel better, I'll tell everyone here that I'm married. And then when they ask me where my husband is or why he's not with us, I'll tell them that we don't actually live together and you don't love me. Will that make you feel better?" I didn't wait for his response. "Oh... and just so you know, I've always kept my marriage vows and will to the bitter end. And I haven't even looked at another man since the day I met you, Bishop!"

He chuckled.

"I'm glad you find this amusing."

"No, just you."

Oh, he was irritating me. "Goodnight, Bishop."

"Hey..." he said before I could hang up on him.

"What?"

"I'll see you Friday."

"I'll believe it when I see it."

Though Michael's insinuations bothered me, they gave me pause. I wondered if I had given the wrong impression to Tim. I just assumed everyone knew I was married. After all, I wore a wedding ring and the whole kids and pregnancy thing should scream, *I'm unavailable.* But I also found it hypocritical that my husband who, for all intents and purposes, had left me, wanted to make sure other men knew I was married. Not that I was looking, or wanted anyone else but him, but it kind of irked me. Regardless, I intended to be careful, just in case. I wasn't going to do it because of Michael, but because I believed marriage was sacred, even if we weren't technically together.

I didn't even have to worry about it the next day. We didn't see our neighbors as we enjoyed the beach and playing in the ocean. Friday was rainy, so we went inland to find our fun. We caught a movie and toured the kid's museum. All day I kept wondering if Michael would really show up. I didn't even tell the kids it was a possibility; I didn't want them to be disappointed again. I didn't want to be disappointed either, so I refrained from calling or texting him all day. I figured, if he showed up, great. If not, there was nothing I could do about it.

I put the kids to bed that night a little sullen. As much as I wanted to be okay with it, I wasn't. He hadn't called, but I was done chasing him. As the night wore on, I became more than sullen—I felt like the raging weather outside. I sat on my bed, listening to the rain beat against the outside walls and windows and watching Mother Nature's light show. Michael loved stormy nights. There was something romantic about a storm, and we'd had our share of romance during many a storm, but those thoughts only added heat to my rage. How could he just throw away everything we had shared? No marriage was perfect, but I had loved ours.

I wasn't sure how long I had been stewing, but when I looked at the clock it was one in the morning. I cursed him for keeping me up so late, and for letting me down again. I wanted to call him and let him have it, but I didn't even think he would care. The baby must have been in a mood, too, it was like he or she was doing somersaults in the womb. I lay still and felt the movements in my body while I tried to let the anger go. I relaxed enough to begin to drift off. That's when my phone's text alert went off. I grabbed the phone and thought, *I'm going to kill him!* First his insensitivity kept me up, and now he had woken me up.

"I'm here," the text read.

To make sure I wasn't hallucinating, I sat up and read the text one more time. After I had assured myself it was real, I crept quietly to the front door and opened it. There he stood, soaked and carrying his luggage.

"I know it's not Friday, but I don't want to hear about it. Just getting here was beyond miserable," were the first words out of his mouth. He didn't even move to come in out of the rain.

I stood there in one of his old t-shirts, not sure what to say to that reception. I hardly even recognized him anymore. He basically looked the same, but his countenance was hardened. He never used to talk to me like that, even when he'd been frustrated. I responded by not saying anything. I started to shut the door. I didn't want him like this, and he so clearly didn't want to be here. The last thing I saw before the door closed were his widened baby blues.

As soon as the door closed, he turned the knob and opened it and walked in. I turned and walked back to bed. I wasn't in any mood to deal with him, especially like this. I guessed he was staying, because I heard his luggage drop to the floor and the door lock. I crawled back into bed and pulled the covers up and let the tears trickle down my cheeks. After a few minutes, there was a knock on my door.

"Hey, Carly," he said as he opened my door.

I wiped my cheeks as he approached my bed and knelt next to it. He was still in his wet suit and tie. His hair was even dripping water on the tiled floor. I lay there with my head on the pillow facing him, trying to see something of the person I loved.

"I'm sorry I'm late. Is that better?" he said gently.

I attempted a smile. "Yes, but I would have added on, 'You're a sight for sore eyes' or maybe 'You look beautiful.'"

He laughed quietly. "You *are* sight for sore eyes and you do look beautiful in my t-shirt I've been searching for."

"Do you want it back?"

"No, it looks way better on you."

I managed a real smile. "I'm glad you're here."

He looked confused as to what he should say, but he ran his finger down my cheek. "Where should I sleep?"

That shouldn't have been a question. "Well you could move Mia in with me and you can sleep with Ashton, or you could sleep on the couch. Or…" I paused and bit my lip. "You could stay in here with me."

His whole countenance registered consternation. I could tell he was torn, and it caused me to be torn up inside. Why didn't he want me anymore? I had kept up my physical appearance both inside and out. So I was pregnant, but the last two times I was pregnant he always told me how beautiful my body was to him.

"I promise I won't bite," I said after a minute of dead air.

He smiled and kissed my forehead. His lips lingered for several seconds, like he was still trying to decide. "Yeah, but I might. I'll just take the couch," he said when his lips left my skin.

Chapter Nine

I WOKE THE KIDS UP QUIETLY THE NEXT MORNING. I DIDN'T WANT THEM TO wake up their daddy. All I needed was him grumpy, because admittedly, I was a little grumpy from the lack of sleep and an overdose of rejection. I quietly sang, "A Spoon Full of Sugar Helps the Medicine Go Down" in my best Mary Poppins's voice. It helped my mood significantly, as did the sweet faces that belonged to me.

As soon as they were coherent, they asked if we would be able to go to the beach. I got up and pulled open their curtains to show them that the sun was shining. They began to cheer. I quickly went back to their bed and hushed them.

"I have a surprise for you, but you have to be very quiet after I tell you. Okay?"

They nodded their heads yes.

"Okay." I smiled. "Your daddy's here."

Mia squealed. I picked her up. "Shhh. He's sleeping, silly. We don't want to wake him up."

"Okay," she whispered back through her big grin.

I looked at Ashton. "Are you excited to have your dad here, little man?"

He thought about it for a minute. "Do you think he'll take me out on my boogie board?"

I stroked his beautiful blond hair. "I'm sure he will, but let's give him some time to rest first."

He smiled at me, before I pulled him into a Mia-and-Ashton group hug with Mommy. We all quietly got ready by putting on our bathing suits. To my ensemble I added my new cream lace cover-up. I looked in the mirror and swore I looked more pregnant than I did the day before, despite the black swim suit. I guess it was inevitable. I fed the kids and packed the cooler.

I kept looking over at Michael on the couch. He hadn't even stirred. I'm sure he was exhausted, and I almost felt sorry for him. He had to fly into Atlanta and then drive down here in the pouring rain. I guess his flight had been delayed. He looked so peaceful, and a lot like my Bishop. I fought the urge to go to his side and run my hands through his dark mop and kiss his lips. Instead, I wrote him a note and told him we would be at the beach and there were eggs in the fridge and wheat bread, just like he liked.

The kids and I set up our chairs and umbrella. We slathered on the sunscreen and commenced our day in the sun. I could still smell the rain from the previous day. It was a lovely scent mixed in with the salt air. *I could seriously live down here*, I thought. It was a great morning too; we mostly had the beach to ourselves. It was an hour before it started to fill up around us. Our new-found friends set up next to us.

Tim was in awe of the storm from the previous day.

"There's nothing like a southern thunderstorm," I said.

"Agreed." He smiled at me nervously and ran his fingers through his rust colored hair. "My kids and I are planning to take a dolphin tour later. Would you like to join us?"

I was about to decline, but I didn't have to. My husband arrived and hovered over us. Tim looked up at him, unsure of why this guy was standing there glaring at him.

I looked up to Michael and then back to Tim. "Tim this is…"

"Michael, Carly's husband." Michael wasn't amused at all. He looked threatening standing there.

Tim looked flustered.

Michael grabbed the chair on my right and placed it on my left in between Tim and me. He sat down and kissed my cheek. "Good morning."

"Good morning, Bishop," I smirked.

He looked over to Tim. "My wife and I have other plans for the day."

I was a little embarrassed by Michael's territorial behavior considering he'd spent the night on the couch. Tim was red with embarrassment, too. So maybe Michael was right. Tim didn't stay around too much longer, and

Michael got an evil grin on his face. We didn't get to talk about it, though, because the kids barraged him with hugs and kisses.

They begged their daddy to come play with them and to take them into the water.

"I'll be right there. Give me a minute to talk to Mommy and put some sunscreen on."

They happily went back to digging in the sand.

Bishop looked my way all smug. "Do you see what I mean?"

"What are you talking about?"

"That guy was totally coming on to you."

"He was asking the kids and me to go on a boat."

"All while looking you up and down."

"Bishop, I look like a beached whale." I rubbed my ever expanding mid-section. "I think I grew overnight."

He looked me over closely, leaned closer and smiled. "Yet, you still have one of the best bodies out here."

I rolled my eyes. "You know you're a big hypocrite, right?"

He grinned and handed me the sunscreen.

"Fine, come and sit in front of me. I'd just as soon let you burn, but I don't want to hear you complain for the next two days."

He sat in front of me and removed his shirt. I took a deep breath. I know it sounds dumb, but I loved his back. He had a strong, muscular back. Not like a body builder or anything like that; it was masculine and it looked like it could bear weight. And I had always loved the way my hands felt across his skin. I poured the sunscreen in my hands and lightly approached his back. At first touch, I felt him tense up. It had been too long since we had touched in such a way. As I began to rub in the lotion, I could feel him relax at my touch.

"How's the baby?" he asked.

"Active. I think we may have another soccer player on our hands."

As I made it to his shoulders and neck, he commented, "You know it wouldn't hurt my feelings if you rubbed my neck. I think I slept on it wrong."

Now he was pushing it.

"Ha." I closed the lid to the sunscreen and handed it back up to him. "I think you can get the rest."

He turned his head toward me, grinning. "So that's a no on the back rub?"

I began to shake my head at him, but I noticed his hair. "Did you dye your hair?"

He turned away from me and ran his fingers through his dark locks.

"Well…you know, I was just trying to get rid of the gray."

I stroked the back of his hair. "I liked the gray."

He looked back to me again with a questioning gaze.

I shrugged my shoulders slightly. "I found it quite sexy, but I'm guessing your girlfriend doesn't."

He turned all the way toward me. "I don't have a girlfriend."

"Just checking." I turned from his gaze and grabbed my novel. "Have fun with the kids." I threw on my shades, laid my chair back, waved at the kids and then smiled at my husband.

He grinned and left me to enjoy my book.

Once in a while I would peek up and watch the people that I loved more than life. It was way more interesting than the cheesy romance novel I brought with me. I loved seeing them play together and laugh and have fun. It was as if, for a moment, my Bishop had returned. I was also reminded why I was so attracted to him. He was a man's man; rugged, with hair on his chest, and his always slightly-grown-in beard was completely swoon-worthy. Just watching him pick up the kids and run with them both in his arms reminded me that this was what I wanted my kids to have. My dad was a great guy, but he was a very genteel sort of man, that was absent a lot. I had never even been camping until after I was married. Bishop laughed at me the whole trip because of my lack of experience. I wanted my kids to have a dad that would play with them in the backyard and teach them about sports and take them fishing and camping, but also someone that would tell them stories and hold them when they were frightened, someone that would kiss owies better. Bishop had been the best of both worlds until last year. Now he, too, was absent.

In the midst of my reflection I was bombarded by kiddos pulling on my hands. "Daddy says you should be playing with us, too," they said in stereo.

I looked up and saw Bishop motioning to me with his finger to join him. I set my book down and braved taking off my cover-up. I looked down. Yep, I was definitely pregnant. As I walked toward him, he lowered his sunglasses and eyed me.

"See, beached whale," I said.

"I was thinking more like beach babe," he replied.

I rolled my eyes at him, but I liked that he actually looked at me. We then proceeded to have the best day we had had in forever. Michael set up a game of seashell toss. We played that until the kids got bored. By that time, it was time for lunch anyway. We picnicked on the beach. Michael took Ashton out on his boogie board while Mia and I worked on a princess castle. The boys eventually joined us and stormed the castle, adding alligators and motes.

If anyone were to look at us, they would think, *happy family*. And at that moment, we were. I didn't know if it was temporary, or the start of working our way back to a permanent state of happy. I tried not to over think it and enjoy the day, but each time I looked at my husband, it was hard not to think about it. I hoped he could see how much we loved him and needed him in our lives. As much as I loved our children, it didn't make up for what Michael took from me when he left.

Several times Michael caught me looking at him. I didn't turn away, and neither did he. Sometimes he smiled, and other times he looked thoughtful. I so badly wanted to know what he was thinking, but now wasn't the time to ask. Today was the kids' day.

By the time dinner rolled around, we were all beat. We gathered up all of our gear and headed back to the condo. Michael offered to barbecue while I bathed the kiddos. The kids relived their day to me like I hadn't been there. Daddy was the hero of the day, which was more than fine with me. He could play hero every day if he wanted to.

Ashton jumped in the shower first, while I lay on the bed with Mia while she talked a mile a minute about the waves that daddy saved her from or how he made the best castle tops, which I think translated into turrets.

"Does this mean Daddy is coming home to live with us?" she asked.

Her question saddened me. "I don't know," I said honestly. "But let's not worry about it this weekend, sweetie." I didn't want anything to put a damper on these fleeting moments we had with him.

By the time both kids were done, Michael was back from the store and getting ready to start dinner.

"Can I help?" I asked.

He looked up from the grocery bag he was emptying. "The kids and I have it covered. Why don't you just relax?"

So that's what I did. I took a long shower and took my time getting ready. I gloried in the alone time and the co-parenting. Once I removed myself from the much needed shower, I found I didn't need much makeup at all. Mother Nature had done her job admirably. I was so happy to feel normal again, well as normal as you can feel when you're growing a human inside of you. I threw on a white stretchy tee that showed off my tan and some shorts and joined my family.

It smelled fabulous when I entered the kitchen area. They were all out on the deck. I could see the kids setting the patio table for dinner and Michael at the grill. I had missed seeing him at the grill this summer. He used to grill almost every night in the warm summer months. He was a master at it. I wondered if he missed it. I wondered if he missed us. I stood and stared for a moment before I slid the glass door open. I knew I missed him.

I stepped out and Michael turned toward me.

"Hi," I said. Why did I feel so nervous?

He smiled and looked me over from head to toe. "You look great."

"Thanks. Dinner smells wonderful. What are we having?"

As he opened the grill, the kids asked me to admire their handiwork; they were excited to point out the floral arrangement that sat in the middle.

I looked back to Michael. "What's the occasion?"

He almost seemed embarrassed. "Do I need one to buy my wife flowers?"

I smiled and cautiously moved closer to him. I kissed his cheek. "Thank you." For a moment our eyes locked, and for a moment I could see desire in his eyes, but he quickly turned from me, back to the shrimp and corn on the cob and what looked like grilled peaches.

"You're welcome," he mumbled.

I almost laughed at the ridiculousness of his actions. It was almost as if he had to try and not want me, like he had to remind himself to keep his distance. No matter, I joined the kids who were not afraid to show their affection for me. We all sat and waited anxiously for the food. I was starving. I think the baby was, too; I felt a good kick.

"Do you want to try and feel the baby?" I asked my kiddos. They hadn't been able to yet, so they eagerly came to my side. I grabbed their small hands and placed them where I thought they would be able to feel it. Ashton felt it first and smiled, and then Mia felt it and the whole beach knew.

Michael snapped at her for being so loud, and she burst into tears. She didn't do well when anyone found fault in her, whether it was warranted or not. Unfortunately, this was unwarranted. I looked at him and didn't say anything, but he knew I wasn't pleased.

"You're mean," Ashton shouted at his dad.

I was shocked, to say the least, as I watched my sweet Ashton run in. I picked up my still-crying Mia and handed her to her daddy, who stood there stunned and apparently speechless. I ran in after Ashton. Things had been going so well, and I wanted that to continue, but I wasn't sure how to smooth this over. I wasn't sure how to help my Ashton, who was obviously hurting. Clearly, he wasn't sure how to deal with it. I found him on the bed, crying.

I sat next to him and stroked his hair that now, thanks to the sun, looked platinum. "Ashton."

He looked up at me with a tear-stained face. I loved his little face that wasn't so little anymore. His eyes continued to make sure he got anything he asked for, just like his dad. The first thing that drew me to Michael was his eyes. He gifted those baby blues to our son.

"Mommy," he said.

He never called me Mommy anymore. I lay down next to him so that our faces were barely inches apart. I kept stroking his cheeks, waiting for him to speak. I didn't know what to say anymore. I wanted to make it all better. I wanted an extra-large Band-Aid to fix our family, but I was pretty sure they didn't make one that size.

"You looked pretty great on that boogie board today. I think you're ready for the boogie board championship."

"There's no such thing, Mom." But at least he smiled.

"You're probably right. How about a sand castle competition?"

"Mom, you're silly."

"I'm being serious. I think we could go all the way with your sand alligator."

He sniffled some and snuggled into me. I knew this wasn't going to last too much longer, so I relished holding him close to me, even if the circumstances weren't ideal.

"I love you, Ashton Michael Bishop."

"I love you, Mom."

Our moment was interrupted.

"Carly, can I talk to Ashton?"

I sat up and pulled Ashton up with me. Michael stood at the door, holding Mia. Her little arms clung tightly around his neck, with her head against his shoulder. He carried her like she weighed nothing. I could barely carry her at all anymore.

"Sure," I replied.

I kissed Ashton's head and squeezed him once more before pushing myself off the soft queen-sized bed with the hideous floral patterned comforter. I walked toward the door that was filled by the other half of our family. Michael kissed Mia's cheek and went to set her down, but she still held on.

I held out my arms. "Come here, Mia."

"Mia, Mommy shouldn't be holding you right now with the baby, can you please stand up like a big girl and go with her?" Michael asked gently.

She reluctantly dropped to the floor and took my hand, all in a dramatic fashion, like it was tortuous to have to walk. I had a feeling she was going to grow up to be a little bit of a drama queen. I looked at Michael before I left with little Miss. I wanted to warn him to tread lightly, but I felt like I didn't need to by the obvious look of regret on his face.

"I'm sorry," he said.

"We'll wait for you boys outside," I responded.

"We won't be long."

Mia filled me in on the way outside. "Daddy said he was sorry and that he was just tired. Then he let me take the peaches off the grill," she added excitedly. We reached the deck, and she was easily distracted by the sail boats. She switched gears on me. "Can we go on a boat?'

"Not this year, baby."

"Aww."

Thankfully she seemed to get over her disappointment quickly.

I grabbed a shrimp and ate it. I was still starving, and my body was demanding food.

The boys were only a few minutes before they came out with Michael's arm around Ashton. Ashton was cautiously smiling. It didn't quite reach his eyes, but he seemed settled. The table was square, so Michael sat across from me, and the kids were in between. I glanced at Michael as soon as he was seated. He looked troubled and confused. I couldn't help but want to make him feel better, no matter what he was putting us all through.

"Are you okay?" I mouthed.

"Let's eat. I'm hungry," he said out loud. He completely ignored my question.

The kids both agreed and began reaching for the delectable food that was at arm's reach. As I filled my plate, I continued to look Michael's way. He was doing his best to not look at me.

"I want to bless the food," Mia yelled out.

Michael and I both agreed that she could, even though we knew we would be eating much later. She had a tendency to thank God for everything, which was a good thing normally, but not when your blood sugar was steadily dropping. Tonight's prayer even included the little guppies she saw in the water. But heartbreakingly she asked God to please let daddy come home. I couldn't help it. I opened my now blurry eyes. Michael's were open too, and looking at mine. I think if he could have gracefully exited, he would have. He was uncomfortable as he watched me wipe at my eyes. I didn't hear what else Mia rattled on about, but I didn't want the kids to see I had been crying. Michael chose to ignore me again and closed his eyes.

I looked up to the sky and begged to know what to do. I was so tired of this.

Dinner tasted wonderful, but I had been hoping for a much more relaxed and fun atmosphere in which to enjoy it. I let the kids and Michael direct the conversation. I tried to be lighthearted and happy when I addressed my kiddos, but I was tired of trying to hold it together and keep up the brave face. I was almost glad dinner was over quickly.

I began grabbing dishes as soon as it was over and walking them back to the kitchen.

"I've got it covered," Michael said.

"Why don't you take the kids out for ice cream or something?"

"Okay…if that's what you want."

I nodded my head yes.

With the promise of ice cream, it took the kids all of two seconds to slip on their sandals and run to the door.

Michael kept looking between me at the sink and the kids at the door like he didn't know what he should do. "Are you sure you don't want to come with us?" he asked.

"I'm sure. You guys have fun."

"Do you want me to bring you back anything?"

I shook my head no.

The kids were clamoring to leave, but for some reason Michael still looked undecided. I wanted to be alone. I could feel my eyes burning. I wanted to cry in peace. He started to walk to the door, but he quickly changed his mind and came back toward me. I set down the pan I was starting to rinse off. Now I was confused.

He lightly brushed my cheek with his lips. I could barely feel the roughness of his ever present facial growth. The tears didn't wait. A single tear leaked from the corner of my eye. I turned back to the pan and did my best to contain the rest.

"I'll see you guys later," I said overly cheerful.

"We won't be long," Michael replied.

I couldn't look at him. If I did, there would be no stopping the flood that was begging to be let loose. As soon as they left and the door shut, it was like the dam burst. I leaned over the sink and let it all out. In the midst of the anguished cries and heaving, I prayed for strength and courage. Courage to do what, I wasn't sure. Should it be to stay or to walk away?

Chapter Ten

After ten minutes or so, I calmed down enough to finish the dishes and clean the kitchen. As soon as I was finished, I made a beeline for my room. I needed to hide the evidence of my moment of weakness. I was becoming a pro at it. I kept eye drops that got rid of redness handy at all times. I also applied a cool washcloth to my eyes. By the time they returned, I was sitting contentedly on the couch reading my book. I was all smiles as they walked in and greeted me.

Michael directed the kiddos to go and get ready for bed, then he joined me on the couch, pulling out, from behind his back, a chocolate milkshake. "It still looks like you could stand to gain some weight. Doctor's orders, right?"

I smiled and took the Styrofoam cup from his hand. "Thank you." I didn't delay in tasting the sweet treat. It really was what the doctor ordered. I felt better instantly. Or maybe it was the concern and love my husband was showing me that made me feel better. I was guessing the latter.

He smiled. "Is it good?"

"It's perfect. Do you want to try some?" I leaned the cup toward him.

He grinned and took a small sip before standing back up. "You stay here and finish that and I'll put the kids to bed."

"Deal," I said between sips.

Within minutes my pajama-clad kiddos were kissing and hugging me goodnight before marching off to bed. I sat there on the couch and listened to them giggle while enjoying the rest of my shake. Michael always made any story come to life when he read it out loud.

After half an hour, he returned and paused in the hallway that led to the living area. He looked good standing there with his tanned arms and legs peeking out of his cargo shorts and t-shirt. It was like neither of us knew what to do now. It was so sad; months ago there wouldn't have been any question what to do on vacation after the kids were asleep. But now, here we were being all first-date awkward, looking at one another like unsure, pimple-infested teenagers.

I took a deep breath. "Do you still want that backrub?" What was I thinking? Was I just begging him to reject me again?

His eyes narrowed, and he slightly bent his head. He hurried over like if he thought about it anymore, he would chicken out. He sat in front of me, nestled between my legs and threw off his shirt.

Nice, I thought.

I handed him the TV remote. "Choose whatever you want." I went to work on his tense and knotted back and neck. I started at the small of his back and at first touch his body broke out in goose bumps. *I still have the touch*, I thought. I didn't linger long in that area, I knew he carried all of his stress in his shoulders and neck, so that's where I spent a majority of my time. As I kneaded and massaged his back, I held back the urge to kiss his neck and work my way forward. Instead, I tried to pay attention to the action movie he had found, but it was no use. Not even Robert Downey Jr. could help me keep my eyes and thoughts off of my husband. I could tell he was enjoying it, too, and perhaps his mind was elsewhere.

After several minutes he reached up and grabbed my hands. "I think that will do it."

He quickly threw his shirt back on. I couldn't help it. I laughed a little. This was so dumb. We were married, after all. I remember when I was the shy, coy one—the one that had to tell him no, that I was waiting for marriage and there was no way he could persuade me. He couldn't believe he had met such an "old-fashioned" girl, but I sweetly remember him telling me on our wedding night how honored he was and how much he admired my innocence.

"Why are you laughing?" he asked from the other side of the couch where he was now sitting.

I shook my head and picked up my book again. "Nothing at all, Bishop."

I went back to reading. It was apparently the only romance I would be getting tonight and maybe forever. But as I read, I could feel his eyes on me, which made it hard to concentrate. It was also show time for the baby. I knew this kid was going to come out with his or her days and nights mixed up. *Something to look forward to,* I thought. Actually, I *was* looking forward to it. I ached to feel that baby in my arms. As the baby put on its nightly gymnastic routine, I shifted to find a more comfortable position.

"Are you alright?"

"Oh yes, this is the baby's favorite time of day."

He moved closer to me. I set my book down and looked over. He seemed hesitant. He reached out toward my midsection. "Do you mind?"

I took his hand, which still bore the simple white gold band I placed on it over ten years ago, and positioned it to where he would most likely feel the movements. I kept my hand resting on top of his as we waited. It didn't take long for him to feel his baby.

He smiled up at me. "This one packs a punch. I'm thinking boy."

I laughed. "I don't know, I've been thinking girl. She feels feisty, like Mia."

A sexy grin spread across his handsome face. "I don't know if the world can handle any more Bishop women."

"Are we really all that bad?"

The grin was gone, but the sexy was still there, as he leaned in closer and slid his hand across my abdomen and rested it on the other side of me. His face was now an inch from mine. I reached up and ran my hand across his cheek and held it there.

He moved closer and his lips were just about touching mine. "You have no idea," he said against my lips that ached to be one with his.

My heart was racing like it had the first time he had kissed me on the ski slopes in Breckenridge. The anticipation was palpable, and I was impatient. I had waited months for this. I closed the minute distance and let my lips rest upon his. That was all the invitation he needed. He parted my lips hungrily and urgently kissed me as I wrapped my hands up in his hair. For a moment, it was like he couldn't drink me in quick enough, and I gasped as soon as his lips finished with mine only to find their way to my neck. I reached behind his neck too, and pulled him closer.

As his lips explored every inch of my neck and face, I made a critical error.

"I love you, Bishop," I whispered.

He abruptly stopped and moved over. "We shouldn't be doing this," he said through staggered breathing.

I leaned back toward him, still breathing hard, as well. I took his face in my hands. "This is exactly what we should be doing."

I began to kiss his lips again. For a moment, he responded, but then he gently pushed me away. "Please stop, Carly."

I jumped up and looked down at him as he leaned forward, arms resting on his knees, his head down.

"I can't take this anymore. I'm done," I said.

He quickly looked up. "What do you mean, you're *done*?"

"I'm done chasing after you and telling you I love you and humiliating myself. If you want me, you're going to have to choose me."

"Don't you think if this was as simple as making a choice, I would have already done that?"

"It is as simple as that. Every day for the last eleven-and-a-half years I've chosen to love you. Through the good and the bad and everything in between, even these past months when you've been anything but lovable. But I'm at my wits' end. I don't know what I've done, but I don't deserve this." I was so angry I couldn't even cry. I stood there looking down at him as he stared up, not responding. I threw my hands up in the air and then hastily grabbed my book and marched out to the deck. I threw myself on a lounge chair and just focused on breathing in and out as I listened to the waves. I think I was forgetting what it was like not to feel stressed out, angry or hurt. I was trying so hard to just be okay and make it all okay for the kids, but this wasn't okay. I rested my book on my now built-in body shelf and closed my eyes. The only thing I tried to feel was the cool sea breeze as it drifted across me. It wasn't working well. I felt angry and confused. I thought more about my agreement with him to delay any divorce talk until after the baby was born, but I kept wondering if that was wise. It seemed inevitable at this point, and that thought made me cry.

I'm not sure how long I stayed out there, but I never ended up reading my stupid book. What was the point anyway? I knew the ending would be a manufactured "happy" ending. What the books never tell you is what happens after the story, the story where the husband grows tired of his wife and leaves her with three children and a broken heart. The story where the woman is left grappling for answers and pained with self-doubt and an overwhelming sense of loss and failure. Of course, they never made stories like that because who in their right mind would want to read such misery?

My back began to ache from the stiff chair, so I decided it was time to go to bed. I stood up, stretched, and looked over the now empty beach. I heard laughter and the clink of glasses coming from the couple above us. I quickly went in before I overheard anything else. I wasn't in the mood to hear the sound of happy couples. I walked in to find the only source of light on was the hall light. The T.V. was off and Michael was lying on the couch. I wasn't sure if he was asleep as his face was toward the back, but either way I wasn't going to say anything. I walked to bed *alone.*

I woke up to the sound of a blender. Without thinking, I rushed out of the bedroom with visions of food splattered everywhere, or worse, cut off fingers, but thankfully, no one was screaming. I came around the corner with my heart pounding to find Michael and the kids in the kitchen.

Mia was the first to see me. "Mommy!" She ran to me.

I carefully picked her up and snuggled her. "What are you doing up already?"

"I'm not supposed to tell you," she whispered conspiratorially.

"Okay," I whispered back. I kissed her cheek and set her down.

She ran off to her daddy and brother in the kitchen.

Michael looked my way from the sink. "Good morning," he said.

I ran my hand through my hair. "Good morning. What are you guys up to this morning?"

"You're ruining the surprise, Mom," Ashton said.

Michael winked at me. "Why don't you go back to bed?"

I got the hint and turned around and went right back to where I had come from. Okay, maybe not right back. I was pregnant, after all, and I think this baby lived on my bladder. After I was done in the bathroom, I crawled right back into bed and waited patiently. While I waited, I thought more about my husband and the situation I found myself in. When he behaved somewhat like his old self, like he was this morning, it confused me. I was having a hard time reconciling between his dual personalities. I felt like I didn't know what was real anymore.

It didn't take long for breakfast to arrive. Michael carried a tray with an egg-white omelet and toast with one of the white roses from the bouquet he bought last night. He looked so sweet as he approached me. Why couldn't we just be together? Ashton was carrying what looked like a strawberry smoothie of some sort, and Mia carried lemon water. Both my children were beaming. Michael lightly set down the tray on my shrinking lap and the kids placed each glass of liquid on my nightstand.

"For me?" I exclaimed. "I'm so surprised. Thank you!"

I wasn't fooling anyone, but I really was touched by the thoughtfulness. Michael directed the kids to go get their swimsuits on while he talked to me. He carefully sat near my legs on the bed as I dug into the yummy food.

"About last night..." he began.

I swallowed and looked up at him.

"Let's put a pin in it and discuss it when I get back from Birmingham. This is my last day here and I don't want to spoil it."

My shoulders dropped. "Bishop, I'm beginning to feel like a pin cushion." I pointed between the two of us. "We can't keep pushing this off."

He took my hand in his. "I know, and when I get back from this trip, you and I will talk and try to work this out. But for today, let's put it aside and enjoy our last day together on the beach."

Those charming eyes of his made me say and do the dumbest things. That's how I found myself on the beach, confused as ever, pretending that everything was grand. The kids definitely enjoyed the day with their daddy, so I guess my faking-it was worth it. I think Michael could tell, but I knew he was just relieved that he was once again off the hook.

After dinner, the kids quickly became upset when they realized it was time for daddy to leave. He was driving to Birmingham and would be gone again for most of the week. He was reporting on overcrowding in the prison system. It sounded riveting.

Mia begged him to stay and wouldn't let go of his neck. Ashton just stayed by my side, but his whole body reflected that of a sad boy, slumped shoulders and head down. It would be my job, once again, to help them through this. They hadn't behaved this way in some time, but this was the first time in months they had spent this much time with him. I think they thought everything would go back to normal, but unfortunately, this *was* the new normal.

Michael gave them hugs and kisses. "Be good and help your mommy." He came to me and kissed my forehead. He lingered for a moment. "I'll be back for the ultrasound on Friday."

I nodded my head.

"Please make sure you drive home carefully, use the maps I made, and call me or text me when you get home on Tuesday," he added.

I half-smiled. "Don't worry, we'll be fine."

"I do worry," he responded.

I wasn't sure why. Was it out of love or guilt?

Chapter Eleven

After Michael left, the fun factor fell sharply for the kids, but we trudged on. We only really had one more full day, anyway. On Monday, I spent a good portion of the day photographing them on the beach. I think they were getting sick of all my picture taking, but they had lots of years ahead of it. If I could capture every moment of the two of them, I would.

Half-way through the day, I noticed Tim and his children a ways down the beach. I was still a little embarrassed by that situation. I felt like I should apologize, so I took the kids for a walk down his way. He was definitely tentative in his behavior, and rightly so. After our awkward greeting, the kids all began to play together, which gave me the opportunity to say what I came to say.

He offered me a chair next to him, and I took it.

"I wanted to apologize if I gave you the wrong impression last week."

He turned a little red, but he smiled. "I'll admit, at first I assumed you were married, but then you never talked about a husband, so...," he paused, "I was just hoping you weren't."

I gave him an apologetic smile. "I'm sorry, I don't expect to be looked at like that, and to be honest my husband and I are separated, so it's hard for me to talk about him right now."

"Oh," he said. "How long have you been separated?"

"Too long."

"Any hope for reconciliation?"

I shrugged my shoulders and shook my head. "But, anyway, I apologize for his behavior and mine."

"You don't have anything to apologize for. I can understand your husband's reaction. I wouldn't have liked it at all if another man was attracted to my wife."

I blushed. It was time to go. I stood up.

He reached into his bag and pulled out a card and handed it to me. It was his business card. It looked like he owned an insurance agency.

"What's this for?"

"In case your husband doesn't realize what he has."

"Oh." I handed back the card. "I really am flattered, but no matter the state of my marriage, I love my husband, and I made vows I plan to keep."

He reluctantly took back the card. "I hope your husband figures out how lucky he is. And if not, I hope I meet you again."

I couldn't and didn't respond to that. I quickly grabbed Mia and Ashton and walked away as fast as I could. It wasn't that I was tempted, but staying any longer might have given the wrong impression to the very handsome insurance agent from Wisconsin.

What an odd vacation this turned out to be, I thought that night as I lay in bed. I was actually glad to be going home the next day. As I went to turn off the bedside lamp, Michael called. I wished he'd called earlier so he could talk to the kids, but I wasn't going to complain.

"Hi, Bishop."

"Hi," he sounded tired again.

"How was your day in prison?"

"Confining."

I laughed.

"Tell me about your day."

I wondered if I should tell him about Tim. "It was interesting. I'm ready to go home tomorrow."

"Did something happen?" he asked anxiously.

"We're all fine. It's just, you were right."

He chuckled. "Well, of course I was... What was I right about, again?"

"Men."

"I was right about... *Men*?"

I proceeded to tell him about my entire conversation with Tim.

"I should have punched that..."

"Language, Bishop."

"Come on, Carly. It's been almost twelve years, you can quit pretending to be offended by my foul mouth. Plus, it's warranted in this instance."

I laughed. "Fine, but don't swear around the kids."

"I knew you secretly liked it when I swore."

"Stop it. I do not."

He laughed at me.

"Anyway, I hope you don't think I elicited attention from him."

"Carly, the only thing you're guilty of is being gorgeous and a little naïve and maybe too friendly."

"I'll work on that," I teased.

"That would be helpful," he responded.

"Helpful?"

"Do you think this Tim is the first guy I've seen come on to you?"

"Yeah, they've been beating down my door."

"Believe me, some would have if I didn't set them straight."

"Who are you talking about?"

"Do you remember Dave?"

I thought for a second. "The guy that used to live next door to us?"

I hadn't thought about him in forever. He had already lived next door when we moved in five years ago. I thought he moved away about two years ago. I did remember him being friendly for the first few months, but after that he always seemed to avoid us. I never even thought about it until now.

"That's the one. I had to tell him if he didn't keep his eyes to himself, he and I were going to have a problem."

"What were you going to do, Bishop?"

"Never mind, I don't want to go overboard on the swearing…yet."

I laughed. "Thank you for your consideration."

He laughed, too.

In fact, we laughed a lot and talked a lot, more than we had together in months. He recounted several stories of the men he had apparently chased off on my behalf. I had no idea. After that, he bored me with the inner workings of the prison system and then we called it a night. I refrained from telling him I missed him or that I loved him. I meant what I said. He would be the next one to say those things. I was done chasing him.

We made it home without any puking or pulling over, so that's what I called a good trip. It was a pretty quiet affair, as both Mia and Ashton slept quite a bit. I think they were all worn out from their fun in the sun. I was worn out emotionally. I just wanted to have a direction and know where I should focus my attention, one way or the other. I know Michael said we would try and work it out when he got back, but I wasn't sure what that meant. I didn't know what we had to work out. I still didn't even understand why he left in the first place.

Our nightly phone calls continued. He would call the kids after dinner and then he would call me at bedtime after the kiddos were asleep. It was like he wanted my undivided attention, which I was happy to give. We didn't talk about anything of significance, other than Mia's birthday that was coming up in a few weeks. I was trying to decide on an American Girl party or a pool party. He suggested we do a pool party at his parents' house. And he said "we" so I agreed. I liked "we" a lot. Other than that, we talked a lot about his assignment. He hadn't been this open about his work in forever, so even though the subject matter was completely uninteresting to me, I was interested because he was.

He even solicited my advice on what angle he should come at it from. "What do you think would be the more compelling perspective, the prisoners, the taxpayers, or the jail keepers?"

I honestly thought none of the above, but I wouldn't say that to him. "Is there any way you can incorporate all three? This sounds like the kind of story where you need the complete picture, not just one angle."

He thought for a moment. "Hmm. I like that. I'll talk to my editor and see if I can turn this into more of an exposé."

"I look forward to reading it." And I really meant it. I was also looking forward to seeing him Friday morning. I didn't tell him that, but I was missing him like crazy. I felt like maybe he was starting to come back to me. He even called me using his Bluetooth as he drove home late Thursday night and he ended with, "I'll see you in the morning." If I wasn't mistaken, he sounded happy about it.

I woke up early to get the kids ready to take to my in-laws. Jack had every other Friday off, so the kids were going to be helping Papa in the garden. I also commenced the torture of drinking lots of water and holding it for the ultrasound. I swear a man made up that rule, because no woman in her right mind would think of such a thing.

Michael had a call with his editor that morning, so he was planning on meeting me at the doctor's office. I arrived at nine forty-five, fifteen minutes early, and I didn't see his truck anywhere, so I walked in out of the Georgia heat. I signed in and waited. I think I checked my phone every thirty seconds to see what the time was and if Michael texted. As ten approached, I texted him and asked if he was on his way. I thought maybe he got stuck in traffic or something. No response. Of course they had to be running on schedule, and I was called back at a minute past the hour.

"Can I call my husband real quick?" I asked the nurse before she took me back.

She smiled and nodded.

Still no answer.

"Don't worry. We'll bring him back to you as soon as he gets here," the sweet nurse said.

She set me up in the room, and I kept my phone in my hand while she took my blood pressure and pricked my finger and all of the other fun things I had done to me every four weeks. It was all made worse by my overly full bladder and the fact my husband was a no-show so far. I called one more time. Nothing.

It only took a few minutes before Dr. White arrived. "Are you ready to see that baby?" she asked.

I nodded. I was ready, but I wanted Michael by my side, like he had been for Ashton and Mia's ultrasounds. "Could you please have someone check one more time to see if Michael is here?" I practically begged before she got started.

She smiled at me sympathetically. "Of course."

Her nurse came back empty-handed.

Emma looked at me with knowing eyes.

I shrugged my shoulders. "I guess just go ahead." It wasn't fair for me to ask her to throw her schedule off because of my absentee husband.

Within a couple of minutes, I could see my baby on the screen. I kept reminding myself this was a happy occasion. I had been alone for this whole pregnancy, so why should today be any different? But I wanted it to be different. I was hoping Michael would finally get engaged and be happy about this baby we were bringing into the world. Our baby.

"Carly, did you still want to keep the sex unknown?" Dr. White asked.

I thought for a moment and went back and forth in my mind. I really did want to know. I wanted to plan, but I knew Michael's thoughts on the subject. But then I looked over at the empty chair in the room. "Actually, I do want to know."

She smiled. "Well, okay. You may want to start thinking pink."

"A girl," I said through tears and smiles.

"Yes, ma'am. Your little girl looks right on schedule and healthy," she responded.

That was the most important part.

"Could you please make two copies of the pictures and videos?" I hated having to do that, but my hopes from the week had been dashed with regards to Michael's intentions.

She looked at me sympathetically and agreed. She helped me up, told me she would see me in four more weeks, and that I should just keep doing what I was doing.

Yeah just keep doing what I'm doing, I thought. I hit the restroom and scheduled my next appointment. I left with bipolar feelings. On one hand, I was so happy about my little girl, and on the other hand, I was so furious with her father. He didn't even call or text.

As I walked out of the building and into the blinding light, I practically ran into a harried Michael. I took one look at him and glared. I kept on walking to my car.

He turned right around and caught my arm. "Carly."

I grabbed one of the packets containing the pictures and the DVD of the baby and slapped it against his mid-section. "Congratulations. It's a girl."

He took hold of the packet. "I thought we decided not to find out."

I turned and looked up at him. "Well, since there wasn't a *we* there, I decided I wanted to know." I marched off to my car, not giving him any time to respond. I wasn't sure what was hotter, the temperature or my temper.

As I walked toward my car, he easily caught up to me. "Carly, I'm sorry, I needed to…"

I stopped. "I don't want to hear your sorries anymore, and I don't care what you had to do. All you care about is yourself!"

That set his eyes on fire. He grabbed my hand. "Come with me."

He led me to his truck and opened up the passenger side door and helped me in. He slammed the door. He came around to his side and did the same. He turned on his truck and blasted the air.

"Why are we sitting here?"

"Because it's hot outside and I don't want to make a scene."

I went to respond, but he beat me to the punch. His eyes were still on fire and his hands were clenched. "How dare you call me selfish, Carly. For years I have been the laughingstock among my peers because of the crap assignments I've taken so I can play house with you. And now, finally, when I'm back on top of my game, I'm the selfish one."

Oh my gosh. Suddenly everything made sense. He resented me. All I could do for a moment was stare at his hardened and emboldened face. I could see the resentment clearly in his eyes. And as hard as I tried not to, tears filled mine. In an instant, the history of my marriage was rewritten.

"I'm so sorry, Michael. I had no idea. I thought you took those assignments because you loved me and the kids and that we were building a life and home together, not playing house."

His defiant expression never changed. It was almost as if he was happy to see me acknowledge how he had been feeling all along. But he didn't verbally respond, and I didn't know what else to say. It was like my life was suddenly a charade.

I reached for the door handle. "I've got to go and get the kids." They were all that were real to me at the moment, and I needed them.

"Carly, I was offered a six week assignment this morning to tour the country with the Republican Presidential candidate. I accepted." He said it with finality, and with no thought about how that news would affect me or his kids. But after his bombshell, it made sense.

I kept staring out the window. I couldn't face him. "Congratulations. I'm happy for you," I said quietly, though my heart wasn't truly in it.

"I leave tonight."

"Okay."

"I've got a lot to do, so I don't think I'll be able to come by and say goodbye to the kids."

"It's fine, I'll let them know. Goodbye."

I opened the door and climbed out.

"Carly."

I wiped my cheeks and turned to him. He was leaning forward toward me. His features had softened some.

"We'll talk about us when I get back."

I shook my head and shut the door. There was no "us" anymore.

Chapter Twelve

I DON'T EVEN REMEMBER HOW I GOT TO MY IN-LAWS. I PROBABLY SHOULDN'T have driven in my condition. I'm not sure if I had ever cried harder. "The truth hurts" was the biggest understatement in the history of the world. I kept thinking, *why didn't he tell me?* I would have supported him if he wanted to travel more. Had I really held him back? Was I that selfish? A million other questions kept coming in and out. I was a wreck by the time I made it to my destination.

I pulled up in the driveway of my in-laws and tried to compose myself, but it was to no avail. The person I loved more than anyone hated and resented me. I had apparently ruined his life all while thinking I was making it better. What was wrong with me?

Danielle opened the door. "Is something wrong with the baby?" she immediately asked.

I started crying harder.

She gently pulled me to her and hugged me.

"No, everything is fine with her."

"Her?"

"It's a girl."

"That's terrific news, so what's wrong?"

"My marriage is over," I blubbered.

She let go of me and looked up at me with grave concern.

Through my sobbing, I told her what her son had said.

She immediately led me to her bedroom. "The kids shouldn't see you like this."

I felt like such a mess. Danielle sat me down on her bench at the foot of their bed. I had never been in their room, so I felt weird on top of being devastated. She shut the door and joined me. She took my hands in her smallish, age-spotted hands. The dirt under her finger nails indicated she had been enjoying her garden. It was one of her favorite hobbies. I didn't mind the dirt at all. I was grateful to have a hand to hold at the moment. She waited for me to calm down and get my crying under control. It took several minutes, but she waited patiently while rubbing my hands. Not a word was spoken until I had it out of my system. I took a deep, cleansing breath in.

"That's better," she said like I was Mia's age. "I'm not going to get involved in your marriage, Carly. That's between you and my son. But I will say this, I've never known a better wife and mother than you." She stood up and looked down at me. "Now go freshen up, we're going shopping for my new granddaughter."

She left me to use her master bathroom. I washed my face, applied my eye drops and kept a cool washcloth on my face for several minutes. I pulled out my compact and reapplied my make-up. I looked into the mirror and told myself it was better to know. At least now I could deal with it. And as painful as it was, I now knew what direction I needed to go, but first I was going shopping for my baby girl.

Danielle and I spent a soothing afternoon oohing and aahing over the beyond adorable baby girl outfits in the stores. Several of those outfits came home with me. We also stopped by a fabric store. Danielle offered to help me make curtains and bedding for the nursery. I finally let someone know what my plans were for the room and why I needed Michael's baby pictures. I don't know if she was just being nice after the day I'd had, but she seemed genuinely impressed with my idea and design layout. "I can't wait to see it all pulled together," she said kindly.

We ended up staying at my in-laws until it was almost bedtime. Part of me wanted to stay even longer, but I knew I had to face reality. It was hard to think about walking into our house knowing this was the way it was always going to be. The hope of salvaging our marriage had been destroyed today. I was having a hard time getting his cold look and hurtful words out of my head. How could he say we were playing house? He talked like I was this huge interruption of his real life. Had he always felt like that? I guess that part didn't matter, it only mattered how he felt now, and he was loud and clear on that. I guess he had been for the last several months; I was just too in love to face it.

Saturday morning dawned and I was woken by a text from Michael.

"I wanted you to know, I made it to California. I'll try and call later."

I picked up the phone and deleted the message. I had no intention of responding. The baby kicked, and I decided it was time for me to get up. As I sat on my bed, I looked around and everything reminded me of Michael, from the comforter to the deep brown color on the walls. I decided it was time to change things up a little. I didn't know if I had it in me to paint my room in addition to the nursery, but I decided to buy some more feminine bedding and maybe change up the artwork and accessories in the room. I also took down our wedding photos and packed them away with all the pictures that had been hanging up in Michael's old office. I didn't even cry. Okay, maybe a tear or two, but that was it.

By the time the pictures were packed, my kiddos were up, and we decided on French toast for breakfast. Over breakfast, I told them of their daddy's assignment. "Your daddy will be traveling for the rest of the summer. He won't be back until it's almost time to start school."

Mia's face immediately dropped. "He's going to miss my birthday?" she practically cried.

"Don't worry, sweet girl. We are still going to have the best birthday party ever."

Ashton was as pensive as ever. His blue eyes were as sad as I have ever seen them.

I reached over and grabbed his hand. "You and I will hit the tennis courts later today. Okay?"

He sort of grinned at me.

"This is still going to be the best summer," I think I said it more to convince myself.

I kept telling myself I had been doing this single parenting thing for almost four months, and we had all survived. I could do this, right? It's not like I had a choice in the matter, anyway. I kept repeating, *it's not our circumstances that define us, but how we choose to deal with them.* And lots of women had it way worse than me. At least I had family support nearby, and a large trust fund. I knew on Monday I was going to have to call the attorney in Colorado about how I could begin to access that and for a recommendation for a local attorney. That's when a few tears came. I couldn't believe I needed a divorce attorney. I wiped them away and sighed. No use in worrying about it until Monday.

Sunday we were back at my in-laws' for church and lunch. I had a feeling this was going to be a tradition. It was a lovely one, so I hoped it would.

During lunch, Jack surprised us all. "I've filed my retirement paperwork. All I have is the next two weeks, and then I will become a man of leisure."

I looked at Danielle to gauge her reaction. She was visibly happy. She wasn't the excitable, overtly emotional type of person, but her demeanor and countenance radiated happiness. I was happy for both of them. It was quite an accomplishment to have such a long lasting career and marriage.

"Congratulations, Jack. So what prompted your decision?"

He looked over to my kiddos. "I've decided being a Papa is a lot more fun than being an engineer."

Both he and Danielle looked at me lovingly. "We're here for whatever you need," Jack said.

I reached across the table and squeezed both of their hands. "Thank you. You don't know how much that means to me." I didn't tell them I was filing for divorce. I could barely admit it to myself, much less others.

Michael finally called that evening as I was preparing dinner. I let Ashton answer it. I listened to them talk to their daddy as they told him about their weekend and how excited they were about having a baby sister. Mia talked about her birthday party and how sad she was he wasn't going to be there.

Mia brought the phone over to me. "Daddy wants to talk to you, Mommy."

"Tell Daddy I'm busy making dinner and can't talk," I said while draining the pasta.

I knew I couldn't avoid communicating with him forever, but I needed some time.

"Daddy says he'll call you later, Mommy."

I knew he would probably be too busy to make good on that. And sure enough, I was right. He never called back that night.

I woke up early on Monday and made a list of all the things that needed to get accomplished before the baby came. I probably had fifteen to eighteen weeks before that blessed event. First on the list was to call my parents' attorney that handled my trust fund. I would call him during swimming lessons. It also dawned on me, with a third child, I would need a new car. I loved my 4Runner; it was the first car we had bought together as a couple, but it would be a tight fit to squeeze two booster seats and a car seat into that back seat. I needed something with a third row, but I was dead set against a minivan. I would have to do some research on SUV's with third rows and high safety ratings. Maybe Jack could go with me to the dealerships and do some test drives with me. He knew a lot about cars.

Getting a personal bank account was also a must. I had set up a business account, but I was still using our joint account for everything. As I kept writing, I realized how entwined our lives were and the effort it was going to take to sever those ties. For so long, we had functioned as a unit, now we would be separate departments, no longer "playing house" as he put it. I still couldn't believe that's how he saw our marriage.

I held out my left hand and looked at my wedding ring. It was a beautiful white gold band with a small solitaire round cut diamond, simple but elegant. I had always loved the way it looked on my hand. When Michael gave it to me, I remember him apologizing about the size, but that never mattered to me. The only thing that mattered was that he loved me and that it came from his heart. He had loved me once, right? I contemplated removing the ring. I even took it off for a moment, but it made me feel bare, so I quickly put it back on. Why couldn't I fall out of love with him as easily as he had with me? Why did my heart still ache for him?

With those thoughts, I crawled out of bed and started another day by myself. I had a busy day on tap: swimming lessons in the morning and a photo shoot in the afternoon. Michael called on the way to the pool; again, I let Ashton answer it. It was the kids he wanted to talk to, anyway. And I was driving; it was unsafe, right? My car was old enough not to have Bluetooth technology. He did ask to talk to me, but I declined, citing the aforementioned safety reasons. It was a bunch of BS I know, but I couldn't yet.

By the time we got to the pool, I had a text from him.

"Is everything okay?"

What a dumb question, I thought. Of course it wasn't okay, but he didn't really care, so I waited several minutes and texted back. "Yep."

As soon as Ashton and Mia hit the water with their instructor, Shawna, I called Mr. Flinders in Denver.

"I was wondering when I would hear from you," he said. "Tell me how you and your family are."

"Well... I'm expecting again and..."

"Congratulations to both you and Michael."

"Yeah... about that. Do you perhaps have any connections in the Atlanta area? I'm in need of a d-divorce lawyer." I could still barely say it or admit it.

"That is certainly a surprise. I'm sorry, Carly."

Believe me, I was too.

He thought for a moment. "I don't have any direct connections, but I'll check with my associates here and get back to you," he offered.

"Thank you."

"I just need your email address where my assistant can send you the necessary documents to begin drawing on your trust. I will also send you information on the tax situation this will invoke."

"Okay. Thank you, again."

"And Carly, don't forget this trust was set up to prevent Michael from gaining access to it, whether married or divorced."

I sighed. I remember being upset when I found out my parents excluded Michael, but I guess they knew what they were doing and now, even in death, they were still protecting me.

After I got off the phone, I added a task to my list to create a monthly budget, so I knew what amount I should draw each month. I also wondered if I should take on more clients. I quickly decided that would have to wait until after the baby was born and I had recovered. If I was smart, I could live off that trust for many years to come, so I decided working extra was an unnecessary stress I could do without at the moment. I had plenty of others to deal with.

One of my new stresses was coming up with ways to avoid my husband. It was like he knew I didn't want him to call or contact me in any way, so he decided to do just that. I mean, what happened to the 'I'm on assignment and not to be bothered Michael'? But by Friday, I knew I couldn't keep putting him off. His texts were becoming annoying and angry. I couldn't understand why he wanted to talk to me so much.

The phone rang late Friday as I was up watching my new favorite movie, *Something to Talk About*, a movie about a man that cheats on his wife. The wife gets him back, and one of her tactics was using a little food poisoning. I wondered where I could get some of the stuff she threw in his food. I thought maybe a little food poisoning would be good for Michael. Then he could see what it was like to puke and take care of the kids all by himself, all while feeling like death.

I begrudgingly answered as I sat there on my bed with the glow of the T.V. "Hello."

"You answered."

"Looks like."

"Am I interrupting anything? I know how busy you are."

He didn't sound pleased at all, but I found I didn't really care at the moment.

"Actually, you are, but I suppose I can hit pause." I did just that. I didn't want to miss the part where her sister knees the lying, cheating husband in the groin. I bet Melanie would do that for me. Maybe I should call her and tell her about my situation.

"Thanks for taking time out of your busy schedule to talk to me."

"You're welcome."

"You know it's not like I'm not busy, and calling is kind of inconvenient for me at the moment."

"Then don't call. Goodbye."

"Wait, Carly."

"What! I would hate to inconvenience you." *Especially since that's all I have been to you our whole marriage.*

"Please, I didn't call to argue with you. I wanted to see how you and the baby are doing."

"We're great. We're all doing great here."

"Ashton and Mia sound happy. Ashton said you were teaching him how to play tennis."

Did I hear a hint of regret? It was probably my imagination. "They are happy." *No thanks to you.* "We're enjoying all summer has to offer."

"I'm glad to hear it."

"Okay. Well, it's late. Goodnight, Michael."

"Goodnight, Carly."

Chapter Thirteen

Michael kept calling on a daily basis. I gave up ignoring him, but I kept the conversations brief and sterile. I limited the topics to the kids and their activities. I also refused to talk about his assignment. He attempted on several occasions to talk about it, but I either ended the call or switched back to the kids. I wasn't in the mood to play the role of supportive wife, and I figured why bother, I had failed miserably at it.

But for some reason, Michael seemed determined to engage me. When he was in Colorado, he sent several texts with pictures. The texts were reminiscent of when we lived there. We happened to get married there, so he sent a picture of the Brown Palace where we said "I do" and spent our first night as husband and wife.

"Remember this place?" he texted.

"Vaguely," I responded.

It was a lie, I know. I remembered every detail of that cold December day over ten-and-a-half years ago. I remembered the way he looked at me as I walked down the aisle with my dad, like I was the only one in the room. I remembered how both the men in my life had tears in their eyes. I remembered my desire to comfort my dad, but it was overruled by my anxiousness to be given to Michael because I wanted nothing more than to be bound to him and for him to be bound to me. I remembered how he kept a hold of me all night, even if it was just my hand. We even ate holding hands. I especially remembered how impatient he was for the reception to be over and how we almost missed our flight to Tahiti the next morning because... well, just because. Believe me, though, it would have been worth missing.

I wiped my eyes as I stared at my screen. I hadn't cried in a week.

He texted a picture of Coors Field where we had gone to see the Rockies play the Braves. Michael was a huge Braves fan. I didn't really care about either team, but I showed my state loyalty by rooting for the Rockies and wearing their jersey. Michael had worn his Braves shirt. He was unmercifully razzed the whole night, but he had the last laugh when the Braves won.

"Go Rockies," I texted back.

"We'll make a Braves fan out of you yet," he responded.

The text surprised me. Or maybe I was reading more into it than he meant. He was probably just making small talk, and even if we were divorced, we had kids together so we would always have to be in each other's life in some way. I'm sure it didn't mean he wanted to get back together. And besides, things couldn't and shouldn't continue on this way.

As that second week wore on, he began asking me to text and email him pictures of the kids. I was happy to oblige him. I was glad he at least missed his children.

At the end of that second week, I made an appointment with a lawyer. Mr. Flinders had finally gotten back to me with the name of a local attorney. Meanwhile, I had set up my own bank account. I was set to take my first draw from my trust on August 1. I think the lady at the bank thought I was going to have an episode. My eyes kept watering the entire time, as I kept hesitating to sign the signature card and paperwork. Signing those papers meant I was closer to really being on my own. And even though I had always been fairly independent, I had loved being a couple. I remember how giddy I was when we received our first boxes of checks with both of our names on them. I was such a dork.

In the midst of banks and lawyers and, of course, kiddos and the house, I began working on the nursery. Jack came over and helped me move the two book cases and filing cabinet left in the room to the walk-in attic. He also helped me tape to get ready to paint. He felt like I shouldn't be on a ladder.

As we taped, he above and me below, we talked and as always the conversation ended up on Michael.

"How are you dealing with his absence this go around?" Jack asked me.

"Better than I expected. I guess I'm growing accustomed to being on my own. I'm trying to stay busy, so that helps."

Before he laid down the blue tape in his hand, he looked down at me. His eyes were full of concern. He didn't say anything verbally, but for some reason I felt really loved. I appreciated how he and Danielle were staying out of the marriage portion of my life. It was nice to be able to talk without feeling judgment. I had really grown to love them both over the last four plus months. They were part of the reason I was still somewhat sane and why Mia and Ashton were so happy.

There was hardly a day when they didn't stop by or invite me and the kids over. Sometimes Jack would come by after work on his way home and mow my lawn or take out the trash. Those were other things he felt like I shouldn't be doing in my condition. I teased him that women walked across the plains pregnant, but he just smiled and kept on doing what he was doing. Danielle was also helping me with Mia's birthday party. We had been making goodie bags and decorations. Mia was still on the butterfly kick, so we made large paper lanterns with small butterflies attached. We even had butterflies on the straws and a butterfly shaped piñata and cake. Ashton was not impressed at all. It was way too girly for him, so Grandpa promised they would do something manly while we entertained ten or so of Mia's friends.

The day before Mia's birthday party, I had an appointment to meet with the attorney, a Mr. William McRae. He specialized in divorce. *What a thing to specialize in*, I thought. I almost canceled. I didn't know if I could face it, but what choice did I have? With guilt I dropped my kids off at my in-laws. I only told them I had an appointment, but I was dressed nice in a pantsuit. My mother-in-law looked at me like she knew, but she didn't ask. I hugged the kids extra tight before I left. *What am I doing?* I thought.

On the drive over, I kept reminding myself this was the right thing to do and I didn't choose this. I kept hearing the voice of the pastor repeating the phrase, "for better or for worse." And I felt my baby move. I was a wreck by the time I made it to the impressive brick building near the courthouse. I found a parking spot and got out and paid the meter, but hesitated to walk into McRae and McRae. Then I remembered what Michael said about playing house before he left, and I propelled myself forward.

I signed in and sat in their stately looking waiting area. The waiting area seemed too large to me. How many people needed their services? I couldn't sit, so I got up and paced. My fellow patrons must have thought me odd, but I thought they were odd. How could they be so calm about dissolving their marriages? Maybe they were there for other reasons. I didn't know. All I knew was that I had never been so uncomfortable in my life.

By the time they called me back, I was ready to walk back out the door, but I took a deep breath and followed the secretary to Mr. McRae's office. Upon entering his office, he stood up and greeted me. He was a fine Southern gentleman, dressed to a T in a three-piece-suit, his teeth and shoes shined. He had gray hair, but his skin was still smooth and flawless. He shook my hand and introduced himself and told me to have a seat.

His office looked as large as my living room, it even included a fireplace. He obviously did well for himself. "So Mrs. Bishop, tell me about yourself."

I looked at him questioningly. What did he want to know?

He smiled at me. I'm sure he could tell I was a wreck. "Let's start with what you do professionally."

That was easy enough. "I'm a professional photographer, but my favorite title is mom."

He grinned and looked at my ever growing midsection. "How many children do you have?"

"Three—a boy and two girls." I rubbed my baby. "But one has yet to make her appearance."

"When is your due date?"

"November seventh. Hopefully sooner."

He chuckled. "I remember those days."

For a moment I forgot I was in a lawyer's office. He was as pleasant as he could be. It was like talking to a friend. That was until he brought up Michael.

"Tell me how you and your husband met and about your wedding day."

I shook my head. What an odd thing to ask. He kept looking at me as if he was anticipating my reply. So I told him about flight 416 and about that cold day in December so many years ago. I couldn't help but get choked up about some of my most prized memories.

Mr. McRae was a captive audience through it all. I almost felt like I was in a therapist's office, but then he started asking more of the kinds of questions I expected.

"How long have you been separated?"

"Since March."

"Is he still supporting you and the children financially?"

I nodded. "He has been more than good about taking care of us that way."

He wrote several notes in his leather pad, before he finally set down his pen and looked up at me with a smile in his eye. "So, Mrs. Bishop, why do you want to file for divorce?"

I sat there for a moment, feeling small all of a sudden, like a child. How did I put it? A well of emotion overtook me. "I don't want to, but I don't feel like I have any other option at this point," I choked out.

He handed me a tissue. I noticed the large box from which he retrieved it. I supposed this was a common occurrence in this office.

"Mrs. Bishop, is there infidelity?"

"He says no."

"Do you believe him?"

"Yes, I think so."

"Any abuse?"

"None at all."

"Mrs. Bishop, I've seen situations much worse than yours where divorce was the best solution, but yet the parties worked it out. Are you sure this is what you want?"

"Aren't you a divorce attorney?" I asked.

He chuckled. "Yes ma'am, but I'm also a family man. I don't take my job lightly. I need to be able to look myself in the eye in the morning. So I need to make absolutely sure this is what you want. Are you sure this is what your husband wants?"

"He says he doesn't love me and he moved out, so I would say yes, this is what he wants."

"Hmmm," he said. "How old is your husband?"

"He'll be forty next month."

He grinned. "Mrs. Bishop, why don't we just fill out the paperwork and I'll hold onto it until you're sure."

I nodded my head yes, wondering if I was just weak, but it felt like the right thing to do. In my heart, I wasn't ready to fully pull the trigger yet.

I got to my car and breathed a sigh of relief. Relief from what, I wasn't sure. I was still in an unenviable position and marriage. And still very alone. Michael had been gone for three weeks. Our only communication was calls and texts; he hated things like Skype and FaceTime. I wasn't sure why, but that was him. And at this point, it didn't matter, I was still talking to him as little as possible. He had no idea how much he had hurt me with his words and actions, but here I was, not even able to file for divorce.

I tried to forget about it for the afternoon as I finished birthday shopping and picking out the perfect color of paint for the nursery. The walls had been prepped and primed, so now the fun stuff was ready to begin. I had ordered the circular crib two days ago and matching dresser as well as a white chair and ottoman. I was going a little overboard, but I needed a good project, and I knew this was my last baby, so it was my last opportunity to have such a nursery. I had saved up all my photography business money for it since Michael had made good on financially supporting us.

My last stop before I retrieved my kiddos was the printers to get all of my copied photos. I couldn't wait to see this all pulled together, but first I needed to get through Mia's party the next day.

On my way out of the printers, my phone rang. It was Michael. It was an odd time for him to call, in the middle of the day. I think he was in Ohio or maybe Iowa, I couldn't keep track.

"Carly," he sounded worried.

"What's wrong?"

"I just remembered I didn't get Mia anything for her birthday tomorrow, would you mind?"

Really?

"Fine, but how could you forget? She's only talked to you about it every day since you've been gone."

"I know, Carly, okay. Don't you think I feel bad about it?"

"I don't know what you think anymore."

"Well that makes two of us," he said.

I had no idea what that meant. How could he not know what he thinks? But I didn't ask him to elaborate. "Did you have something in mind?"

"She's been talking about an American Girl doll. Did you get her one already?"

"I thought about it, but I've been busy and I didn't want to drive to Alpharetta."

"Oh."

"But I suppose I can. Your mom has the kids right now."

"I don't want to put you out."

Really? I thought. *You've been putting me out for the last several months.* "Its fine, I know she'd love a doll from there."

"Carly, thank you."

"You're welcome. Bye."

"Wait."

"What?"

"Tell me what you've been up to?" he asked.

If only he knew. I wondered if I should tell him. Would it even faze him that I had been to a lawyer? Would he be relieved that I was the one to pull the trigger? Maybe that's what he wanted. But as I was so unsure, I decided not to mention it. "I'm getting ready for Mia's birthday party."

"Tell me something about you. All you ever talk about is the kids."

"Okay... I've been doing photo sessions and working on the nursery."

"Nursery? Did you move the kids in together?"

"Uh, no. I'm using the other bedroom."

"My office?"

"No, your office is at your apartment. Remember several months ago when you moved out?"

Silence. I don't know why I waited for a response, but I did.

"So you weren't even going to ask me if that was okay?"

"Michael, you moved out. You can't have it both ways. And even if you want to move back in someday, and if I'm amenable to that, that room is still going to be a nursery."

"What do you mean, if you're amenable?"

"Do you really think after everything you've done and said to me, all it's going to take is you deciding to move back? This isn't a game for me. I don't play house. And I'm not okay being treated like this."

Silence again. At least he wasn't hanging up like he had been when anything he didn't want to discuss was brought up.

"The day I left... I said some things I regret."

"Well, at least I know the truth now."

"Carly, the truth is relative."

"I don't even know what that's supposed to mean, but I'm tired."

"I know, Carly."

"I should probably go."

"Thank you, Carly. I'll call you later."

"Yeah, I know."

That man was driving me crazy. My whole drive down to Alpharetta I kept cursing him in my head. Every year he would buy the kids something special that was just from him. It was something the kids looked forward to. It was a tradition, and I didn't want Mia to be disappointed. It was the only reason I was fighting traffic on a Friday afternoon. Okay, and maybe a part of me wanted to do it for Michael. I don't know why because he sure didn't deserve it.

I also thought about what he meant about regret and truth being relative. Did he regret what he said because he sounded like a world class jerk? Or was there something more to it? I knew I wasn't going to solve the mystery of Michael Bishop that afternoon, and I wouldn't until he came home, if ever.

The doll was purchased and beautifully gift wrapped in the store. I snapped a picture of both the doll and the wrapped package with my phone and sent it to Michael. This way he could at least pretend with Mia he purchased it. I decided I deserved the best-wife-ever award. Maybe not after the text message that went with the pictures, but seriously I deserved to be a little snarky.

"You owe me."

"Believe me, I know," he replied quickly.

I hoped he did know.

Chapter Fourteen

It was birthday party day. I couldn't believe my baby was five. She was even up before me and jumping on my bed in her swimsuit no less. I grabbed her and pulled her back under my covers to snuggle with her. She wasn't having it; she was way too excited. I guess I *wanted* to get up at six a.m. on a Saturday.

I let Mia watch cartoons on my bed while I quickly showered. I was now at the stage in my pregnancy where I felt like every day in the shower I looked down and saw a bigger belly. I was twenty-five weeks, and whereas my abdomen had definitely grown, I was barely back at my normal weight. I had lost so much at the beginning, from morning sickness, stress and illness, but I was back on track now. I just carried this little girl differently. She was all out in front, where Mia and Ashton had been more evenly distributed. So many things about this pregnancy were different, including me being alone in the shower.

I kept wondering if Michael missed me at all. Did he ever think about all the small wonderful things that made our marriage amazing, or had it really been all for play? Did he ever wake up in the morning and forget for just a second and reach across the bed to touch me, only to find it empty? Did he miss all of my shampoo and conditioner bottles in the shower that he used to tease me about? I knew I missed his single, solitary blue bottle and his green bar of soap. I missed his razor, too; my legs hadn't felt the same since he left. I guess I could buy one of my own, but it wouldn't be as fun as using his because who would complain?

I got out of the shower and looked at our dual sink counter top; it was still half-empty. Just to try it on for size, I placed my lotion bottle on his side. I stepped back, wrapped in my towel, to see how it felt. It looked lonely, so I shifted some candles that way. I left them there as I continued to get dressed and put together for the day, but they began to bug me, so I started rearranging the whole countertop. In the end, it pretty much looked like it had to start. The left side was bare, and my side was just more organized. I shook my head at myself and walked back into my bedroom.

My new five-year-old, in her bright pink swimming suit, was lying on her tummy with her head propped up on her hands, singing along with the characters on T.V. I shook my head and laughed at her. She was the cutest thing ever. I had to snap a couple of pictures of her on my phone.

I wondered if Michael was up yet. I kept forgetting which time zone he was in. Regardless, I decided to text him one of the pictures. What could be better than waking up to that sweet face?

He must have been awake already because within seconds my phone rang.

"Hey," I said.

"Good morning. You're up early," he replied.

"Well, as you can see, I had a little encouragement there."

"Let me talk to her."

I handed the phone over to our five-year-old. She was more than happy to talk to her daddy. She told him everything we had planned, from making butterfly masks, to the piñata, to swimming and, of course, cake and ice cream. Her Mimi was even making homemade peach ice cream for the occasion. She told him about each one of her ten friends that were coming, and she did it all in about one minute flat. The girl had a gift.

She handed the phone back to me. "Did you get all of that?" I asked.

He laughed. "I think so."

"Okay. Well, have a good day."

"Carly, wait."

I paused.

"Why are you always in such a hurry to get off the phone with me?"

"Isn't that what you want?"

"I miss talking to you."

I sat down on my bed, out of shock. Did he say he missed something about me? "Okay. I'm listening."

He cleared his throat, almost as if he was nervous. "I got an exclusive interview with Joseph Xavier on Monday." Joseph Xavier was the Republican nominee for President.

"Wow. That's a big deal."

"Thanks. Have you read any of the articles I've written about his campaign?"

Of course he would ask that. "Uh. Well... No."

"Oh..."

Should I offer to read them? I thought. Was I a bad person for not reading them?

"I think you would like him," he said.

I laughed. "I guess that means you don't."

Michael and I had rarely agreed about anything political. Most of our marriage we had either stayed away from the subject or agreed to disagree.

"I have to remain unbiased, remember?"

"Okay. Sure."

One thing he wasn't, and that was unbiased. Of course, because of journalistic integrity, you would never know which way he leaned, but Michael had an opinion on everything.

"Anyway, if you get a chance, maybe you could read my articles. I would be interested in your thoughts."

"I'll try and read them tonight, after today's craziness."

Why was I such a sucker for him? I was doing so well being an inattentive wife, almost as good as he was at being an inattentive husband. But he sounded happy about my agreeing to read his stuff.

"I'm looking forward to talking to you about my articles tonight," he said.

Which meant I was really going to have to read them.

"Will you please take some pictures of the party and of Mia opening her doll?" he asked before I could hang up.

If I wasn't mistaken I could hear regret in his voice over missing Mia's big day.

I wasn't sure what to think of him after that call, but I didn't have time to think about it. I had to put the final touches on the goody bags and commence all the other Saturday chores, like laundry and bathroom cleaning. While scrubbing the toilet, I felt a wave of resentment thinking about him living in a hotel room with maid and room service, but then my kiddos called out, "Mommy." That made it all worth it, right? Without a doubt, yes.

We ended up leaving early for my in-laws. Mia couldn't contain her excitement and Mimi and Papa were more than happy to have them over, and I was more than happy to have the adult company. I couldn't say it enough, my in-laws were saints, and I would be forever grateful to them.

When we arrived, Jack came out immediately and helped me carry in the myriad of boxes and bags that contained all of Mia's birthday presents and decorations. Jack had taken it upon himself to be the surrogate in his son's absence. I knew he wasn't pleased with Michael, and from what I could gather, they weren't really taking to one another. I hated to see that happen. Jack was missing his son and the relationship they used to have. It wasn't only me Michael had cut himself off from. Many times, in the past summers, Jack and Michael would take a Saturday to fish or catch a Braves game or just mess around in Jack's shop. I wasn't ever sure what truly went on in there, but it was male bonding at its finest.

Jack was now doing the same things with Ashton. In so many ways, it did my heart good to see Ashton so happy with his grandfather, but there was always a little ache in my heart because it should have been his father or, better yet, the three of them together. It should have been Michael with Ashton when he caught his first fish this summer or when he built his first birdhouse. Michael should be playing catch and wrestling on the floor and teaching Ashton how to whistle. Jack thought so too, and I don't think he kept it to himself.

Jack and Danielle were trying to stay out of my marriage, but Jack always asked me if I had talked to Michael. I think he figured as long as we were talking, there was still hope. On several occasions, Jack expressed how he hoped Michael would be smart enough not to let me go. And like me, he couldn't wrap his head around his son's confusing and sometimes juvenile behavior.

Today, though, we were all smiles for Mia and her big day. There would be no talk of absent fathers and husbands. No talk of how much I hated doing all of this without him and how I felt so empty. I would, yet again, rise to the occasion and fake my way through it until I actually felt happy. I would remind myself over and over again that I could do it and that this was my reality. There was no sense in crying over it, at least not in public.

We spent the remainder of the morning making the pool area look like a butterfly-palooza and finishing up the food for the party. By one p.m., our guests began to arrive making Ashton and Jack disappear into the wild blue yonder. Jack was going to give Ashton his first golf lesson.

"I need a good caddy now that I'm retired," he teased Ashton.

Ashton had no idea what that entailed. "I can do it, Papa," he said excitedly.

Jack winked at me. He was too much of a softie to ever make Ashton carry his golf clubs around. Instead, I could picture him letting Ashton drive the cart around. That and lots of ice cream cones.

Danielle and I proceeded to herd eleven little girls through lunch, crafts, swimming (with the help of a life guard) and cake and ice cream. Last but not least, we did presents. Mia was not happy about saving that for last, but I knew she would have been no good for any other activities had we done that at the beginning. She received some very fun gifts from craft sets to Barbie Dolls, but the crowning jewel was from her daddy. I had her open that last, and it was a good thing, too, because that was all she had eyes for. Daddy became the hero, even though I had done all the work. I snapped picture after picture and sent them to the luckiest, most idiotic man in the world, my husband.

The party was a success, so much so that Mia conked out clinging to her doll while Danielle and I cleaned up. In my frustration, and admittedly some jealousy, I expressed the unfairness of the situation. "It was me who spent hour upon hour baking, cutting, pasting, and shopping. I was even the one who had to buy the dumb doll. But is it me that receives the accolades and the shouts for joy? No. It's Michael!"

My mother-in-law kind of chuckled at me as we took down the butterfly-clad lanterns. "Honey, it's the plight of all mothers. Someday, when Mia's a mom, she'll understand and your dues will come."

"Has that day come for you?" I asked.

She looked at me thoughtfully. "Not yet."

I walked over to her and put my arms around her. It took her a second to reciprocate, but she did. "If I haven't said it lately, thank you. You're the best grandmother and mother-in-law a girl could ask for. I wouldn't have survived these last months without you. My life is better because of you."

She patted my back a couple of times and let go of me quickly. She didn't say anything. She went back to taking down lanterns, but I did see her wipe at her eyes. I made a mental note to talk to Michael. He needed to tell his mom what a good mother she was. She deserved her dues, and I think they were way past due.

By the time bedtime rolled around, this pregnant lady was tired. I tried my hardest after the kids went to bed to read Michael's articles, but I couldn't keep my eyes open. I was happy Michael texted, "Sorry, I can't call. Late night rally. Sleep well."

I didn't even have the energy to text back, but I guess Michael took that as not a good sign. Several minutes later I was woken up by another text.

"Is everything okay?"

"Just exhausted. Goodnight," I managed to text back.

"Goodnight," he texted back almost instantly.

I smiled to myself and went back to sleep.

We weren't able to connect until the next afternoon. He called while we were still at his parents' for lunch. He took a turn talking to the kiddos, before I went out by the pool where he and I could talk alone. I managed to squeeze in reading his articles before church. First he wanted to revel in his delight about Mia's reaction to the doll. I tried not to let it grate on my nerves. I tried to remember what Danielle had told me.

Maybe he could tell I was annoyed with my short replies of, uh huh's and yeah's. "Carly, I just wanted to say thank you for taking care of the doll and... everything else." He redeemed himself some with his profuse thanks. "I hope you're taking it easy today, I worry that you're overdoing it."

"Feel free to come back to Pine Apple anytime and jump in," I snapped at him.

"Carly... I'll be back in twenty days. You understand how big this assignment is for my career, right?"

I did understand that, and under different circumstances I would have even been supportive of it, but after everything that had happened, I knew this wasn't just about his career. If I thought for one second he was doing it for the betterment of our family and out of love, I could get on board with that, but I knew this assignment had nothing to do with any of that.

I didn't respond. I wasn't sure how to. Sometimes just saying nothing at all was the best answer.

He cleared his throat. "Did you read my excerpts online and in the Wall Street Journal?"

"Yes."

"And...?"

"They were very well executed. I can see why you were chosen for an exclusive. You did a very good job of keeping it neutral." Which I'm sure Mr. Xavier appreciated. So many were excoriating him in the media. It's one of the reasons I hated election season. The nastiness on both sides was ridiculous.

"But...?"

"What do you mean but?"

"I know there's a but in there. I can hear it in your tone."

Maybe he still knew me.

"Okay. I just found them cold and impersonal."

"That's the way it should be. How else can you keep it unbiased?"

"Michael, the man has a fascinating story. He's the first man running for president in modern times that will not be bringing a first lady with him to the White House if elected. He's also an amazingly successful business man who was a virtual unknown in political circles until the last couple of years. To top it off, he has an incredible rags-to-riches story. There's a very human element to his campaign that is missing in your articles."

"It's not as easy as you think to walk that line."

"I would never say it is, but I know you, and if anybody can walk that line, it's you."

"So you're saying I can do better."

"I'm saying I believe in you, Michael."

He paused, he did that a lot now whenever we spoke. "One more question before I have to go. Why don't you call me Bishop anymore?"

"Probably for the same reasons you never call me 24B anymore. Good luck tomorrow."

"Thanks," he said quietly. And that's where we ended the call.

I sat for a moment on the patio chair before going in, trying to solve the mystery to Michael's behavior. I knew one piece; he resented me for a perceived lack of success and fulfillment in his career and maybe life in general. I knew he said he regretted what he said and that truth is relative, but there was some truth there; I had felt it in his behavior toward me during the past year. But the more I pulled away, the more he didn't seem to like it. He was like a walking dichotomy, but the truth was, I wasn't going to be patient much longer. He couldn't have it both ways. He either loved me and our family or he didn't. There was no in-between or middle ground there.

Chapter Fifteen

"Carly, you'll never guess who Joseph Xavier was friends with?"

"Well, hello to you, too. Who was he friends with?"

"Your dad."

"No."

"Yes. Your dad helped him with his business arrangements in Mumbai and Hong Kong. Through the process, they became friends."

"How did you find this out?"

"During my interview with him, we got to talking about his business dealings outside of the US and why he felt like that would be a help to him in foreign policy matters. One thing led to another and he mentioned a Derek Rogers. I asked him if he was talking about the same Derek Rogers that died in the Consulate bombing and he said it was the very one. I told him I was married to his daughter. He knew your dad well enough and remembered him enough to ask Carly or Melanie?"

"Really? So did you say Melanie?"

"Funny. I told him I married the better of the two and he knew right away which one."

Poor Melanie, she always felt like second best. She was closer to Michael's age, a couple of years older than him. I think my dad was a different person and father to her. From what my mom had told me, I think he had a lot of growing up to do, and he drank too much in the early days of my parents' marriage. I think that may have a lot to do with her attitude toward men and life in general. I know my dad tried to make amends with her later in life, but Melanie was stubborn and unforgiving. I think for her, it was too little too late.

"You're lying," I said.

"I swear to you, I'm not. He referred to you as enchanting and the apple of your father's eye. He recalled the pictures your dad had of you in his office."

I laughed. "So did you set him straight on the whole enchanting thing?"

"Why would you think I would say something like that?"

"Oh, I don't know. Why do you think?" He was so dense sometimes.

"Carly, I told you this is about me, not you."

"And that's a lie. This is about me. I saw it in your eyes the day of the ultrasound."

"Carly, I told you I regret the things I said that day."

"Michael, this is about what you didn't say that day or didn't have to say."

"Please, do we have to get into this tonight? I don't want to do this over the phone."

I didn't respond. We were never going to move on, one way or the other, until we had this out. I was tired of skirting around the issue, but I suppose over the phone wasn't the best way to go. Except that's all the contact I had with him these days.

"Carly?"

"Yes?"

"He said he would love to meet you. He wants to arrange something when he comes through Georgia sometime next month."

"I would be honored."

"Okay. You'll have to go through a security check."

"I think I'll pass."

He laughed. "Okay, I'll let him know. And I'll let you know when to look for the article. It should be in several publications."

"Goodnight, Michael."

When I got off the phone, I decided not to think about the never-ending nowhere conversations I kept having with my husband. Instead I focused on how cool it was that Joseph Xavier knew my dad and that he knew of me and wanted to meet me. I hoped that would work out. I also decided I should call Melanie; it was time to be honest with her about what was going on over here. It had been so easy to keep it from her. She never wanted to talk to my kids. She barely made an effort to call me. I was usually the instigator, unless she had something to really brag about like a famous client or something. She had done some pretty swanky remodels for some of Hollywood's elite that had mountain homes in Colorado.

As soon as she picked up, the sarcasm in her voice was clear. "So, is this my long-lost Southern belle of a sister?"

I refused to take her bait. "Hi, Melanie. How are you?"

I let her prattle on about all of her clients and complain about each one and then about all of the inept subcontractors she had to work with. And of course it was too hot, and she was peeved at me for not calling sooner. I reminded her she could pick up a phone just as easily.

"Well I would hate to disturb paradise over there," she quipped.

"Why would you say something like that? You think my life is perfect?"

"Well isn't it? Married, two kids. You're living the dream."

"Yeah, it's dreamy over here. Listen, I'm going to go."

"Trouble in paradise?" she almost sounded happy.

"If you must know, Michael and I are separated and I'm pregnant, due the first part of November."

I think she was taken aback and, of course, annoyed I hadn't told her sooner, but seriously what did she expect? I knew how she felt about my family, how did she refer to them? My "offspring." And Michael was either my "boy toy" or the "y chromosome that occupied the same space as me."

After hanging up, I questioned why I called in the first place. I guess it was good for her to know that my life was anything but perfect, but I got a full fifteen minute lecture on the evils of men and how all they were good for was their sperm, and even that was questionable. And of course, she always knew this would happen. She never liked him in the first place.

After those two phone calls, I broke out the leftover birthday cake. The baby applauded that decision. She put on quite the routine in response. I was happy to feel her move. She and her siblings were what kept me going every day, and they were reminders that, though life wasn't perfect, I was blessed.

We finished off July and headed into August. The baby was on track, and the nursery was painted. I was just waiting for the furniture to be delivered. In the meantime, I began to work on my black and white picture collage on the back wall of the nursery. So far, I was so in love with it. It was a compilation of mine, Michael's, Ashton's, and Mia's baby pictures. Some of the pictures were only of toes or belly buttons or hands or smiles. I loved going through all of the pictures. Mia and Ashton were the most adorable babies, and Michael was, too. His and Ashton's photos were almost identical except for the hair. And Mia's and mine were similar, as well.

Jack had helped me paint. He offered to do all of the painting because he thought it was bad for the baby, but I insisted on helping with a promise to wear a mask the whole time. I loved to paint, and the project helped me keep my mind off of me. The walls were a slate grey. I know it was an odd choice for a nursery color, but paired with the collage, white furniture, and pops of peach that would be added in through bedding, curtains and throw pillows, it was going to be stunning. I couldn't wait for it to be done.

August also meant I was emancipating myself, at least financially. I received my first draw and started paying all bills and living expenses from my own account. It was weird and a little disheartening, but I felt like I needed to be prepared.

Michael continued to call every day, sometimes even more than once. I kind of got the feeling he was ready to come home, meaning home in the general sense, not as in *our* home per se. He sounded tired, and every time we talked, he would mention how many more days until this tour was over.

His article came out, and I had to say, he rose to the occasion. It was unbiased, but yet it humanized my dad's old friend. The guy had such an interesting life. He was born to a single mother on welfare, but he ended up being the valedictorian in his South Carolina high school. He went on to Yale and married his college sweetheart, Marilyn. They had four beautiful daughters together, but sadly she passed away from leukemia a few years ago, just as his political aspirations were beginning. He was obviously very much in love with her, and from all accounts, she was a wonderful person. His daughters now took turns traveling with him.

Michael was pleased. His article had been picked up by the *Wall Street Journal*, *New York Times*, and the *Washington Post*, as well as several smaller markets. He was back on his A game, as he put it. I was happy for him, but it came at a high price, at least for me. I wondered if I was just expendable baggage in his mind, but I was about to find out. He was due back in town August twentieth, the day after his fortieth birthday.

I was nervous about seeing him again. Our conversations had been going well, but again, we weren't talking about anything that had to do with our status as a married couple. He hadn't even mentioned when we would see each other when he got back. I wasn't even sure what do to on his birthday. It was so sad too, because I had the most fabulous plans for his fortieth birthday. I had been planning for it for months, well that was until it became clear that this separation was going to be for an extended length of time and maybe permanent.

I awoke on the morning of his birthday and texted him a simple, "Happy Birthday."

My fabulous in-laws came and took my kids for the day and night. They were headed to Chattanooga to the zoo and the aquarium. The kids were super excited, and I was excited to get some time to work on the nursery. I was twelve-and-a-half weeks away from my due date, but with school starting at the beginning of September, and all the activities that go along with that, I wanted to be finished soon. The furniture had arrived, and Jack had helped me set up the circular crib that would go in the center of the room. I had found a circular peach patterned throw rug for it to sit on. It looked perfect against the dark hardwood. I had always wanted a circular crib, but I never had a room for it to work in. Now at last I did.

My husband never responded to my text, but at this point in our marriage, I didn't even think twice about it. Instead, I cranked up my alternative music playlist and went to town on my beautiful baby nursery. I began by finishing up the curtains my mother-in-law had helped me with; I just needed to add the trim. Then I hung the hardware and the curtains. I stood back and admired my handiwork. I had to say they were fabulous.

By mid-afternoon, I was able to focus on the collage that was about a quarter of the way done. The trick was rearranging the pictures to make it pleasing to the eye, while at the same time making it look randomly coherent. There was a lot of putting up pictures and taking them down, but in the end, I knew it would be worth it. I also knew I needed to finish it soon; getting up and down in this almost twenty-eight-week pregnant body wasn't very fun.

I was having a great afternoon with me, myself, and I, as I sang along to my tunes and basked in the glory of my art. It was then that I had the ever living heck scared out of me. With my back turned to the door, and in deep contemplation about where the next picture should go, I felt a tap on my shoulder. I jumped up higher and faster than I thought was possible in my current state.

"It's just me," Michael said.

I smacked him. "Don't ever do that to me again! What are you even doing here?" I was still clutching my chest. I could feel my heart pounding; the scare even made the baby move.

He didn't look happy at all. "Well, I came home early to surprise you, but instead I was the surprised one." He immediately handed me some papers. "That's one heck of a birthday present to come home to," he barked.

I was so confused. I looked at the papers. It looked like a bank statement. I looked up at him like, so what?

He took the papers back. "There's a lot of extra money in there."

"Well, that's just terrible. I'm so sorry." I was still very confused.

"Carly, that's our account and you know what? Not one bill has been paid or debit transacted in almost three weeks, except for one, which I'll get to in a moment. At first I thought maybe you were so busy you forgot to pay the bills, but I checked, and all of our accounts are current, so it makes me wonder, how is that possible? But first," he held up a copy of a cancelled check "let's talk about the divorce lawyer you paid."

I held on to the crib for support. I wasn't expecting this today, and I just realized my stupidity. I must have accidentally used the joint checkbook to pay that bill. I hadn't meant to.

He was furious, though I couldn't really understand why. What did he expect after all this time? The way he was looking at me, with his handsome face that I hadn't seen in weeks, got my ire up. Who did he think he was?

"You know what, Michael, I did go to see a divorce lawyer and I cried practically the entire time, so much so that Mr. McRae told me I wasn't ready and he politely sent me on my way. And I opened up my own account with my own money so that I could take care of the kids and myself, so when you decide to leave for good, I'm prepared! Does that answer your questions?!"

I had been so good about not crying, but all it took was him coming home, and here I was crying like a baby.

He stepped closer, his eyes wide, but softened. I would even say worried. He reached out and touched my arm. "I thought we decided not to make any final decisions until the baby was born."

I yanked my arm away from him. "I'm not stupid! I know the only reason you haven't pulled the trigger is because you feel guilty because I'm pregnant. And even knowing that, and knowing how you feel about me, I was still too weak to do it myself!"

I hated admitting my weakness in front of him, not to mention telling him how much I still loved him. I turned to walk out of the room; I didn't want him to see me like this, but before I knew it, I was in his arms, and he was stroking my hair. I didn't wrap my arms around him; I was so stunned to be in them that I wasn't even sure this was really happening. He hadn't shown me true affection in months.

"Carly," he whispered in my ear. "You're not weak. You're one of the strongest people I know. And I'm not just staying because of the baby... I've missed you." He sounded like he didn't want to admit that to me or himself.

That only made me cry harder. I finally gave in, put my arms around him, and sank into him. I felt like I had come home.

He kept a hold of me while stroking my hair gently until I had it all out of me. Once I calmed down, he released me and half-smiled. I don't think either one of us knew what to say. So he missed me and I missed him, but that was far from solving our issues. Not even him saying "I love you" would fix it, but it would be nice to hear, even though I knew it wasn't going to be said today, or probably in the near future.

He took a look around the room. "You've certainly been busy."

"I can't take all the credit, your parents have helped with a lot of it."

He walked toward the unfinished collage wall and touched some of the pictures. He pointed to the ones of Mia and Ashton and recognized out loud who they were, but then he pointed to his own. "Who is this?"

I walked to the wall and smiled. "These are you." I pointed. "And these are of me."

He kept touching them like it couldn't be true we were ever so small. "They look like Mia and Ashton," he said as he continued to touch and stare.

I smiled. "Yes, they do."

He turned his attention back toward me. "Where are my pictures that used to hang in here?"

I pointed to the closet. "I boxed them up along with some of the other things you left."

"Can I have them?"

"If you want them."

He walked over to the closet.

I sat back down on the floor and began to rearrange the pictures again. I heard him rifle through the closet.

"Hey Carly, what's all this other stuff?"

"What other stuff?"

He carried out a fairly large box and set it next to me.

"Oh, I had forgotten I put that in there." I looked up at him. "This was supposed to be part of your birthday present. So, I guess, happy birthday."

He sat down on the floor next to me, eager to go through the box. He almost looked like a kid at Christmas. First he pulled out three vinyl records that I had searched high and low for. He loved old records, and he loved the three bands Journey, Led Zeppelin, and Rush.

"Where did you find these?" he asked while looking them over.

"Let's see, eBay, flea market, and an online marketplace."

His smile was huge and genuine. He set the records carefully down and resumed rummaging through the box. He pulled out each item. There were twenty six items that ranged from the sentimental to the silly. But each one reminded me of him. There was a signed Braves hat that I had to stand in line for hours to obtain. Then there were little things like his favorite candy; he loved Three Musketeers bars. Again, just things about him I loved.

"So what were you going to do with all of this stuff?"

I was almost embarrassed to tell him. I bit my lip. "Well, I had planned on giving you one gift every day for the forty days leading up to your birthday and then on your birthday surprising you with… well never mind."

He looked at me, then at the partial present, and then back at me. He was smiling, but it was a closed mouth kind of smile. I couldn't tell what he was thinking, but he kept looking at me. All of a sudden, it was like a light bulb went off in his head. He sat up straighter and his blue eyes brightened. "Let's go out tonight."

"Like on a date?"

He grinned. "It is my birthday, after all, and my folks already have the kids."

I thought for a second. "I don't know."

He reached over and touched my cheek gently. "Come on, Carly. Just you and me."

I went back and forth in my head trying to decide whether this was a good idea or not. Normally going on a date with your husband was a good thing, but we really needed to work a lot of things out, and I thought maybe that should come first.

"Carly?"

His eyes got to me. Darn him. "Okay."

"Great," he said as he gathered up all of his gifts into the box. "I'll pick you up at six."

I nodded. He leaned over and kissed my forehead and thanked me. He took his box along with the box of pictures. "I'll see you in a few hours," he called back as he walked out of the room.

Just when I thought I knew what to expect from him, he did the unexpected. He came home early to surprise me, he asked me on a date, and he held me while I was crying. Did I even dare say he was acting like my husband? At least I knew better than to get comfortable with that idea. We had been separated for five months, and there was a lot of water under that bridge. Regardless, I got up, went downstairs, and started to get ready for my date.

What do you wear when you're pregnant and on a date? That was the question. I searched through my closet over and over again. I tried on several outfits from the casual to the dressy. I kept thinking how ridiculous this was. Why was I so nervous? I don't even think I was this nervous on our very first date. I only remember being excited. Our first date came right after Christmas, just a few weeks after we had met. He flew to Denver and stayed with my cousin, Kyle. Well, kind of; the few nights he was in town we practically stayed up all night talking, except for the second night when we had been skiing all day. I had never felt so connected to anyone. I wondered if we could get that back.

I finally decided on a black poly-cotton dress that hit me above the knee. My legs were still looking semi-sexy, so I thought I might as well show those off as my mid-section was looking pretty pregnant. First I showered and relaxed under the warm water. It was nice to be able to shower without the worry of kiddos knocking on the door. I hadn't had that feeling in a while. I was missing my babies, but I was taking advantage of the alone time that had been scarce.

I dressed and carefully fixed my pixie haircut. I brushed it forward and let it fall sexily around my face, just like Michael liked it. I was still sporting a great summertime tan, so just a little lip gloss, mascara and blush did the trick. I tied a cute pink scarf around my neck, threw on some sling-back heels and called it good. While I waited, I read Michael's latest article about the role of media in presidential elections. It wasn't his finest, but it was good. They couldn't all be Pulitzer Prize level.

At five minutes before six, the door unlocked and Michael came in. I don't know why, but I expected him to knock. I guess that was silly since he had a house key and his name was on the mortgage…and I was carrying his baby.

I stood up.

He waited in the entryway looking extremely handsome. He was wearing a nice pair of dark jeans, a white rolled-up shirt and a tan vest. I loved vests. He was obviously able to work out on the road, his arms were still toned and his chest was broad. His seven o'clock shadow was perfect, as always. For a moment, my breath was taken away.

I walked toward him, and he grinned as he looked me over.

"You look radiant," he said before he kissed my cheek.

"Thank you, handsome."

"Are you ready to go?"

I smiled and nodded. He opened the door, led me out, and locked it. He reached for my hand, and we walked down our porch steps hand-in-hand. I hadn't seen him this happy in months. I wasn't sure what had happened, but I liked it. He walked me to the passenger side of his white Silverado and helped me in.

Before he shut the door, he placed his hand gently on my middle. "Looks like she's coming along nicely."

She kicked in response.

He smiled.

I smiled back.

He shut my door and went around and climbed into the driver seat.

"So where are you taking me?"

He looked over and winked. "You'll see."

As long as it involved food, I didn't care. I sat back and enjoyed the company. We talked easily all the way to a cozy restaurant called Wild Flour Bistro. It was in the next town over in a lovely setting. I made a mental note to add it to my list of photo locations; it was a downtown district, and there was a brook and park nearby. As we got out, I could smell something superb; I hoped it was coming from the restaurant. Mixed in with that aroma was the smell of honeysuckle. One of the many reasons I had come to love living in the South, even when it was humid, was the smell of honeysuckle.

We walked hand-in-hand into the restaurant, glancing and smiling at one another. It had been too long since we had been out like this. If we stayed together, I would insist we date more. It's something we should have been better at. Michael told the host his name and that he had made reservations. We were promptly seated. I looked around at the little restaurant, and the word that kept coming to me was *eclectic*. None of the tables or chairs matched in a conventional sort of way, but oddly it all came together. And apparently the menu changed daily. They only offered four to five different dishes to choose from. When the server brought out our water, I noticed the goblets were each unique. It was kind of fun.

Michael decided on the pan-seared duck breast with sautéed broccolini, and wild rice topped with a mushroom-sour cream sauce. I chose the citrus glazed grilled salmon on a bed of wild rice with grilled asparagus spears sprinkled with toasted almonds. Definitely looking forward to trying both.

"Here are the rules for tonight," he said after our server left.

I raised my eyebrow. "Rules?"

He slyly grinned. "My birthday, my rules."

I rolled my eyes.

"Rule number one, no phone calls."

"But what if the…"

"Ah, ah, ah," he said while waving his finger. "I already called my mom and talked to the kids, everyone is doing fine. I told them you would call them in the morning."

I smiled. "Okay."

"Now that we have that out of the way. Rule number two, no talking about the kids or work." He paused as if he was waiting for me to object.

"Is that all?" I said.

"Rule number three, I reserve the right to add rules as we go along."

"Then I reserve my right to object." I winked.

He picked up my hand and kissed my palm. I always loved when he did that.

"Of course," he replied.

We both sat for a second and thought about what to say. The things I really wanted to know at the moment were probably not the best to bring up on an evening out, especially since it was his birthday. I wanted to know where our relationship was going and if I should be calling back Mr. McRae.

I wanted to know if he still loved me and wanted to be with me, but I settled on, "Read any good books lately?"

As a matter of fact, he had. He read a physics book all about string theory. I had no idea what he was talking about, so he elaborated. I still had no idea what he was talking about, but I supposed that didn't matter.

When he was done showing off his high IQ, he smiled at me. "What about you?"

I smirked. "I just finished this riveting tale all about breast-feeding. You should check it out sometime."

His eyes sparkled when he laughed. I missed that laugh. I missed him.

Throughout dinner it felt like old times, the way we talked and laughed. The conversation was all over the place from music, to movies and remember when's. I told him about the new bands I was loving, and he, of course, countered with why the bands of old were far superior. The conversation gravitated toward when we were dating and right after we were married, when we were free to do as we pleased and when. Back then if he had an assignment, it was common for me to just pack up and go with him. Those were great times and I'll always cherish them, but I was happy when we settled down some. I was especially happy when we started a family. He, on the other hand, seemed to long for those days again.

As we were waiting for our check, he reached over and placed his hand on mine. "What were you going to surprise me with today?"

I set down my goblet of water and thought for a second. "Do you remember that bed and breakfast you wanted to go to in Estes Park last year?"

His smile faltered as he sat up straighter. He definitely remembered. I wondered if he remembered what a spectacle he made out of himself when I told him it wasn't a good idea at the time. I had never seen him behave that way before.

"Well," I bit my lip. "I booked a long weekend there for just the two of us."

His eyes lit up a tad. "Do those reservations still exist?"

I shook my head no. "That boat sailed a long time ago."

He dropped his head slightly and let out a deep breath.

I had canceled them back in June when I realized this wasn't going to be fixed anytime soon.

He began to verbally respond, or at least I thought he was going to. He definitely looked like he had something to say, but he was interrupted by the waiter with the check. I used that as my opportunity to use the ladies' room. Three glasses of water and a baby on my bladder was an uncomfortable combination.

By the time I returned, the check had been paid. Michael stood up, put his arm around me, and we left.

When we reached the passenger side of his truck, he stopped before he opened my door. He looked to me at his side. "Thank you for making this a better birthday than I deserve. I want you to know that the thought and preparation has not been lost on me. I regret that I prevented you from seeing your plans through." His hands came up and he took my face in them, his eyes bearing down into mine. "You're incredible." He leaned in closer.

I held my breath, but my head kicked in instead of my heart. "What are you doing?"

He grinned. "Has it been so long that you've forgotten what this is?"

"It has been too long, but…" I placed my finger on his lips that were seductively grinning at me. "I don't kiss on the first date."

His eyes narrowed. He dropped one hand and placed it on my belly. "Need I remind you, *Mrs.* Bishop, this isn't our first date, and you're carrying *our* child."

I wickedly grinned and placed my hand on top of his. "Believe me, I don't need a reminder."

He stepped back, still smiling, but definitely disappointed. "So I guess that means my favorite birthday present is off the table tonight."

I felt the heat rise to my cheeks and my heart pick up a little at the thought. He had no idea how tempting that idea was to me, or maybe he did. "As much as I would like to… I don't think we should sleep together until we know that we plan on sharing a bed permanently."

"It's like déjà vu," he quipped.

He had definitely heard a variation of that line before we were married.

I shrugged my shoulders. It was for the best. I wanted nothing more than to be connected to him in that way again, but I couldn't until I knew for sure where his heart was. And from what I could tell, he didn't know. I couldn't stand the pain of opening myself up to him like that just to have him walk away.

Without another word, he opened my door and helped me in. As I watched him walk around the front of the truck, I could tell he was walking slowly. When he reached the front, he stopped deliberately and looked straight at me through the windshield. He looked bothered. After a moment, he purposefully turned back around and came back my way. He was acting strange. I followed him with my eyes as he walked to me and opened my door.

"Uh, did you forget something?" I asked.

He stepped closer and took my face in his hands again. "No, I remembered something."

"What?"

Without a second thought, his lips were on mine. He began to tenderly kiss me.

I let myself fall into it as my lips parted. For a moment I forgot we were separated and that he didn't love me anymore because his kiss said something entirely different. He kissed me softly and repeatedly for a minute or two as he gently touched my face. I'm sure the people around us thought, "Get a room already," but at the moment I didn't care. I just wanted my Bishop back.

He gently extricated himself from my lips and leaned his forehead against mine as he still held my face in his palms. "I remembered how much I regretted not kissing you on our actual first date. I couldn't sleep that night thinking about what I had missed out on. I didn't want that again tonight." He kissed my forehead, shut my door, and walked quickly around, this time to the driver's side.

I tried to rapidly wipe away an errant tear or two before he noticed.

"Are you tired? Do you want to go home?" he asked.

Suddenly, I had a thought. I smiled brightly. "No. There's something else I want to do. Will you will take me to Johnsons?"

"You want me to take you to the grocery store?"

"Yep."

"Okay…"

I think he was pretty disappointed on the way over, but I hoped he wouldn't be for long.

As soon as he parked, I looked over to him. "Wait here, I'll be right back."

He shook his head at me.

I quickly hopped out and made my way in. I grabbed a little cart and headed to the bakery section. I hoped they had what I was looking for, and thankfully, they did. I placed a small double layered red velvet cake in the basket. Then I went in search of candles, a lighter, and plastic forks. I even grabbed some sparkling water. At checkout I asked if they could put it all in a paper bag with handles to hide the purchase.

I walked as quickly as I could back to my waiting husband. It was the first time in weeks I had any hope that maybe he would continue to be my husband. I couldn't help but smile. As I approached his truck, he had the windows down and he was scrolling through his phone.

Before I opened the door, I raised my eyebrow at him through the open window. "Hmm…I believe you just broke rule number one."

He immediately threw his phone in his console. He reached over and opened the door from the inside. I set my bag down; he tried to peer in, but I quickly closed it.

"Rule number four, no peeking."

He smiled. "Okay, so now what?"

"Riverbottom Park."

He had no problem complying, but he was definitely intrigued. Riverbottom Park was near his parents' place. It was a lovely place for a stroll or a picnic. There was a great spot right by the river where the willow trees hung low and the scent of wildflowers infused the air. It was one of the first places that Michael had taken me when he brought me home to meet his parents for the first time. It had been in the spring, and it was so green compared to back home in Colorado. I think I instantly fell in love with the Southern charm of it all. After we had Ashton, it was an easy choice to make to settle down here.

We pulled into the parking area near the playground. There were just a handful of cars, which wasn't surprising since it was close to nine p.m. Michael looked over to me for direction.

"Do you still carry a blanket behind the back seat?"

He nodded his head yes.

"Perfect. Grab it," I said as I exited the vehicle with my bag.

He met me with the blanket in hand, and we began to walk toward the river. It was a little difficult, in heels, walking on the uneven grass with only a speck of daylight left in the darkening sky. Michael kept steadying me and several times he offered to carry the bag, but I refused. We landed in our favorite spot on the bank of the river. Michael laid out the blanket, while I kicked off my shoes and untied my scarf. It was still quite warm. Michael helped me sit down, although I wasn't in need of that particular service yet, but it was nice all the same. As soon as we were both situated, he looked at me like, "Now what?"

I looked out over the water and sighed. I loved this place. "Do you remember the first time you brought me here?"

He wickedly grinned, leaned over, kissed my neck, and whispered against it, "I do."

Goosebumps erupted as he continued to softly kiss my neck.

"I wish we could go back to those days, don't you?" he quietly asked between kisses.

I sighed. "Those were amazing times and I loved every second, but so many wonderful things have happened since then and we have so much to look forward to."

He abruptly stopped kissing me, sat up straight, and looked out beyond.

I took his hand. "What's wrong?"

He squeezed my hand, but quickly let go. "Nothing. So what's in the bag?"

I gave him a quizzical look. I could tell something was off. He smiled, but it was wistful. I didn't know what else to do, so I asked him to close his eyes. His smile turned wry at the request, but he obeyed. I waved my hand in front of his face to check before I emptied the contents of my bag. I took out the cake and placed the four and the zero candles in the center before I carefully lit them. Thankfully, at the moment there wasn't a breeze. Then I began to sing 'Happy Birthday' and without prompting, he opened his eyes.

At first his smile was thin, so I sang even louder and he couldn't help but grin broadly. I finished on a long drawn out note, then held the cake close to him.

"Make a wish, Michael."

He thought for a moment as he searched my eyes. I got the feeling he was torn on what to wish for. His eyes were sullen as they reflected the candle light. I looked deeply into those troubled baby blues of his, trying to figure out what was going on with him. It wasn't like Michael was a happy-go-lucky kind of a guy, but he used to be happy, or maybe content was a better word. He was anything but content at the moment, and hadn't been in some time. I wished I knew what to do to make it better. Or, sometimes I wished I could just smack him and say, get over it already. Your life is great.

He easily blew out both candles.

I leaned over the cake and kissed him once on the lips. "Happy birthday," I whispered.

His eyes were still searching as I lowered the cake and took out the candles.

"Forty," he sighed.

"Forty's the new twenty, you know."

"Spoken like someone several years from turning said age."

I rolled my eyes and handed him a fork. "Honestly, I don't think forty will bother me. In fact, I look forward to it. I think women in their forties exude a sexiness and confidence that only comes with age."

"Talk to me in six years."

I dug into the cake with my fork, retrieved a large bite, and held it up in front of his face. "Smile and eat your cake."

He reluctantly grinned and opened his mouth.

I shoved the cake right in.

"Mmm," he said as he chewed slowly.

I joined him and took a bite myself. It was pretty good. Not as good as homemade, but it would do. We ate silently for a moment, looking out over the river. It was completely dark now except for fireflies and moonlight. I kept wondering what he was thinking about and if he would ever really open up to me again. I wondered if this was the last birthday we would celebrate together, or if we were on the road to reconciliation. I kept waiting for him to choose, but I was becoming impatient.

"I had an early flight from Dallas. I think I'm ready to call it a day," he said without warning.

"Okay." I didn't even try to hide my disappointment.

I covered the cake back up and placed it in the bag. Michael stood and helped me up. He gently pulled me to him as I stood, and he held me for a moment. I held on tight. I didn't want to let go, but he kissed the top of my head and did just that. He lifted up the bag and the blanket and left me standing there in the very warm evening air feeling lost and confused.

Chapter Sixteen

You know when they say be careful what you ask for? I think whoever that was knew what they were talking about. Michael's bipolar behavior over the weekend was perplexing to say the least. I desperately needed to know why he was acting that way and what I should do.

Let's cover the chain of events. He came home early to surprise me, stormed over to the house because, surprise, I wasn't just sitting around twiddling my thumbs waiting for him to do whatever he was going to do. Then I found myself in his arms, and he claimed to miss me and asked me out. We had a lovely dinner and shared a passionate kiss; he even implied he wanted more, but we headed to the park for what I thought would be a continuation of the romantic evening, and perhaps the beginning of reconciliation, it was then that he became distant again.

We had a silent drive home, until the end when he mentioned how busy he'd be that weekend, finishing up a couple of articles and getting ready for his assignment in Phoenix the following week. I reminded him he hadn't seen his children in almost two months, so he stopped by Saturday night and took them to pizza; I wasn't invited. Sunday he declined an invitation to his parents' house for lunch, and all I got was a phone call telling me he was off again and he'd see me Friday when we would meet with Mr. Xavier for dinner.

I knew his parents wanted to stay out of our marriage, but I felt like I didn't have anyone else to talk to, so while the kids were swimming after my doctor's appointment on Tuesday, I told them about everything that had happened the previous weekend and asked for their take on it. They were both reluctant, but I think they could tell I was in desperate need of advice.

"Honey," Jack began. "Danielle and I have been talking."

Danielle looked solemnly over at him. This wasn't good.

He reached over and took my hand. "Honey," he repeated. "This can't go on. It's not good for you or the kids. I thought my son would get his head out of his as... butt and realize what he was throwing away, but I just don't know where his head is at."

"So you think I should file for divorce?" my voice faltered.

I looked at Danielle, and she had tears in her eyes. She looked like she couldn't speak. Jack's face was red with anger. "We don't want to see that, but we'll support you one hundred percent if that's what you decide, and we won't blame you one bit. You don't deserve this."

I tried to keep my tears at bay. I didn't want the kids to see me crying again. They'd already seen way too much of that. I quietly told them of my meeting with the lawyer. They didn't seem surprised. They just reiterated they were here for me, regardless, and how sorry they were. It was a depressing conversation, but at the same time empowering. It was like I needed someone to give me permission. I decided that weekend, when Michael was in town, we were having it out once and for all. He was going to either agree to work on our marriage and make it a priority by seeking counseling and taking the necessary steps to come home, or I was filing for divorce.

The thought made my stomach twist in knots, but my in-laws were right, this wasn't good for anyone, especially Mia and Ashton. I spent the rest of the week taking the kids school clothes and supply shopping. Mia was so excited to be starting kindergarten, and she was even more excited to be in the same school as Ashton. We had to get the perfect pink backpack with butterflies on it, of course, and the prettiest lunchbox we could find. Ashton was surprisingly excited, too. I had Jack to thank for that. He was the best grandpa around.

Ashton didn't want kid lunchboxes and backpacks. "I'm a man now," he informed me. He could catch and gut his own fish, and Jack had taken him to the shooting range, so now he had shot a gun and, of course, Papa let him drive the golf cart. He was growing up to be a true Southern boy. Too bad his daddy was missing out on it all. What was worse was that Michael didn't even seem to care. Ashton ended up, to my chagrin, with a camouflaged backpack and lunchbox. I would have preferred Legos or Star Wars, but hey, if it made him happy, I was okay with it.

At night, while the kids slept, I worked on my wall. It was getting so close to being done. As I worked, I talked to the baby. I told her stories about how her daddy used to be and why I fell in love with him. I talked to her about my parents and how much I missed them and all the interesting places I had lived around the world, including Japan, Finland, Iceland and even a tiny island called Micronesia. I told her funny stories about Mia and Ashton and how I couldn't wait for her to get here to meet them. I promised her, no matter what, we would be happy and I would take care of them.

Thursday, I finished the wall at around midnight. The only spaces I left open were for the little girl that was growing inside of me. I wanted all of us to be represented on the wall. I sighed as I thought it might be the last and only place where we would all truly be together. I fell into the new, white, oversized chair in the corner of the room and sank low into it. I had been having such a hard time sleeping. I knew this weekend my life was going to change. I knew it needed it to, but I was scared.

I had a thought as I sat there. I went and grabbed my laptop and came right back to my new favorite spot in the house, that chair in the nursery. I curled up and watched the baby move as the laptop came to life. The baby was big enough for me to see hands and feet protruding out. I contemplated how life was so amazing and how incredible it was that a human could grow inside of me. As soon as I could, I got on the internet and typed in blog.thegirlinseat24b.com. It had been ages since I visited the old site. As soon as I saw the page come up, I teared up, seeing the cover photo of Michael and me sitting next to one another on our flight to Tahiti. I remember asking the stewardess to take it. We looked so young. What did I even know at twenty-four? I guess the only thing I knew was, I was in love. I touched the screen lightly and brushed over Michael's happy face. He looked like he was in love, right? I scrolled through several other pictures of us; we looked so happy. It looked real, and I could still remember how it felt; those memories felt so real, my heart ached.

I looked at the pictures of me with my babies. Michael had written beautiful posts about the day each of our children were born. When Ashton was born, his blog centered around what it was like to become a father for the first time, how proud he was to have a son, and everything he was going to teach him. When Mia was born, he wrote about what an honor it was to raise a girl and how he wished she would grow up to be exactly like her mother. He talked about how amazing I was, how he couldn't believe that I still loved him, and that "lucky" didn't even begin to describe him.

What happened? How did a love like that turn into resentment? Was there any hope for us at all? I was about to find out.

Michael was supposed to meet me at the house where a car and driver was picking us up to drive us downtown to one of those ritzy hotels for dinner. My in-laws came over in the afternoon; they hadn't seen their son since the weekend I was in the hospital, and they thought this would be a good opportunity. They were also going to stay and babysit for me. With them there, I could shower in peace. I had mixed emotions coursing through me as I showered. I was excited on one hand, that I was getting to meet a man who was possibly the future president of the United States—a man who had been a friend of my dad's. I mean, how often does one get a chance like that? On the other hand, I was sick to my stomach thinking this could possibly be it for my marriage. There was no more sitting on the fence.

As soon as I turned off the water, I heard my phone ring on my bed in the room. I wrapped a towel around me quickly, but it quit ringing. *Oh well*, I thought as I dried off. I was getting too big to be running to the phone, or anywhere for that matter. At almost thirty weeks pregnant, whoever it was could call back if it was that important. I carefully did my makeup and blow dried my hair to just the way I liked it, or just the way Michael loved it. He was such a stupid man. I dressed carefully in my evening gown. It was a beautiful, long Valencia gown in sunset red. I thought it was exquisite, or as exquisite as it could get in my current state.

On my way out to the living room, I grabbed my phone. Two missed calls and messages from Michael.

"Carly, please call me as soon as you get this message. My flight got delayed in Huntsville. I'll probably have to meet you at the hotel, but I need to talk to you first."

"Carly, please call me. It's important that I talk to you."

I wondered what the urgency was. I quickly tried to call him, but it went straight to voice mail. I left a quick message of annoyance. He hardly called me all week and now, suddenly, he wanted to talk to me, and of course, he was running late. The driver was going to arrive in forty-five minutes. There was no way Michael was making it to the house on time. The flight from Huntsville was less than an hour, but we lived forty-five minutes from the Atlanta airport.

I looked in my full-length mirror once more and added a light sheen of lip gloss. I slipped into my nude heels and walked out, completely out of sorts.

"You look like the most beautiful princess ever," Mia said as I walked into the living room. That boosted my mood significantly. I smiled and kissed the top of her sweet head.

Jack came over and kissed my cheek. "You are stunning, my dear."

"Thanks, Jack."

He touched my cheek and smiled. "You know, I would really love it if you would call me Dad."

I smiled back. "Really? What if, you know... you know..." I didn't want to say divorce in front of the kids. And it's not like I didn't want to call him Dad. I would love to. Jack was like a father to me.

"That won't change how we feel about you."

I hugged him tight and kissed his cheek. "Thank you, Dad." I almost choked on the words. I hadn't said them in so long, and my feelings for Jack were overwhelming. I owed him so much. I looked at Danielle. She had a thoughtful look as she looked up to me from the couch. She didn't ask me to call her mom, but that was okay. I was happy with how far we'd come these past few months.

At five-thirty, the doorbell rang, and there stood a very large intimidating man in a black suit and glasses.

"Mrs. Bishop?"

"That's me." I wasn't sure for how long, but he didn't need to know that.

"Right this way, ma'am."

I turned around and gave hugs and kisses and loves. I also profusely thanked my in-laws for once again babysitting, then I was off.

In front of my home was a black Mercedes limo with windows so dark I could see my reflection clearly. The man who called himself Heath opened my door and helped me in. It wasn't my first limo ride, I had done it several times before with my parents. In fact, most of my growing up I was driven around by people other than my parents. My dad said it was always safer to have natives drive you in their own countries; accidents were less likely that way.

I tried to relax in the wide seat. I was told to help myself. There was water, soda, and alcoholic beverages. I didn't dare drink anything. It would be my luck to get stuck in traffic with a baby on my full bladder. I kept checking my phone. Michael never called. I made small talk with Heath, but I mostly stayed quiet inside my own thoughts.

We arrived at the hotel and drove into an underground parking garage. There I was met by the Secret Service. Mr. Xavier, as a potential next president, was already being guarded by the Secret Service. I was gently patted down; I could tell they were uncomfortable touching a pregnant woman, but I understood. They also looked through my small purse and checked out my phone.

"Ma'am, you will need to keep your phone shut off during the entire meeting," the female agent instructed me.

"Where is your husband?" asked her male counterpart.

"His flight was delayed; he should be joining us later."

They both seem to take my word for it. I was glad because they gave off this threatening vibe.

I was finally escorted to a private table set in the back. It looked like we would be by ourselves, other than wait staff. Mr. Xavier immediately rose as soon as he saw me. His face broke out in a huge grin. He was a tall, distinguished-looking man. He had thick salt and pepper hair and bright eyes. I believe he was sixty years old, but he could easily pass for fifty. He was quite attractive, and even without speaking he exuded charisma.

He held out his hand. "It's such a pleasure to finally meet you, Mrs. Bishop."

"Oh, please call me Carly, Mr. Xavier."

"Joseph, please."

"Okay." I smiled.

He pulled out my seat for me and helped me sit down. "So, where is that husband of yours?"

"Delayed flight. I'm sure he's on his way." I did my best to keep the annoyance out of my voice.

He sat across from me, his eyes alight. "It really is so nice to meet you after all this time. I must say, though, I didn't know you were expecting. Your husband never mentioned it, and considering."

That wasn't surprising, but I was confused by the last part. "It's a pleasure to meet you sir. And kind of you to take time out of your hectic schedule for me."

"Please, I've been sir'd enough to last me a lifetime."

"I bet you have. Could you please explain what you meant by 'considering?' "

He laughed. He had a hearty jovial laugh, kind of like a Santa. It was contagious, but why was that funny?

"Well, considering your husband will be working for me and the nature of his work, this is quite a sacrifice for you and your family. You must be the world's most understanding wife, which isn't a surprise," he answered.

I shook my head. I was speechless. "Mr., I mean Joseph, I'm afraid I have no idea what you're talking about."

His eyes widened and his skin reddened as he nervously laughed, "Well, now that the cat's out of the bag I guess there's no going back. I'm sorry, though I assumed your husband would have told you that he accepted an offer to write my biography. He'll be traveling with me through election day."

Now I really was speechless. I reached for my glass of water and took a few sips. I tried to keep my composure. How could Michael keep this from me? Our baby's due date was the day before Election Day this year.

"You know I can have him home in a moment's notice, if needed," he offered when I didn't respond.

"That's very kind of you," I managed to say.

"How far along are you?"

"My due date is November seventh."

His eyes widened in surprise. "Again, I have a private plane, and it will be at his disposal."

I nodded my head and smiled. This was a new low for Michael. How do you accept a new job and not tell your wife about it? Especially when it involves you being gone the remainder of her pregnancy with a high probability of missing the birth? I had to remind myself to stay calm and not freak out, this was not Mr. Xavier's fault, but I so wanted to scream. Instead I smiled. What else could I do?

Mr. Xavier kept looking at me so intently. He had kind eyes, like Jack. There was a nice peaceful feeling surrounding him. I wasn't sure what to expect; he was all over the T.V. and news, but sitting here with him, he seemed so normal.

In the meantime, the waiter came out and handed us our menus and told us what the specials of the night were. Unfortunately, nothing sounded good. My stomach was churning over the rage I felt toward my husband at the moment. How dare he not tell me! I just ordered some pasta dish with shrimp and asked for some lemon to go in my water.

Once the orders were taken, Joseph turned his attention back to me. He kept looking at me like I was a long lost friend. It was kind of sweet. "Please, let me say up front how sorry I was to hear about your parents. They were good people."

I nodded my head in agreement. They were the best.

"I'm so sorry I wasn't able to attend their funeral, but we had just found out about my wife's illness."

"I'm so sorry for your loss," I replied.

He smiled sadly. "To lose a spouse is not something I would wish upon anyone."

I had to hold back the tears at that sentiment. I knew he meant in death, but I was losing my husband all the same, and I felt like something was dying.

"But," he said, "We must rise to the occasion and make the best of what we have been given."

"That's a very good motto. Maybe you can use that in your next speech or perhaps on a bumper sticker."

He laughed. "You really are enchanting."

I blushed. "Thank you."

"I can't tell you how happy I am to meet you. And I'm even happier to find you still married, and obviously happy by the looks of things." He looked toward my stomach.

Oh, if he only knew. I really was going to kill Michael. He better hope his plane crashed. I kept smiling.

"Maybe I shouldn't say this, but you know your dad was so worried about you marrying Michael."

I sat up even straighter. "No. He never mentioned it."

He laughed again. "Well, I guess I'm just full of surprises tonight for you."

He had no idea.

"He was worried Michael was a rolling stone and he was full of wanderlust." He paused for a moment as if he was contemplating whether he should go on.

I was more than interested to hear what he had to say. So I smiled pleasantly, hoping he would get the cue.

He smiled in return and took the hint. "He feared you may lose your luster in Michael's eyes and that he would break your heart. I think he thought Michael very undeserving of your love."

Suddenly, a new layer of the mystery of Michael's behavior unraveled. I wondered why my dad never said anything, why didn't he caution me if he was worried? Probably because he knew I wouldn't have listen, but he was right. I couldn't help it, a tiny tear fell.

"Oh, I'm sorry," he said as he handed me a real handkerchief. "I'm sure you still miss your parents."

He had no idea, but that wasn't why I was crying.

I took the handkerchief and began to dab my eyes. "I'm sorry."

"No need to apologize. I hope someday my daughters will shed a few tears for their old man."

I smiled. "I'm sure they will."

"Speaking of my daughters…"

In the middle of his sentence, Michael arrived. He looked worried, as he should be, when he looked my way.

Joseph stood up again like he was greeting an old friend. "Michael, my boy. You finally made it," he said as they shook hands. "I was almost hoping you wouldn't. Your wife really is enchanting."

Michael lied while glancing down at me. "Yes, she is."

I glared back at him while Joseph returned to his seat. He wasn't scoring any points with me.

Michael sat down next to me and kissed my cheek. "I'm sorry I'm late."

I didn't respond, and thankfully I didn't need to. Joseph started right back where he left off. "I was just explaining to Carly that her dad gave me the best advice for my sons-in-law." He looked to Michael, "I know you've heard it straight from the horse's mouth, but it's worth repeating." He looked directly back at me. "Your dad said, 'I told my son-in-law before he married my daughter, if you love her the right way, she'll make you her world. And if you don't, I will take you out of this world.' Best line ever."

I looked over to Michael, who looked very uncomfortable. He had never mentioned that speech, and he obviously didn't take much stock in it anymore. He wouldn't even look at me. He cleared his throat, "It was a great line."

Joseph beamed at us. "I'm happy to see you were smart enough to listen to it. Derek would be so pleased to see you still together."

That was enough. I stood up. "Excuse me while I use the ladies' room."

Michael and Joseph both stood up. I smiled at Joseph and then turned and walked away. I was followed by the female secret service agent who had patted me down earlier. It was odd, but it kept me from losing it. It reminded me that decorum was needed, but once I was in the bathroom, I stood at the sink and held on. I breathed in and out, in and out. I desperately wanted to leave, but I knew I couldn't. Instead, I silently prayed for strength. I stayed as long as I could, before I rejoined the small party of men, half of which I could do without at the moment. He knew, too, as I walked back and he helped me with my chair. His face was red and his eyes implored me to keep up the act. They should have said sorry, but that was too much to expect from him.

Joseph, on the other hand, had no clue, so either I'm a phenomenal actress and should seriously take up poker, or he was clueless. And if that was the case, I wouldn't be voting for him for president. Joseph looked my way. "I was just berating your husband here for not telling you about his new job and even more importantly, for not telling me that you were expecting."

I looked at a very stiff Michael. Now his eyes pleaded. He cleared his throat, "I tried to call you from the airport."

I didn't respond to him. I put on my best fake smile and looked to Joseph. "You know Michael is like that rolling stone my dad talked about and I've just learned not to get in his way. I want him to be happy. This is a dream come true for him and I would never even think of standing in his way."

From under the table Michael reached for my hand that rested in my lap. I pushed it away.

Joseph looked to Michael. "You certainly are a lucky man."

Michael smiled nervously and nodded his head in agreement.

I had never been so happy to see food arrive. I was so ready for this evening to end, so I could have the nervous breakdown I more than deserved. I barely touched my food, but I blamed it on the pregnancy. Joseph didn't even think twice about it, but I knew Michael knew.

I stayed mostly quiet and let them yammer on about ideas for the biography and who Michael would be meeting with, people like his daughters and business associates, etc. Joseph went on and on about Michael's talent and how impressed he was with the write-up Michael had done about him.

Michael tried and failed to score some more points with me. "It was Carly's idea to add a more human element to it."

Joseph's eyes sparkled at the tidbit. "You make an excellent team."

I used to think so, too.

Thankfully, Joseph could only spend ninety minutes with us. He had a fundraiser to attend.

Joseph approached me. "Would you mind if I hugged you?"

"Not at all."

"You are more lovely in person than I could imagine and beautiful doesn't even begin to describe you."

"Are you trying to earn my vote?" I smiled.

He laughed that booming laugh of his and shook his head. "Delightful is what you are." He looked to Michael. "I think you're a fool to agree to this assignment and leave this at home."

I didn't even bother looking at Michael's reaction to that.

"You know," Joseph said. "You're welcome to join us at any stop. Just say the word and I'll arrange it."

For some reason, I was interested to see Michael's reaction to this piece of news. I was surprised to see that he looked genuinely happy about the idea.

I looked backed to Joseph. "Again, very kind of you, but my children will be starting school soon and I'm not sure how my doctor would feel about me gallivanting across the country."

"Yes, of course. But you're welcome if you change your mind," he replied.

"Thank you again for meeting with me," I said. "It was quite enlightening. And best wishes to you."

We all said our goodbyes, or see-you-soons in Michael's case. Joseph asked an agent to escort us to the car, but Michael chimed in that he drove and could drive us home. I desperately wanted to decline, but doing so would be very bad form. Just once, I wanted to hone in on the main character from *Something to Talk About* and vilify my husband publicly. I wanted to have my moment of vindication, but tonight would not be the night.

As we walked toward the lobby, Michael reached for my hand again.

"Don't touch me," I said very quietly with razor precision.

He backed off, and I walked very briskly out to the front of the hotel where we waited for the valet to bring Michael's truck around. We only waited a couple of minutes, but it was dead silent between the two of us. The truck was brought around and the doorman helped me. Michael tipped the valet and got in. As soon as he drove off, he started to speak.

"Not a word," I said succinctly. I looked out the window and fumed. I was done crying and mourning for something I could never have back. I should have believed him back in March when he first said he didn't love me. He meant every word. No man that loved his wife would do this to her.

"Carly, we need to talk about this," Michael said halfway home.

"No, the time for talking is long past."

"What does that mean?"

"It means I finally understand and believe you and I'm going to give you what you've wanted all along." I twisted my ring off my slightly swollen finger (you've got to love being pregnant in the hot, humid summer) and dropped it in the cup holder that sat between the seats in the console.

"Carly!" he said as he looked down at my wedding ring and swerved. "I don't want your wedding ring!"

"No, I'm sure you don't, but you want what that represents—your freedom."

He didn't say anything, he just took the next exit.

"Where are we going?" I asked

He didn't respond. He kept driving until he found an empty parking lot. He pulled over and threw the truck in park and turned my way. "So what are you saying? I have to choose between you and my job?"

I practically laughed. "We both know that choice has already been made, but…" I choked. "I would never ask you to make that choice. I couldn't bear to see the resentment in your eyes. I love you too much for that." I swore I would never say those words to him again unless he spoke them first, but I guess it was okay since this was the end game and I would never say them again. I wiped my eyes as Michael looked on, bewildered, with a crinkled brow. I picked up my wedding ring, took his hand, and placed it in his palm. "Take it. Go be happy. Make your mark on the world."

He slowly, but surely wrapped his hand around the band that looked so tiny in his large hand.

I turned and leaned my head against the cool glass. "Please take me home now." I deserved my breakdown in the privacy of my own home.

"You know," he yelled. "You changed."

I turned slowly toward him and stared at him blankly. It was an odd thing to say.

"Ever since we had kids, your life began to revolve around them. I became second best," he shouted as he pointed toward his chest. "Even though I was the one sacrificing my career and aspirations to support you and them."

I shook my head in disbelief. Did he really feel this way? "Michael," I cried, "I'm sorry you felt that way. I honestly loved you more after we had kids. To me, they've always been a reminder of what our love created. I don't know what more I could have done to show you how important you were to me and that I loved you more than anyone, including our kids. I'm sorry I failed in that regard." I sat up straighter. "But yes, Michael, I did change. It's called growing up. And you know what? You changed, too. And you don't get to blame me for choices we made *together*. If you were so unhappy, you should have said something a long time ago."

His eyes were as hard as steel, and they bore into me, but I wasn't turning away. Several times it looked as if he was attempting to say something, but the words never came.

I sighed. "Please take me home now." I turned back toward the cool glass and silently let the tears fall against the window.

Michael took his time leaving, but I didn't say anything while we sat there for several minutes. What was left to say? It was over. My heart ached, but at least I felt peace; I was no longer teetering on the fence. I had received the insight I had been seeking. Michael and I had seen our marriage from completely different points of view. My dad had been right about Michael.

The remaining twenty minute drive home was deafeningly silent. The only movements seemed to come from my abdomen. The baby seemed out of sorts. I gently placed my hand on her, and a wave of sadness washed over me. I wondered if Michael would even love this baby at all. I just needed to be home.

I had never been so happy to see my house. And it was only my house now. As soon as he stopped, I began to open the door.

"Carly."

I paused, but didn't look at him.

"Can I come by and see the kids tomorrow before I leave?"

"Yes."

I proceeded to leave again.

"I'll still try to make it home in time for the birth."

I turned toward him with tear-stained cheeks. "Please don't."

"Why?"

"Because…I don't want you there." I knew he didn't want to be there anyway.

"You're going to do this by yourself?"

I wanted to say that's what I'd been doing this whole time, but there was no sense in beating a dead horse. "I was planning on asking your mom to be there with me."

He gently grabbed my arm. "Hey. What about your rule? That only medical personnel and those that were there at conception could be in attendance."

"That man doesn't exist anymore, and after tonight, I'm not sure if he ever did," I eeked out.

Michael's hand released my arm, and if I wasn't mistaken, I saw tears well up in his eyes.

I couldn't take it anymore. I turned and left. I don't even know if I shut the truck door in my haste. I ran to the safety, love, and protection my home and children and in-laws provided.

I ran toward my new reality.

Chapter Seventeen

It didn't take long for the shock to wear off and for the crushing reality to hit me. Sure, our marriage had been over for months and, whereas a certain amount of peace came with knowing, there was still overwhelming grief and sorrow that followed. That first night, I lay on the couch with my head in Danielle's lap, like a child. She let me cry while she stroked my hair. She didn't say a word. Jack, on the other hand, decided to take matters into his own hands. He left straight away to Michael's apartment. I asked him not to, but he felt like his son needed to be talked to.

He was gone for a couple of hours, and he looked furious when he returned. I don't know what he thought he was going to accomplish by going over there. Michael had made up his mind a long time ago. I was the foolish one that kept trying to hold on. Sure, I thought there was some sadness on his part, but more than anything, I was sure he was relieved. Jack didn't say what had happened, and I wasn't asking. I knew Michael didn't want me; I didn't need to hear it repeated. They stayed until almost midnight and mostly just listened to me. They tried to offer me comfort and tell me I was a good wife to their son and he was the one seeing things incorrectly. I wanted to believe them, but I really did feel like a failure.

As soon as they left, I changed out of my now very wrinkled evening gown. At first, I thought what a wasted purchase it had been, but in reality, it was worth every penny. This night had helped me to see the ugly truth, and it had given me clear direction. I'm sure Joseph Xavier had no idea what he'd helped set in motion. I hoped if he was elected president, all of his dinner meetings didn't end so explosively. I wondered if Michael would tell him we were getting divorced. He obviously never mentioned we were separated. I think he'd used me to his advantage in that way, and it had worked like a charm. Michael would now have his fame and probably fortune, too. I could picture him hitting the talk show circuit when the biography came out. I thought it might be time to quit watching T.V.

I walked up to my children's rooms and watched them sleep for a moment. I wanted to reach out and touch their sweet heads, but I didn't want to wake them. Mia was holding the doll her daddy had given her. The doll I'd given her, but told her it was from her daddy. It made me wonder what birthdays and holidays were going to be like now. I supposed they'd be the way they had been the last few months, just me and the kids. But if he thought I was going to take up the slack for him again, he had another thing coming. I wouldn't be his wife anymore. The tears formed again. I really needed to stop that.

I went and curled up on the chair in the baby's room. It was such a serene place. No matter what else was happening, I was happy to be having this baby, my baby. I couldn't even think of her like she belonged to both Michael and me. Of course, he made it possible, but he never wanted her. It was then I decided to change the divorce papers to ask for full custody of the kids, not joint. Michael could have visitation, but honestly, he had been absent for some time; and from what he'd said tonight, he may have resented them, too. That made me the angriest. They were his children. Children he had wanted, by the way. But it was me that would be here while he was off making his mark; it was me that would be wiping their tears when I told them that Daddy wasn't ever coming home. Some hate started creeping in.

I barely slept, which didn't leave me in a good enough mood to see Michael the following morning. He actually knocked on the door. I almost asked for his house keys, but I thought I'd just have the locks changed someday soon. I didn't say anything to him as he looked sheepishly at me. I motioned for him to come in, and then I called the kids down. They both ran to Michael as I walked to the kitchen.

I heard Michael explain to them how he would be gone again for a long time. I expected to hear moans and cries, but instead it was more like *Okay Dad, see you later, guess what Mimi and Papa took us to do and do you want to see the stuff Mommy bought us for school?*

Wow, they were much more resilient than me, but how sad. Michael did agree to see all of their new school stuff. I heard them all walk upstairs. Meanwhile, I cleaned the kitchen.

Within minutes, they were all coming back down. "Why don't you guys go play out back while I talk to your mommy," I heard Michael ask them. They agreed and both tore through the kitchen out the back door. *If I could bottle that energy*, I thought. I needed it today, too.

I stood at the sink, filling the dishwasher with this morning's breakfast dishes.

Michael came and leaned against the counter on the other side of the dishwasher and watched me. "How are you this morning?"

I rolled my eyes as I scrubbed a syrup-laden plate. "I'm tired."

"I'm sorry about that."

"I'm sure you are." No. No, he wasn't.

"Carly, please."

"What do you want, Michael?"

He pulled a check out of his shirt pocket. "I wanted to give this to you."

My hands were wet, so I didn't take it. "What is it?"

"It's a check."

"For what?"

"For you and the kids."

"We don't need your money."

"Carly, I want to make sure you and the kids are taken care of while I'm gone."

"By writing a check?"

"Just take the money, Carly."

"Let me repeat, I don't *need* or *want* your money."

"And where are you getting all this money to take care of everything?" he threw at me.

"Where do you think?"

Realization dawned on his face. "You didn't need to touch that."

"Well, here's the thing, I did, because our children deserve at least one parent that puts them ahead of their career and themselves."

He slammed the check on the counter and stormed off. He didn't go very far before I heard his footsteps cease. "Carly, I know you won't believe me, but I'm sorry. I never set out to hurt you or the kids. I'll be in touch."

I couldn't look at him, but I called out, "Michael."

"Yes?"

"I need an address where my lawyer can send the divorce summons by certified mail." I tried so hard not to choke on the words, but it was still hard for me to say.

"That's going to be tricky."

"I want this settled as soon as possible, preferably before the baby's born."

"Is that even possible?"

"It can be done in thirty days if no one contests, so please make sure to get me that address."

"Again, it's going to be tricky and I'll want to get my own attorney. It could take some time."

"Please," I begged. "Just make it quick."

"I'll see what I can do."

He didn't sound very convincing. A quick and easy divorce was the least he could do for me, but I feared he was yet again going to disappoint me. I didn't get it. Why wouldn't he just want it done and over with? I guess it probably made no difference to him. He had been living like a bachelor, and this was only an inconvenience for him.

Once he left, I looked over at the stupid check he left. I picked it up; it was written from his stinking secret account. I shoved it into the sink drain and flipped on the garbage disposal. Juvenile? Maybe. Satisfying? Definitely.

I decided to tell the kids after church while we were at my in-laws. I needed the support. I practiced all night, and that morning, what I would say. My tactic was going to be to help them see things weren't really changing at all. The only real thing was that there would be no more hope of it working out and, of course, my marital status. I decided I would keep my last name. It would make things simpler and, in my mind and heart, I was Carly Bishop. Dumb tears!

After church, I faced my toughest test yet as we set the kids down. Mia sat on Mimi's lap and Ashton sat on Papa's on their family room sectional. Boy, did I wish I had someone's lap to sit on.

I took in a deep breath. "Ashton, Mia." I took their small hands in mine. "You know how Daddy has been living somewhere else for a long time now?" They both nodded their perfect little heads. "Well, Mommy and Daddy have decided that um... well... that we are just going to keep things that way." It sounded completely lame.

"Why? Don't you love Daddy?" Mia cried.

That did it for me. I began to cry, too. "Baby, I love your daddy very much, but sometimes even when people love each other, they can't be together."

"Are you getting divorced?" Ashton asked.

I nodded my head yes.

Ashton remained emotionless. Mia asked what divorce meant. I tried to explain it in five-year-old terms, but it still sounded terrible. She howled. I grabbed her and held her tight as she cried into my chest. By this time, my in-laws were both tearing up, too.

"Ashton, son. Are you okay?" He sat there with his big blue eyes wide and doe like. "Come here, honey."

He hopped off his Papa's lap and he stood next to me. I pulled him to Mia and myself.

"Don't worry, Mom. I'll take care of you and Mia and the baby," Ashton said stoically.

I squeezed him harder. "You're the best son a mom could ask for, but I think I should be the one to take care of you and your sisters."

"We'll be here to help, too," Jack said.

I whispered, "Thank you."

"This will all be okay," I promised.

It would be, right?

Monday morning I woke up determined that I would, by sheer force of will, make it okay. The first step was to call Mr. McRae.

"I'm surprised to hear from you, Mrs. Bishop. I thought for sure you and your husband would work things out."

"Well that would take a miracle at this point."

"I'm sorry to hear that."

Believe me, no one was sorrier than me. "I wanted to make some changes to the filing. I'm going to ask for full custody."

"In that case we need to ask for child support and alimony."

"I don't want either."

"Mrs. Bishop, as your attorney, I need to advise against that tactic as well as telling you that asking for full custody will probably send this to court."

"I don't want his money and I don't think he will have an issue with the custody." He'd practically ignored them for the last several months. I didn't see that changing anytime soon.

"Hmm... Well, you're the boss."

"Thank you, Mr. McRae."

"I'll have my aide prepare the paperwork and we will file the petition on Thursday. The summons should be ready to go by Friday. I just need an address for your husband."

"That may be difficult." I explained the situation.

"Well, we have sixty days before the petition expires."

Sixty days was out of the question in my mind. I wanted this done as soon as possible. "I will make getting that address priority number one." This was going to be done by the time my baby was born.

Michael hadn't called at all, so I wasn't sure the best way to get a hold of him or what his schedule was like. I decided to email him. I knew he checked his email several times a day on his phone. And, honestly, it was better than talking to him.

Michael,

I just wanted to let you know that the divorce petition will be filed on Thursday in our county and the summons will be ready on Friday. Please send me an address where my lawyer can overnight the summons to you. All you need to do is sign for it as proof of receipt.

I also need you to sign the title for my 4Runner so I can trade it in. If you want, I'll pay you half of what the trade-in value is. I need a bigger car now, with the three kids.

Please get back to me about how best to make both of these items possible.

Carly

By the time I was done talking to my lawyer and emailing Michael, I felt like I had already had a full day, and it wasn't even ten in the morning. I decided we needed to do something fun. School was starting the following week, and summer was fading away. The end of summer was always a little depressing, but it was made more so by our circumstances this year. The only good thing was that it meant I was closer to having this baby. She was due ten weeks from today, which hopefully meant seven or eight weeks until she was born. Ashton had been nine days early and Mia was three weeks early, so I was hoping this little one would do her mommy a favor and follow her siblings' examples.

I decided to take the kids to the science museum; they had lots of hands-on projects and experiments the kids could do, and it was too hot to be outside in my condition for long periods of time. Already, I wasn't looking forward to the start of fall soccer, but Ashton loved to play, so I would do my best. Plus, I had Jack to pinch hit for me.

I never got a response from Michael that day, and he never called the kids. Only Mia asked when he would call. "I'm sure it will be soon. He's just getting used to his new job," I told her. I hoped he didn't make me a liar.

Tuesday was my doctor appointment, which turned into a therapy session as I spilled my guts about what was going on. Emma was sympathetic and supportive. She offered her and Jace's help, which included taking Ashton to and from soccer practice.

"As long as you're there to catch the baby, that will be help enough," I responded.

Speaking of my little bundle of joy, she was looking good. Her heart rate was strong and steady and I measured correctly. The doctor's office visits would now be every two weeks instead of four. It was getting closer.

That more than anything was why I was so anxious to have things settled. I knew this would be an ongoing process, even after we were divorced. We would always be connected by our children, but I didn't want to have to keep worrying about the actual divorce part. Plus, I think I would only really be able to start to heal after it was finalized and I could move on. Move on to what, I wasn't sure, but I would figure it out. I always did.

Michael didn't call until Wednesday night after dinner. I handed the phone to Ashton to have him answer it, but he refused to speak to his dad. That was a problem. I handed the phone to Mia instead, who was eager to talk to him. She caught him up on all her days and what she had been doing. "I named my doll Jilly, Daddy. And I took her to the museum with us." I wasn't sure that doll ever left her side; she had even joined us for meals.

I assumed Michael asked to talk to Ashton because Mia said, "Ashton doesn't want to talk to you. He says you don't love us or Mommy anymore because you're getting divorced. He's mad at you."

Ashton had never said that to me. I knew those two shared secrets, but I guess I hadn't expected them to talk about this. That was naïve on my part. I quickly grabbed the phone from Mia. "Hey guys why don't you head into the family room. You can start the movie we rented, while I talk to your daddy."

I walked into the living room. "Michael, it's Carly."

"What the hell, Carly! Why did you tell the kids we were getting divorced and that I didn't love them!" he yelled.

I tried to remain calm. "First of all, I don't appreciate your tone, nor do I deserve it. Secondly, I did tell the kids about the divorce, but you should know me better than to think I would tell them you didn't love them."

"I'm sorry, but why did you tell them we were getting divorced?"

"Because we are and they deserve to know the truth so they can start to deal with it."

"You should have asked me what I thought first, before you said anything."

"When? It's been days since you've contacted us."

Silence. We were back to this routine.

"Let me talk to Ashton."

"I don't think we should force him. He'll talk when he's ready. And you telling him you love him isn't going to help."

"Why not?"

"Ashton needs you to show him, not tell him."

"I can't really do that right now."

"Then you have a problem."

More silence.

"Anyway, did you get my email? I really need…"

"I'll respond to you tonight," he cut in.

"Okay. Thanks. Goodbye."

"Do you have a minute?" he asked quickly.

"For what?"

"I thought you would be interested in what I've been doing. I've got to interview…"

"Honestly, Michael, I don't want to hear about your job or anything surrounding it. Maybe in ten years or so when this doesn't hurt so badly, I'll read your book. Maybe. So goodnight."

"Carly," he interrupted. "Did you tell the kids I don't love you?"

"Oh, they're pretty smart. I didn't have to."

Chapter Eighteen

So what Michael meant when he said he would respond was that he would only respond to half of the email. First he berated me for even thinking that he would want half of the trade-in value. "Do you really think I would stoop that low?" he asked. Then he sent me several links about safety ratings and he offered his opinion. He assumed I would want an SUV; he didn't see me driving a minivan. He knew how much I loved the 4Runner, and he informed they made a model now with third row seating. He suggested I take a look at that. "Take my dad with you," he wrote. Then he told me I could send the title to Joseph Xavier's campaign headquarters in South Carolina; they would forward it to him, and he would overnight it back to me. He sent the address and that was it.

"Thank you. But did you only read half of my email?" I wrote back.

I got a very quick response of, "No."

I let it drop for the night; he was grating on my nerves. As I sat in bed, I realized just how yucky I felt about him. I had been trying so hard for months to remember that I loved him and not to be negative, but did I need to do that anymore? Okay, I knew I shouldn't be negative, at least for my own good, but I needed to start to let go. I had hung on so tightly to the idea that it would work out between us that I never stopped to think about really letting go and what that meant. I knew it meant I would eventually have to forgive him, but that was going to take time and a lot of it. But what else did it mean? I decided to sleep on it.

I woke up early and lay there and felt my baby move in the early dawn light. I was so anxious to meet her. As she moved, I was reminded that I was on my own for this one and what that meant. I knew I needed to move on, so I decided I was going to start by focusing my energy toward other facets of my life. Yes, Michael had been my world, but this was the dawning of my own world. The canvas was being redone; the kids were now the backdrop and I would learn to fill in. The first brushstroke was going to be my art.

I threw the covers off and decided we were going shopping. The kids weren't going to be thrilled with the idea or what I had in store with the new clothing we would be purchasing, but they would survive. I needed something to take my mind off of their daddy, and this was a start.

I dragged the kids from store to store trying to patiently deal with their whining as I searched for the perfect outfits for our photo shoot that would happen the next day in the soft morning light. It only took thirteen stores, one temper tantrum, four potty breaks, some sweat, tears and ice cream, but in the end, I was completely satisfied. I had the perfect beautiful flowing white gowns for Mia and myself and a very handsome white linen shirt and natural color pants for Ashton. That night I also made a muted pink flowered headband for Mia.

The next morning I tried my hardest not to think about the fact that this would be our first family pictures without Michael, but I was finding it difficult, especially as I gazed into Ashton's eyes. *Just breathe and take one moment at a time*, I thought. So that's what I did, I took a deep breath and positioned my babies in the flowered meadow, and together, with the help of a remote control, we took several shots with lots of different poses. There were shots of them hugging my belly, shots of them kissing it, shots of them with chalkboard signs that read "big brother" and "big sister" on them. I even took some shots of only me in the romantic light of morning.

Beyond wanting to capture this moment in time for my family, I wanted to showcase my abilities on my website. I had decided to start a blog called Studio Outtakes on my website. My hope was to increase my social media presence and to give myself another outlet. I already had quite a few followers on Facebook, but I hoped this would increase traffic and communication.

As I uploaded and sorted the photos that night on my laptop, I was pleased with the results at first glance. I quickly whittled down the one-hundred-plus shots to a more manageable forty. It was then that my phone rang. I knew who it was, no one else ever called this late. I almost didn't answer it. I was beyond annoyed with him. I wanted a quick divorce, and he was making that difficult. I talked to my lawyer about it today, and he said if Michael could get his own attorney here, that attorney could act as his representative and the summons could be delivered there. It sounded like the best option since Michael made it sound like it was going to be impossible for him to receive certified mail.

"Hi," I said curtly.

"Am I interrupting something?" he asked.

"Yes."

"I can call back," he offered.

"That's okay. I wanted to tell you I talked to my lawyer today and he recommended you get your own attorney here, that way he could send the summons to your attorney on your behalf. This way the petition won't expire while you're gone. I think it's a good plan."

Insert a long pause.

"Michael?"

"I'm here."

"So, can you do that?"

"Carly, this is really a bad time for me. I don't want to pick some attorney out of the yellow pages. Can't this just wait until I get back?"

"No, it can't! I want this done and over with. I haven't asked anything of you and I'm not even asking anything of you in the divorce! I'll even get you some good recommendations, just please do this one thing for me!"

"Carly, please don't cry. I didn't mean to upset you."

I couldn't help it. The anger wouldn't let the tears subside. I don't even know why I stayed on the phone and let him listen to me cry. And now I would have to restart my calendar of how many days it had been since I cried over Michael. It was only at one day, so it wasn't much of a record, but still, I had to start over.

"Please," I begged again.

"Carly... I don't..."

"You don't what?" I asked.

"I'll do some research, but it will have to be next week," he hastily answered.

"Fine," I sighed.

Chapter Nineteen

WITH ENDINGS CAME NEW BEGINNINGS. SUMMER VACATION WAS OVER AND my marriage was too, but on the bright side, school started and I had received tons of positive reviews and posts over the weekend on the maternity shoot I did of myself and the kids. Some of it was even a little embarrassing and overboard. I hadn't meant to seek for all of the compliments. I honestly was posting the pictures to showcase my abilities, but I've never had so many people tell me how beautiful they thought I was. But hey, at thirty-one weeks pregnant, I'd take it. There were also several comments about the written part of the blog. The blog centered around new beginnings and how I felt about my children, those born and unborn. I didn't mention anything about divorce or Michael. I wanted to keep it positive and about me and the kids. I was trying to move on, even though I felt like I was horrible at it.

I'll admit, I had pictured Michael being the one kissing my belly or gently placing his hand on it as he smiled at me like we alone shared a wonderful secret. Then I switched to picturing myself kneeing him in the groin for everything that he had and was putting us through. I had to remind myself that I had been with him for almost twelve years and that I wasn't just going to be able to magically move on from that.

So many things were just glaring reminders, like all the paperwork I had to fill out for Mia and Ashton at the start of school. It was the first year I would have to fill out different addresses for each parent. I also had to write under the "Any special circumstances we should know about?" section that my husband and I were currently going through a divorce (or at least trying to, if the idiot would ever pick a lawyer). I was so depressed by the time I finished filling out paper after paper that I decided we were going out to eat and inviting Mimi and Papa.

I wanted to thank them, anyway. Jack had come early to the house that morning and helped me take the kids to school for their first day. Ashton and Mia both loved it, so much so they each took one of his hands as we walked to the elementary school in our neighborhood. I didn't mind in the least. He deserved every bit of attention those two paid him. Without him, I don't know what I would have done; especially where Ashton was concerned. He and his dad were too much alike, they could both be brooding and quiet and apt to bottle in emotions. Even with Jack's help, Ashton was still upset with his dad. Every day I asked if he wanted to talk with his dad when he called, and each time so far he'd declined.

On the walk back from school, when it was just Jack and me, we discussed Ashton and his unwillingness to talk to his dad. His advice was to give it some time and that Ashton would come around.

"Does it sound terrible if I say I don't want to talk to him, either?" I asked.

Jack chuckled.

"I just wish he'd hurry up and get a lawyer already, so we can all move on with our lives."

"Hmm…" Jack said as we approached my house.

"What's that supposed to mean?"

"I probably shouldn't say."

I stopped at the mailbox at the end of my drive. "Well, now you have to tell me."

He looked thoughtfully at me with those kind brown eyes of his. He hemmed and hawed as we stood there. "I just got the feeling when I went over to knock some sense into my son that he wasn't sold on the whole divorce thing."

"You're kidding me, right? That doesn't make any sense at all."

Jack pursed his lips together. "I don't think it even makes sense to Mike. I think he's the most confused out of all of us."

I shrugged my shoulders. It was time to stick a fork in our marriage; it was done, and I was sure Michael thought so, too. He had wanted this back in March. Now it was just an inconvenience, that was why he was dragging his feet, not because he wanted to stay married. If only I would have listened then. Oh well, I guess this way I'd never wonder.

But Jack's comments were only the beginning of the weird and odd things that started happening in my life. First, we began to receive a lot of extra mail. Michael began sending postcards to the kids from each city and state the campaign stopped through, some days the kids would receive two or three cards each. He didn't write much on them, maybe a fun little fact or two about the place, but each card ended with how much he loved and missed them.

Those postcards were probably the only thing that kept me from metaphorically and physically wringing his neck because apparently he had time to write postcards, but not to find a lawyer. Every day I would ask him about it, and every day he was working on it, or so he said. Again, I was so thrilled that he was making an effort to stay connected to the kids, but really, how hard was it to find a lawyer? It took me no time at all.

The postcards also opened the door back up for Ashton. He finally agreed to talk to his dad after a week of receiving those little notes. My little man even got a little choked up when he said, "I love you, Dad." Even I teared up. There went my streak again. I was up to four days this time. It wasn't huge streak, but I figured for a pregnant hormonal woman, it was pretty good.

I, too, started receiving extra deliveries. Not postcards or mail, but large packages. First, it was a car seat. Not just any car seat either, it was top-of-the-line and quite expensive. It was called a Carcoon. It was supposed to be the safest car seat around. Then I received a baby swing that looked as space-aged as the car seat, but it too was highly rated and expensive. I had a feeling Michael was determined to make up for the money that my garbage disposal ate. Yes, he wasn't thrilled at all when he'd found out where that check had ended up. My last package was a beautiful dark wood high chair with cream colored padding that matched the kitchen beautifully.

I had no choice but to call him and thank him every time a package arrived. It was like he did it on purpose. I had threatened on a few occasions that I would refuse to speak to him until he got an attorney, but he always had some excuse for why that wasn't possible: everything from he was just plain busy to he'd interviewed this one or that one and there was always something wrong with them.

"A divorce lawyer isn't a lifelong commitment. Just pick one already!" I admonished him.

"I just want to make sure I do this the right way," he said.

"Is there really a right way to get divorced?" I responded sarcastically.

"I suppose not."

I begged him to hurry. I was already thirty-three weeks by this point. That's when the really bizarre stuff began to happen. I put pictures of the nursery up on my blog and wrote about my inspiration for the photo wall and how we would all be represented as soon as my little one made her entrance into this world. Before I knew it, I was a hit in the social media arena, at least for a brief moment. My pictures were being pinned over and over again on Pinterest. I had several shares on Facebook. I was being bombarded with requests for quotes to do similar designs for other people. My nursery even ended up being the window picture for my new friend Laura's baby boutique.

Still pregnant, I couldn't accept any jobs to design rooms, but I kept everyone's info and told them I would get back to them at the first of the year. I wasn't sure I wanted to go into that line of work, and I wasn't sure how I could with a newborn, but I wanted to keep my options open. I was a single mom after all, well practically. I was still working on the single part.

I was so excited about all of the attention that I even told Michael about it the night he called after my thirty-four week appointment. I think I blathered on for ten minutes about the requests and how much everyone loved it. I rambled on about how I was already booked for photo sessions through March. My plan was to do my last one in a couple of weeks, and then I was off through the end of the year. The words just kept falling out of my mouth about how happy I was about it all and how I couldn't believe it. Inadvertently, I started talking out loud about how I would juggle the baby and work. I ran through the logistics in my head and out loud.

"I guess you have it all figured out," he interrupted. He sounded melancholy.

"Yeah, I guess so. I guess it's working out for both of us. You got your dream and I... well... I'm getting direction."

"Direction?" he questioned. "This isn't your dream?"

"No... I had to wake up from my dream."

"Carly..."

"Never mind. Anyway, did you find a lawyer?"

"As a matter of fact, I did. Your lawyer should be contacting you tomorrow."

"Well...good. There's still a chance we can get this done before the baby comes."

"I have to run," Michael said abruptly.

He didn't even say bye. I set down my phone and thought, *hmm*. That was weird. But hey, at least he finally got a lawyer. It only took a month, but at least now we could move forward and the healing could begin for me. That was a nice thought...

Mr. McRae called the next morning after I dropped the kids off at school. "Mrs. Bishop, your husband has obtained an attorney."

"Yes. He informed me last night."

"Oh, good." He sounded relieved. "Then you know that he's contesting the divorce and has asked for a stay until he can return."

I had to sit down on the couch. I couldn't believe what I was hearing. "On what grounds?" I spluttered. "I wasn't even asking for anything except the house, and he's already moved out."

"Well, ma'am that's part of the problem. He insists on paying alimony and child support. He also won't agree to give you full custody."

I rubbed my head. "I'm so confused."

"Mrs. Bishop...can I speak off the record?"

"Sure."

"After talking to my brother, I get the feeling he doesn't really want to proceed."

"He chose your brother for his attorney?"

"Yes, ma'am. It's unusual, I know, but...did you hear what I said about him not wanting to proceed?"

"I did and I just don't believe it. And regardless, *I* want to proceed. Do you think the stay will be granted?"

"He makes a good case for it."

"AHHHH!" This wasn't happening. "Sorry."

"It's alright, ma'am. I'll be in touch, but I really think you need to talk to your husband."

"Oh, believe me, I will." I wasted no time dialing his number after I hung up with the attorney. Three rings and no answer, four rings, still no answer, voice mail. "Michael Jonathon Bishop, I have no idea what you're playing at, but I swear you are going to make me go into labor! Why do you hate me so much?" I cried. "You left me and your kids and now that I'm trying to move on, you won't let me. Why?" I didn't know what else to say, so I hung up and threw my phone on the couch. I lay back and screamed into a pillow. I felt like swearing, but instead I cried. I had forgone my no-crying-about-Michael calendar, so I couldn't tell you how many days it had been since I last cried over him. All I knew was it was a good thing he was away or I'd be having this baby in jail.

Within minutes, I received a text. "I just got your message. I can't talk right now. I'll call you tonight after the kids have gone to bed. Carly, I don't hate you."

I threw the phone against the soft cushions. I continued to lay there. *Fine*, I thought. *I'll take alimony and child support.* It didn't mean I had to spend it. I would just start trust funds for the kids with it. And as far as custody went, I would change it to joint, but with me having physical. That was fair, right?

I got up and texted Michael back my compromise and asked if that would work.

"Please, Carly. I'll call you tonight."

"Do you know how much I hate you right now?" I texted back. I had never told Michael I hated him. I wasn't sure I had ever said that to anyone.

"Probably not as much as you should," he texted back.

At least he got that part right.

Well, there went my day. I ended up on the couch watching my mantra movie, *Something to Talk About* and added in the *The First Wives Club.* Maybe not the best movies, but it was cathartic to watch women get even with husbands or ex-husbands who had treated them like dirt. I was jealous.

Considering I had been lying around all day, I was sure tired by the time I picked up the kids. I was still walking every day to drop them off and pick them up. It seemed like every day it got a little harder. Thankfully, it was the last week of September and the weather was no longer scorching, now it was just balmy. I was growing steadily, and felt like the baby had dropped some. It was at that stage where I was going to be uncomfortable regardless. The emotional roller coaster didn't help, either.

No matter how bad my mood was, it was always made better when I saw my two kiddos walking out of school with big smiles on their faces. Mia loved kindergarten, and I could tell by Ashton's countenance he liked second grade, even though he didn't gush like Mia. For a minute I forgot about their asinine daddy.

That's when Mia decided to bring him up. "Did Daddy send us any postcards today?"

I sighed, "Yep."

They both took off running toward the house, leaving me to call after them to slow down. I didn't move that fast anymore. They slowed down, and I slowly caught up. As we walked home, I noticed signs that the leaves were about ready to change colors. It reminded me that I should probably start thinking about Halloween costumes, and maybe if I was feeling ambitious, I could get out my autumn decorations and we would dress up the front porch. As difficult as this year had been, it had sure flown by.

Jack's truck was in the driveway when we arrived. He was waiting on the porch. Ashton had soccer practice, and Jack was my savior, as always; he had been taking it upon himself to take Ashton for me. It was good male bonding time, as he put it. The kids ran up the porch and greeted Papa with hugs and kisses. I took my turn, too.

"Hi, Dad," I said as I kissed his cheek. It seemed so natural to call him that now.

"You look tired, my dear."

"Good, because I am." I smiled.

He winked at me. I loved him.

I quickly got the kids a snack of peanut butter and sliced apples at the breakfast bar. While they ate, I asked Jack if I could talk to him in the living room for a moment. As soon as we were situated on the couch, I quietly told him about the news I received earlier that day from my attorney.

"So what do you think?"

A Cheshire-cat grin erupted from his lined face. That was not the reaction I expected. "It's about time."

"About time for what?"

"About damn time for my son to start fighting for his family."

"Come on. You know that's not what this is about. And besides, I want a divorce."

He took my hands and sincerely looked at me. "As you should," he said. "But don't expect Mike to make that easy for you. I would be disappointed if he did."

My head dropped slightly and my eyes fully opened. That statement took what wind I had left right out of my sails.

Jack smiled at me sweetly and lifted my chin up. "Chin up, my dear. I'll be disappointed in you if you don't give him the run of his life." He kissed my forehead, just like his son had on many occasions, and then he called after Ashton to get his gear.

I sat there, puzzled. I was starting to question reality again. *I used to be such a sane person*, I thought. In a split-second decision, I decided I needed to get out of the house. Being cooped up all day had not done me any good. "Mia," I called. "Do you want to go to the store with Mommy and get some flowers and pumpkins for the porch?"

She came running out of the kitchen and enthusiastically agreed to that plan. We left at the same time Jack and Ashton did. I think Ashton was happy he dodged the bullet on the whole shopping trip. "Will you get me a big pumpkin?" he asked as we all walked out the door.

How could I say no to his sweet smile and beautiful eyes? "I'll see what I can do."

As I buckled Mia into her booster seat, I was reminded I would be giving up my car this weekend. I loved this car. I'd had it longer than the kids. They were both brought home in this very backseat. Each time, I sat in the back with them. I was so paranoid when they were babies, and I supposed I would be again. I was sad to see the car go, but we needed that extra row. I had decided on another 4Runner, but this time I was getting leather and more seating. The car was being delivered this weekend to the dealership, so I only had a few days left with this old gal. I decided when I got home to take some pictures of her and pull out a few from the past. It would be the perfect spotlight for my next blog.

On the way to Home Depot I looked in the rearview mirror at Mia. "Honey, what do you want to be for Halloween this year?"

"A butterfly," she said as if it was obvious.

I wasn't surprised in the least, but I thought I should at least ask. Her request was easy enough. I could make butterfly wings, and I would buy a leotard and some tights. I would ask Ashton tonight what his plans were. I figured I better get on it, there was a possibility this baby could be born before All Hollow's Eve. Honestly, I hoped so.

Mia and I filled up a large flatbed cart full of mums, pumpkins, baskets, urns and cornstalks. I even picked up some paint samples for my master bedroom. I knew I wouldn't be painting it anytime soon, but I wanted to get some ideas. I had already changed out the bedding to an all-white ruffled set. It was completely beautiful and impractical with little ones, but I loved it. By the time we left the store, it all barely fit in the back of my car. Mia had cornstalks tickling her head.

We got home at the same time as Jack and Ashton. Jack was a dear and insisted on carrying my items to the porch. He berated me for lifting the said objects in the first place. I grinned and reminded him again that women walked across the plains pregnant.

"Yes, but they weren't carrying my granddaughter."

I smiled and kissed his cheek. "Thank you."

The rest of the evening kept me busy with dinner, bathing children, and bedtime. I was wiped out by the time I settled into bed. That was the baby's cue to begin her nightly party. I saw many sleepless nights in my near future. I'll admit, I was fearful being on my own after the baby came. I knew I wouldn't be the first woman to go it alone, but how do you take care of a baby all night and then get up and take care of the older children and the house and meals and everything else that needed to be done? I knew Jack and Danielle would help, but I couldn't ask them to stay overnight or come over every morning. I was going to miss someone to burp the baby after I fed her, or waking up to see Michael walking back and forth with her and talking to her like he had done with Mia and Ashton. Instead, I would be cursing him from afar as he would be sleeping peacefully at his apartment or in a hotel room. I really did hate him.

Just as that horrid feeling was coursing through me, he called. I debated again on answering, but he and I were having it out; he was going to give me the divorce I deserved, and he was going to give it to me as soon as possible.

"Hi, honey."

"Are you serious?" He'd never once called me honey. He found it cliché and overused.

"You can't blame a guy for trying."

"No amount of sweet talk will help you."

"Come on, Carly."

"No, Michael. Just tell me why. Why, after all of this? Why do you have to make this difficult? This is what you wanted."

"I never said I wanted a divorce."

"You left me and you said you didn't love me anymore! No need to get hung up on the fine details!"

"Carly, I know. I know I've screwed everything up and none of this has been fair to you and you have every right to hate me, but I don't think we've given this a fair chance to work out."

"We? Did you just imply that I didn't give this a chance?"

"Okay, let me rephrase that. *I* didn't try the way I should have. And I know I have no right to ask, but I'm asking you for time. Time for me to at least try."

I set the phone down for a minute. I didn't know whether to scream or cry or both. I took a big, cleansing breath and counted to ten. That didn't work, so I counted to ten again. I tried to be calm. "Michael, that time has passed. How could I ever trust you again after everything you've put me and the kids through? Please, can we just cut our losses and compromise on the terms of the divorce? Like I told you before, I'll take alimony and child support and we can have joint custody, as long as the kids stay with me during the week, except for my baby until she's at least weaned."

"Wait a second, why do you keep saying my baby? I've noticed that lately."

"Because this is *my* baby!"

"Maybe you need a biology lesson."

"We both know you didn't want this baby and I coerced you into having sex in the first place and you haven't even tried to be a part of this process other than sending some very nice gifts, so let's just call it like it is. My baby."

He almost laughed. "You really think you needed to coerce me into having sex with you? How long have you known me?"

"But you haven't, we haven't…"

"Not because I didn't want to. Carly, not a day has gone by since I've known you that I haven't wanted to. I didn't because you deserved better. You deserved to be loved by a man that…a man that was better than me."

I didn't speak. What could I say?

"And you're right, Carly. I didn't want this baby at first, and I've had a hard time adjusting to the thought. But these last few weeks as I've watched her ultrasound over and over, and as I've looked at the photos you've taken, it's made me realize I want our baby. *Our* baby, Carly."

I tried to cry silently. Did he know how much he was killing me? "Michael, let's just compromise on the divorce terms."

"Carly, I know that in the end, there's probably nothing I can do to change your mind, but I'll be damned if I don't at least try my hardest. The stay has already been filed and if that doesn't work, I'll contest it as far as I can."

I sat there completely confounded. So many emotions, so many words and thoughts swirling through my head, but none could escape.

"Goodnight 24B."

Chapter Twenty

THE NEXT COUPLE OF WEEKS BREEZED BY AS I KEPT MYSELF OVERLY BUSY. I had to, or I would have to stop and think about the fact that Michael thought he wanted to work things out, and I just couldn't think about it because I knew how that ended, and I somehow always came up on the losing end. I'd already given him more chances than he deserved. The problem was, he wasn't giving up. I tried to ignore him, but he wouldn't let me. He took to leaving long messages on my phone or writing me emails. I even started getting postcards. The subject matter varied as did the volume of the content, but it was always something every day.

He left a message about my car that went something like this, "Carly I just saw the pictures and your blog about our car. Remember when we first bought it and we thought we should break it in that weekend and go camping up above Gunnison? Remember how it rained all weekend and we ended up spending the whole time in the back. Best camping trip ever."

Okay, I had to give him that one. It *was* the best camping trip ever.

Or what about this message? "Hey, Carly. I was just thinking. As soon as this election is over, which can't get here soon enough, and of course after you've recovered, we should book a family trip. How does a Disney Cruise sound? Do you think that would be too much for the baby? Probably, right?" He paused for a moment, then said, "We could take a skiing trip to Colorado. Let's go for Christmas. The kids would love to have snow for Christmas and I wouldn't mind some quality time with you by the fireplace. I'll look at some options and email them to you."

That was bizarre. He had always hated the thought of a Disney Cruise when I had mentioned it before. The fact that he even considered it was weird. Not like I was even considering it now. We were still getting divorced in my mind.

And he wanted frequent updates now on the pregnancy and baby. He was now going online and reading about exactly what the baby should be doing and what kinds of changes my body should be going through. He was also suggesting names, but I already had one picked out; I just wasn't telling anyone, and he wasn't getting a choice. He wasn't even going to be there.

His latest message was about how everyone on the tour bus, including Joseph and his daughters, were completely in love with my photography, and they all wanted me to take their family pictures. Joseph was even asking if I could take some for his biography, and if he could swing it with the publisher, he wanted me to do the front cover. Michael made sure to mention how I was his screen saver and how everyone was enamored with me, too.

When I wasn't busy ignoring my phone ringing and listening to voice messages, I was working on costumes. Ashton had decided he wanted to be a grandpa. Jack was so flattered, he handcrafted a small cane for him. I sewed matching plaid shirts for Jack and Ashton so they could both wear them on Halloween. Both kids were going to look adorable. I was hoping to have three kids to dress up, so I bought a newborn pumpkin outfit, just in case.

At my thirty-six week appointment, Dr. White told me the baby's head was in the correct position and everything was looking great, she just needed to cook a little longer.

"Make sure your in-laws are on speed dial," she warned me. "Also, practice your breathing techniques since your plan is to go natural again and make sure your bag is packed."

I nodded my head in acknowledgement. I had already been practicing my breathing in anticipation. It had worked for the first two, so I was hoping I could survive it again. Albeit, without my coach this time.

My mother-in-law was pretty nervous about being in the delivery room with me, but she agreed to do it. I considered calling Melanie and asking her if she wanted to come and stay for a while and be there with me, but I didn't see that ending well. I pictured myself more worried about her, and I could just hear her commentary on how awful the whole process was and on the gross factor. I could imagine her puking and maybe even becoming faint. That was a no-go.

I'll admit, I teetered on asking Michael if there was any way he could make it, but I couldn't bring myself to do it. I still planned on divorcing him, even though his stay was granted. I couldn't be with somebody who could just, on the turn of a dime, decide that he was tired of "playing house" with me, and it wasn't like he was professing his undying love to me. He only wanted to *try* and work it out, which in my mind meant he still wasn't fully committed to the idea. But with all that said, I missed him; maybe I always would. I knew I would miss him in the delivery room and with all that came after, but I had to move on. I had to move forward without him, right?

At thirty-six weeks and two days, I finished up my last two photo sessions until the New Year. My first one of the day was a newborn session, and it made me even more anxious to hold my own daughter. As I held the one-week-new baby boy, my maternal senses went into overload. New baby scent is intoxicating.

My final shoot was an engagement session. The couple was so in love and so young.; he was twenty-three and she was twenty-two. They looked like children. I had the urge to warn the girl that this phase didn't last, but I remembered what it was like to be in love like that. I hated it when people would offer their unsolicited advice. Maybe I should have listened, but we each had our own journey, and even though my journey was not ending like I had planned with Michael, I would never say I regretted it. There was too much love, and too many of my greatest joys and loves had come out of this relationship for me to ever regret it. So, I congratulated them and wished them all the best. I took the loveliest pictures I could. I tried to use my lens to capture just a hint of what they felt for one another at this moment in their lives. I thought maybe one day, when they had their first argument, like we all do, that they could look at these photos and remember how in love they were and that love was the greatest force on earth.

The combination of those thoughts, coupled with my exhaustion as I was editing the photos that night long after the kids had gone to sleep, made me forget not to answer my phone when Michael called.

"Carly. I wasn't expecting you to answer."

"Yeah, me neither," I said sleepily.

"Are you alright? You don't sound well."

I thought for a moment. I was going to say I was just tired, but come to think of it, I didn't feel very well. I felt a little nauseous and my back ached, which wasn't surprising. I had done too much up and down earlier that day, taking pictures.

"Honestly, I'm not feeling all that hot. I should probably go to bed."

"Maybe you should call the doctor," he sounded worried.

"No. I just overdid it today. It was my last day, so I'll just try and take it easy the next few days."

"Are you sure? I worry about you."

"Maybe you should have thought about that before you left me to tour the country." I put my hand to my mouth. "You know what, I'm sorry. I shouldn't have said that. I'm just tired."

"It's true, Carly. I shouldn't have left you and I regret it, but the election will be over in a month and then I'll be home. There's even a chance I could see you next weekend. Joseph is thinking about doing a campaign stop through there, even though he will hands down take Georgia in the election. If he does, could you meet me with the kids?"

"Yeah, I guess so. Listen, Michael, I really need to lay down."

"Carly, are you sure you're okay?"

"I'm sure."

"Okay. I'll call you in the morning. Please answer."

"Okay, Michael."

I immediately turned off my laptop. I didn't even bother walking to my room. I pulled an afghan over me and fell asleep on the living room couch. I was awoken at six a.m. as I turned over. I heard the faintest pop and felt a warm, wet sensation. I jumped up as quick as I could. My water broke. I had never had that happen on its own. I then realized this was too early. I was only thirty-six weeks and three days. Panic set it in. I immediately dialed Dr. White's after-hours number; her service said they would notify her and she would call me. As soon as I hung up with the service, I called my in-laws and woke them up.

"We'll be right over," Jack said with a mixture of excitement and worry.

Emma called within a few minutes. "Don't panic," she said. "Yes, she's a little early, but I'm not too worried about it. Are you having any contractions?"

There weren't any to report yet, which was odd to me. She instructed me to relax and get to the hospital as soon as I could. I know it sounds stupid, but the first thing I did was jump in the shower. I knew it could be a long day and I didn't want to feel gross on top of everything else. Besides, my water wasn't gushing, it was like a small trickle, and I was out and dressed by the time my in-laws got there.

Jack woke up the kids and brought them down. He didn't want me walking up the stairs in my condition. When I saw my children, it reminded me I should call their daddy. The thought made me cry. I wanted him there. I was scared and I needed him even though he was the bane of my existence at the moment, but he was somewhere in Virginia. I think. As I got my phone to call him, the front door flew open, like just thinking of him made him appear out of thin air.

There he stood, disheveled in jeans and a tight brown t-shirt. The kids immediately ran to him and clung to his legs. "The baby is coming, Daddy," they excitedly announced.

He held them to him, but his eyes never left mine.

We both stood there for a moment as time seemed to pause.

"Why are you here?" I cried.

He smiled warmly. "Because this is where I'm supposed to be."

My in-laws each swooped in and took a child. Mia and Ashton were not happy to be taken away from their daddy, but we needed a moment.

Michael quickly made his way to me and wrapped his arms around me.

I instantly felt better, but I started to cry even harder. "You know I still hate you," I said against his chest.

He laid his hand against my head gently. "I know, but I'll take it as a good sign. You wouldn't hate me if you didn't love me."

True, but I wouldn't be acknowledging that I still loved him, especially not now when I felt panicked and scared. "By the way, my water broke."

He loosened his hold of me and looked me over. "I guess we better get to the hospital then."

"She's early."

He kissed my forehead. "Everything will be okay. Where's your bag?"

"In my room, by your old dresser. The car seat is there, too."

He quickly went to retrieve the items. I was joined by the rest of our family. Danielle looked visibly relieved that she didn't have to go. Jack had a sly grin on his face; he was certainly happy with the turn of events. The kids were a mixture of excitement and whininess. They wanted to go to the hospital, and they were not happy to have their daddy leave them.

Michael came back out and picked them both up. "I need to be at the hospital with Mommy, but as soon as the baby is born, Mimi and Papa will bring you to the hospital." He kissed them both. "I love you." I think he almost cried as he expressed his feelings for our children.

Jack kissed my cheek. "Don't worry, my dear. Everything will be okay."

"Thanks, Dad," I replied.

Michael did a double take when he heard me call his dad, Dad. Jack placed his hand on his son's shoulder and gave him a look of pride mixed with warning. He didn't even say anything.

"I'll take good care of her," Michael said to his dad.

"See that you do."

I was getting anxious to leave. The water wasn't gushing out of me by any means, but I was worried that was a possibility; I was pretty sure maxi-pads weren't meant to hold copious amounts of amniotic fluid, and I was worried about her being this early.

"Carly, we need to take your car. I had to take a cab here."

I nodded my head and told him the keys hung in the laundry room like they always had. They were just a different set of keys to a different car. As we left, I felt like I was kind of in a dream state. I wasn't expecting to deliver this early, and I certainly wasn't expecting Michael.

"How did you know?" I asked him after he threw my bag and the car seat in the back seat and walked me around to my door.

"I remember you felt sick the day before you went into labor with Ashton and Mia and I had a feeling." He placed his hand on my cheek. "And I was thinking about coming home, anyway. I've missed you so much."

I shook my head at him and refused to give him any inkling of a smile. I wasn't going to let him sweet talk me. "What about your job?"

"It will be there when I get back. But let's talk about it after we get you to the hospital."

He helped me in and hurriedly shut my door and ran around to the driver's side. As he was backing out of the garage and looking back, he commented. "Nice ride. Definitely worthy of a camping trip." I'm sure he was referring to our camping trip for two in the rain.

I looked at him like he was crazy.

He grinned widely and devilishly at my response.

Two could play this game. "If you want to take the kids, I'll let you borrow *my* car."

He laughed. "That hurts, Carly."

I rolled my eyes. He had no idea what hurt was.

He picked up my left hand and held it while he drove. "Any contractions?"

"Not yet. Does that seem odd?" I responded as I rubbed my abdomen with my right hand. "I'm worried."

He glanced over at me. "From what I've read, I think it's normal. Try not to worry."

"From what you've read?"

"I'm a pregnancy expert now. I even read the riveting tale on breastfeeding you recommended."

I couldn't help it. He broke through and made me laugh. He was really making it hard for me to hate him this morning. But not impossible. "Maybe you should nurse this one then," I suggested.

He smiled. "I missed you, Carly."

I closed my eyes and laid my head back and sighed at that sentiment.

"You don't believe that?" he asked.

I didn't respond right away. I kept my eyes closed and tried to focus on what was going on inside my body. "I don't know what to believe anymore. The last time you told me that, we had a few great hours, but then you became more distant and you took a job without telling me and then you left... *again.*"

He gently rubbed my hand with his thumb. "There is no excuse for what I've done to you and our family, but..."

"Mmm!" I broke in. Contraction. I squeezed his hand tighter and breathed in and out. It was sharp, but short lived.

"7:10." Michael timed it. "You okay?"

I nodded my head. I knew from experience that was nothing compared to what I had to look forward to.

Michael brought my hand up and kissed it. "We're almost there."

I closed my eyes again and focused on breathing. I wasn't sure I wanted to be talking about our relationship status this morning; I didn't want to bring negative feelings with me into the delivery room. I reminded myself I had wanted him to be here, and now he was. Regardless of what happened to our marriage, today we were having a baby, and that was a joyous occasion.

Michael got the car parked. "Do you want me to get a wheel chair? Or I can carry you."

I shook my head no. I still felt okay and there was still no gushing water, and I hadn't had another contraction. We walked in slowly. Michael carried my bag in one hand and held onto me with the other. I noticed how firmly he grasped. I also realized he was wearing his wedding ring. I wondered if he had ever taken it off. It reminded me of how empty my ring finger had felt the past couple of months. So many times I thought I had lost it only to remember I had given it back. I wondered if he kept it, and if he did, where it was. Not that I was ready to wear it again, or ever, it was just one of the many things I wondered about.

We got checked in quickly as I was pre-registered. Libby, the nurse assigned to me took us back to a delivery room. She looked to be in her fifties, and she was as pleasant as she could be. *Fabulous*, I thought. The nurse you get makes all the difference.

She placed a horrid blue gown and absorbent pad on the bed. "Okay, you know the drill, I'm sure. Take all of your own clothing off. When you're done getting dressed, you'll need to stay in bed since your water has broke."

I looked at the absorbent pad and gown and thought, *oh, I hope this goes quickly*.

She left us so I could change. I picked up the blue gown and headed to the bathroom.

Michael grabbed my hand on the way. "I don't think today is the day for modesty, *Mrs*. Bishop."

I looked up into his sincere blue eyes that were smiling down on me.

"I'll be right back," I replied.

He let go of me reluctantly. "I'll be here," he said quietly.

I knew I'd changed in front of him a million times, and I got it, I was pregnant with his baby, but I wasn't ready to expose myself like that to him. It's not like I was prudish, I most certainly wasn't, but I didn't want to feel vulnerable around him. Does that make sense?

By the time I made it back to the bed and situated myself, the whole not changing in front of him seemed pointless. Libby came back in and pretty much exposed me by running a test to make sure it really was my water that broke; she also checked for dilation. I was at two inches and fifty percent effaced. She hooked me up to all sorts of monitors, all while Michael looked on and smirked at me. He was so annoying.

At least he was useful. He came and held my hand as she put in my IV. That was the worst part for me. I stared at him and tried to breathe normally while she looked for a good vein. I noticed he looked tired, but he looked good. I was happy to see the gray back in his hair. It was even showing up in his facial hair now. His eyes looked happy and settled. They hadn't looked like that in a year. As she went in for the kill, I closed my eyes and squeezed his hand.

After I got stuck, Michael looked to Libby. "Is everything okay?"

"So far, so good," she chirped. "Dr. White will be in shortly, so try and relax."

My contractions were too few and too far in between, so that's all there was to do. Michael sat on the bed next to me and rubbed my neck. His hands felt good. I tried to relax under them to the rhythmic sound of my daughter's heartbeat. I couldn't believe I was finally going to get to meet her today.

Michael's stomach interrupted the reverie.

"You should go get something to eat," I admonished him.

"You know that always makes me feel guilty."

"I know, but I also know how unbearable you become when you haven't eaten."

He continued to rub my neck, which felt heavenly, but I knew he needed to eat—for both of our sakes.

"Seriously, go get something." I looked at the monitor that was showing no contractions. "It's going to be a while."

I missed his hands immediately, but they quickly found my face. He caressed me softly and gazed at me for a moment. "I'll be right back."

He leaned closer. He came ninety percent of the way and stopped.

"What are you doing?" I asked.

He moved to ninety-five percent. "Are you going to ask me that every time I try and kiss you now?"

He didn't wait for my response. His lips barely brushed mine. He was testing the waters, and they weren't all that warm, so he just kissed me once and stood up. "Someday I hope I'll be worthy enough for you to come the other ten."

I shrugged my shoulders. I didn't know what I would do, or should do.

Not long after he left, Dr. White came in.

"Was that Michael I just saw in the hall?"

I nodded my head in the affirmative.

"When did he get back?"

"This morning, just as I was about ready to leave for the hospital."

"So?" she asked.

"I don't know what to think. He won a stay on the divorce until the end of the year, and now he comes walking in acting like prince charming saying he misses me."

My heart monitor started speeding up.

Emma grinned. "Calm down there."

I smiled. "Anyway, what about the baby? She's early."

"She definitely jumped the gun, but like I told you on the phone, I'm not too concerned. Most babies born at this time are just fine. She may have to spend an extra day or two in the hospital, but most likely she'll be able to go home when you do, so try to relax."

Everyone keeps saying that to me. Do I look tense?

She looked over the nurse's notes and then at the monitors. "If your labor doesn't start soon, though, I'm going to want to start Pitocin."

I grimaced. I knew that could make labor more painful.

"I know how you are about natural childbirth, but with your water broken, we need to be careful about infection. Time is of the essence, and it won't make you any less of a woman if you need something for the pain this time."

"Okay," I sighed, but I prayed my labor would start on its own.

"So for now we're just going to monitor you. Try and rest if you can."

When she left, I lay back against the pillow and said a silent prayer amidst the beeping of the monitors. I prayed everything would be okay with my baby and that I would know what to do about her daddy. I wanted to know what would be best for our family. Having him around muddied the waters for me. It was so easy to hate him from afar, but having him back, and acting like my Bishop, clouded my judgment.

Michael was barely gone twenty minutes. I opened my eyes and turned toward him as he opened the door. I could see him light up as he looked at me. What was I going to do with him? I also noticed the plastic bag in his hand and I inquired. He came back over and sat next to me on the bed. He pulled out a crossword puzzle book, a couple of magazines, a bottle of lavender lotion, and some pink nail polish.

I held up the lotion and nail polish. "Are you trying to get in touch with your feminine side now?"

He grinned and took them both out of my hand. "In a manner of speaking."

I raised my eyebrow at him.

"You're my feminine side."

I shook my head at him.

"I ran into Dr. White. She was a little cold."

"What did you expect?"

He breathed out heavily. "I'm sure everyone thinks I'm the world's biggest jerk."

"I'll second that motion."

He leaned forward and rested his forehead against mine. "I know this doesn't make up for anything, and it sounds hollow, but I'm sorry. I'm going to be a better man."

I didn't get to respond as our nurse walked in. She smiled at the two of us. "That's what I like to see."

If only she knew, I thought. She came and checked my vitals and the monitors and informed us the baby was looking good. She sat down with us for a while and tried to get to know us better. She wanted to know what number this was for us and how long we had been married. I let Michael answer—it was a touchy subject. I felt like we could subtract the last year, but Michael proudly told her almost eleven years.

She looked at me in amazement. "You must have been a baby when you got married; you look way too young to have been married that long."

"I *was* a baby. I was barely twenty-four," I responded.

She looked between the two of us. "You both look so familiar. Have you delivered here before?"

I shook my head no. Ashton was born in Colorado, and Mia was born in a hospital in Atlanta.

"Hmm..." She kept trying to place us. "This sounds weird, but I'm thinking an airplane."

Michael and I both looked at each other.

"Did you ever read a blog called, 'The Girl in Seat 24B?' " Michael asked.

Her eyes beamed as she threw her hands up into the air. "I loved that blog. I can't believe it's you. Oh, my goodness, you are the cutest couple ever. My girlfriends and I were so jealous of you. I used to beg my husband to read it to get some pointers."

Yeah, well, she wouldn't want him taking pointers from Michael now.

She directed her attention to Michael. "Why did you quit writing? You don't know how disappointed we all were."

Michael rubbed the back of his neck. "I still write, just not that."

"Well, you should," she said as she got up to leave. "Just wait until I tell some of the other nurses on duty who's in here. They'll be so jealous."

That hadn't happened in a long time. It was a little awkward now, under the circumstances. After she left, things were quiet for a couple of minutes. I thought about that blog and how much it had meant to me, and I wondered something. "All those things you wrote about me. Was any of it true?"

"Every... last... word," he spoke slowly as he ran his finger softly down my cheek.

A couple of tears fell. He wiped them away. "Only happy tears today, okay?"

I nodded my head yes.

Time seemed to be going slower. I hated that all I could do was lay there. I wanted to walk around to see if I could get my labor to start, but with my water broken, that was against the rules. I was so anxious to meet this baby; I wanted her in my arms, as soon as possible.

To pass the time, Michael sat next to me on the bed and we did crossword puzzles together. We hadn't done that in ages. We took turns being across or down. We raced each other to see who could finish first. So far, we were tied two-two. I don't even remember when we stopped doing crosswords, but I had missed it.

Around noon, Dr. White came in and examined me. I hadn't progressed at all.

"It's time to get the ball rolling," she said. She ordered Libby to begin the Pitocin drip into my IV. Emma knew I wasn't thrilled with the idea. "We'll start with a slow drip to see if that does the trick," she said as if that would appease me.

"I'm surprised I need this kind of help. My labor has always started on its own before."

She smiled at me. "Every pregnancy is different. This isn't a sign that something's wrong. Just relax."

Michael tried to be reassuring after Emma and Libby left.

It was anything but reassuring. I was frustrated and lashed out. "I should have known this wasn't going to be a typical delivery. This whole pregnancy has been so different."

He held my hands again. "I know, Carly. You don't know how sorry I am for that. I wish I could go back and recapture everything I missed."

I was trying so hard not to be upset with him, but when he made comments like that, it reminded me of all the hurt and pain he had caused me and my children this past year, and especially during this pregnancy. I knew this wasn't the right time and place for it, but when was it ever going to be?

I felt the urge to smack him, but instead I shook my head. "Why the sudden change of heart, Michael?"

He began to rub my hands he still held. He nervously moved to the edge of my bed from the chair he had been occupying. He looked at the monitors that were keeping track of the baby's and my vitals. I could tell he was trying to gather his thoughts, and I let him. I had waited this long, and it looked like we had plenty of time at the rate my labor was progressing.

After several minutes he looked my way and into my eyes. "Carly, when I met you, you turned my whole life upside down. Before you, I thought I would never get married or have children, and then, in an instant, you changed that. Everything suddenly became secondary to you. I wanted to do everything I could to make you happy, even if it meant putting my career aspirations on the back burner."

"I never asked you to do that," I interrupted.

He reached up with his free hand and touched my cheek. "No, you didn't. You wouldn't, but I wanted to because I thought that's what you wanted. I knew you didn't want to be constantly traveling around like you had growing up and I didn't want to be away from you. So we made choices *together*. And for a long time I was happy about those choices, but then..."

I kept waiting for him to elaborate.

He searched my eyes while rubbing my hand and touching my face.

I shrugged my shoulders. "I became undesirable and lost my luster as my dad feared."

He scooted closer and wiped the corner of my eyes, where the tears were beginning to form. "No. That's not what happened."

"Please don't lie to me. You told me you didn't love me and you left me. You didn't even care about how much you were hurting me or the kids or even your parents. You hid money from me and rented apartments and accepted jobs, all without any regard to my feelings. All that didn't happen overnight, so don't try and spare my feelings now!"

Libby came rushing in. My blood pressure and heart rate were spiking. By this point, I was full-on bawling and Michael was trying to calm me down.

"Is everything okay?"

"No, everything's not okay." I was tired of pretending.

Michael looked up to Libby. "Could we please have a minute?"

She nodded and walked back out. I'm sure she thought I had lost my mind. As soon as she exited, Michael wrapped me up in his arms. At first I tried to push him away, but he gently persisted, and I finally gave in.

He soothingly rubbed my back and began to whisper in my ear. "Listen to me, Carly. You are the most desirable creature on this planet. It was me that became undesirable. I felt worthless and I began to doubt myself. I let that fester and I wrongly placed the blame on you and the kids."

"Why didn't you just talk to me?"

"Because I was confused and ashamed. I knew I shouldn't feel that away about you. But things kept getting worse at work and I felt trapped."

"You feel like I trapped you?"

He pulled me tighter. "No. I did that to myself. You are the most freeing and wonderful thing that has ever happened to me. And I'm sorry I lost sight of that. And I'm sorry for the pain I've caused you and our family. I know there isn't a way to make up for this past year. And I know I don't deserve you, but I don't know what I'll do if I lose you. My work, my life means nothing without you. I love you, 24B; and I'm going to do whatever it takes to prove that to you."

My crying ceased, but he still didn't let go. It had been so long since I had heard those words. I wanted to believe them, but... "Michael, I don't know if I can ever trust you again or forgive you. What happens the next time you become unhappy? Are you just going to walk out on us again? How can I take that risk or subject our kids to that again?"

He released me and sat back, but took back my hand. His eyes were wet, too. "Carly, I know it's a long shot, and I've given you no good reason to want to work this out, but if you give me some time to show you how much you mean to me and how much I love you, I'll prove that I do."

He kissed my hand. "Please," he begged.

I didn't know what to say or do as I looked into his sincere, tear-filled baby blues.

Chapter Twenty-One

I DIDN'T HAVE TO ANSWER RIGHT AWAY BECAUSE IT WAS FINALLY SHOW TIME. A contraction came on full force. I squeezed Michael's hand tightly.

He quickly realized what was going on and turned toward the monitor that measured the intensity of the contractions. "Almost there," he said. "Slow and steady, Carly."

I tried to regulate my breathing pattern, but I was caught off guard, and the emotions weren't helping.

"Focus on me. Deep breath in…now let it out." He smiled. "You can do this."

After sixty seconds, it was over. I took a deep cleansing breath in.

Michael kissed my forehead. "Good job, Mom," he said. He retrieved the lotion. "I think now it's a good time for this. Or would you rather I paint your toe nails?"

"Are you serious?"

"Yes," he laughed. "I noticed they weren't painted and I remembered how important that was to you when Ashton and Mia were born. Though I can't figure out why."

I smiled. "It's a woman thing."

He winked. "Then painted toenails it is."

I just my head at him as he pulled out the bubble gum pink nail polish and proceeded to paint my toes. This was a first for us, and the gesture meant a lot to me. Libby came in as Michael was finishing up my right foot. She looked relieved to see that I was no longer upset. She was downright giddy over what she called the sweetest thing she had ever seen. "If all husbands could be like Michael," she exclaimed.

Michael rightly set her straight. "No one deserves a husband like me, especially my wife."

Michael and I looked at each other. I didn't bother to see what Libby's reaction was to that statement. I didn't know what to do with this man. If it was a matter of just being in love with him, then it was a simple choice, but this was anything but simple, and I wasn't sure love could or should fix this. How do you even begin to rebuild a trusting relationship after this? I didn't have time to contemplate it because another contraction hit as strong as the last one had, ten minutes previous.

Michael handed the nail polish to our sweet nurse, and she finished up my left foot while Michael held my hand and talked me through it again. As much as I really did hate him, I was so glad he was there. While I loved his mom, she never could have replaced Michael in this situation.

My labor continued like this for a couple of hours. Contractions every ten minutes, but unfortunately I still wasn't progressing very fast. I was now at a three and seventy-five percent effaced. They upped the Pitocin which increased the intensity and left me worn out, and I wasn't even to the worst part yet.

"Honey," Michael said as he fed me ice chips.

I looked at him strangely. Honestly, that was not a word he ever used.

He gave me a knowing smile. "I really think you should consider the epidural this time. Dr. White said it may even speed things up if you can relax."

"I'm really tired of people telling me to relax."

He set the ice down and took my hands in his face. "Carly, you're in control here. I'll support whatever you want to do, but honey, you're already exhausted."

The ever present tears started up again. "I don't want to do anything that will hurt the baby."

Dr. White entered during our conversation. "If it makes you feel better, I've had an epidural for both of my deliveries, and women have them every day with no complications. I really do think with the amount of Pitocin you have in you, this would help, but it's your decision. I'll give you some time to talk it over."

I leaned my head against Michael's shoulder. He wrapped his arms around me.

"What do you think?" I asked.

He thought for a moment. "I think it's time for you to let go. You don't always have to be so strong."

"Yes, I do."

He chuckled a bit and kissed my head. "I love you."

"So you say."

He didn't respond to my rebuttal. What could he say? He could say he loved me until he was blue in the face, and I still might not believe it.

"So what do you want to do?"

A doozy of a contraction came before I could respond. It was strong enough that I hurt Michael's hand.

"I'm sorry. You should take off your wedding ring."

He had with Ashton and Mia. Apparently, I became like the Hulk when in labor.

He brushed my hair back and looked lovingly into my eyes as he held up his left hand. "I don't plan on ever taking this ring off."

I closed my eyes and sighed. I couldn't think about that right now. "I think I'm going to get an epidural." I opened my eyes to find him smiling at me.

He kissed me quickly, with no thought on how I would feel about that. "I'll go let Dr. White know."

I nodded my head, lay back against the bed, and closed my eyes, waiting for the next wave of pain. I rubbed my abdomen. "It won't be long now," I whispered quietly to my baby.

I wanted that baby in my arms more than anything at the moment. I knew I wasn't the only one anxious to meet her. Jack and Danielle had called at least four times to get an update. Ashton and Mia were beyond ready to come to the hospital. I hoped the epidural really would expedite things. I wanted the kids to be able to come today; to have the three of them together was going to be amazing.

Michael wasn't gone long. He informed me they were calling up the anesthesiologist. He took up his position by my side, and we went through two more rounds of contractions before the anesthesiologist arrived. Libby also came in to assist and prep. As they completely undid the back of my gown, I wondered why I even put anything on. Michael was right, there was no need for even trying to be modest today.

They had Michael hold me still against his chest, and when the next contraction hit, they apparently inserted a needle in my back. Michael said I didn't even want to know how big it was. All I knew was I felt so much better that I wanted to kiss Dr. Madsen. *I love anesthesiologists*, I decided.

From then on, Libby was almost a constant presence in my room as they monitored me. Both Libby and Emma encouraged me to try and sleep if I could. Before I closed my eyes I looked at Michael. He sat on the bed and stared at me sweetly. "You should get something to eat." He had skipped lunch.

He reluctantly agreed. He kissed my forehead and lingered. "I'll only be gone a few minutes."

"That husband of yours sure loves you," Libby commented.

I didn't disagree. Instead, I closed my eyes, tried to rest, and tried not to think about it. I focused my thoughts on the baby girl that would finally be joining our party. I'm not sure when Michael returned; I was tired enough that I drifted off. I woke up to Michael staring at me and Libby checking the monitors. The contractions were finally closer together. It was weird, but in a very good sort of way, to feel the pressure of them, but not the pain.

"I'm going to check you again," Libby announced. "Seven centimeters and one hundred percent effaced," she happily reported.

Both Michael and I lit up at the news. It really wouldn't be long now. Michael called his parents to give them a report. "It shouldn't be too long now," I heard him say. It was already five in the evening. It had been a long day, and I'm sure the kids thought it was an eternity already.

While we waited, Michael brought out the lotion and rubbed my upper back, shoulders and neck. He really did have the magic touch.

As he rubbed, he commented. "If I haven't said it lately, you really are beautiful. I almost changed the screen saver of you after the salacious comments I received from some of Joe's campaign workers. Even Joe is taken with you. If he wasn't such a decent guy, I think you could have a shot at being First Lady."

I couldn't help but laugh. "You're such a liar, Michael Bishop."

"Carly, I'm not lying. You have no idea the effect you have on people."

"Does he know about us?"

Michael stopped rubbing. I looked toward him. His countenance was thoughtful. "I told him about a month ago. He told me I was a fool and I quickly agreed with him."

"Maybe I'll vote for him after all." I smiled.

He grinned. "You may want to rethink that. He's the one that suggested I file for the stay."

"Why would he do that?"

"I don't know. I think he felt sorry for me. He hinted that perhaps his marriage had a rough patch that had to be worked through, but he wouldn't discuss it, and I didn't press."

"Aren't you writing his biography?"

"Some things should be private, don't you think?"

I nodded my head yes. That was one thing I always admired about Michael; he was never one to dig for dirt and smear people. There were too many people out there willing to tell all, even about themselves.

A little before seven I began to feel what they called breakthrough pain. The contractions were close and strong, and I was feeling them. I also felt the urge to push. The delivery room became a flurry of activity as Libby and two other nurses readied for the delivery. Michael and I smiled at each other. This was it. Michael helped position me and held my hand. As soon as Emma was there and ready, I was more than ready to push, and thankfully, I was really good at pushing. In two pushes her little head was delivered, and as soon as her mouth and nose were suctioned out, I heard the most wonderful sound, her cry. For a brief second I glanced at Michael. I was surprised to see tears in his eyes. I was already crying. I had been waiting for this for so long.

It didn't take much for the rest of her to be delivered. As soon as they pulled her tiny body out, Emma rested her on my chest. She was perfect. She had lots of dark hair, and was mad as heck, and was letting the world know. I was so thankful she was breathing on her own. I couldn't touch her enough. Michael placed his hands on her as well. I could tell she was definitely smaller than Ashton and Mia.

"Do you want to cut the cord?" Emma asked Michael.

"Yes," he said eagerly, but not before kissing me. "I love you. Thank you." I think he was crying more than me. He had never reacted that way before.

As soon as her cord was cut, the nurse took her and wrapped her up, placed some ointment on her eyes, and took her to be cleaned and weighed there in the room.

"So, what are you naming this sweet thing?" Libby asked.

I looked at Michael. "Her name is Danielle Rogers."

Michael's eyes widened. Rogers was my maiden name and now my middle name. I wanted her to have a piece of me. It only seemed right, but I quickly added, "Bishop." He was visibly relieved.

"But I'm calling her Dani," I informed both my husband and Libby.

Libby began cooing at my little Dani. I was already missing her from my arms. "You should go over with Dani," I instructed Michael. I was a paranoid mom. I needed him to watch over our daughter, even though she was in the room with us. I never wanted her out of our sights. Not that I couldn't hear her. I think the whole floor could. She and Mia were definitely sisters. While they cleaned her up, I had the fun of delivering the placenta, but thankfully, no stitches this time. Libby called out that Dani weighed six pounds and one ounce and was eighteen inches long, just a little thing. Ashton was almost two and a half pounds bigger than her and Mia had been a pound bigger than her. No wonder I didn't need any stitches. Bless her.

Those moments right after birth seemed to be so surreal; there was so much going on around me, it was kind of hard to take it all in. I loved that feeling of not being pregnant and being able to breathe normal again, but none of it really mattered until that baby was in my arms.

When both she and I were cleaned up and I was free to sit up, Libby carried over my now-swaddled and capped daughter. She was really ticked. I think she must have liked it in the womb, but as soon as they placed her in my arms, she quieted, and I swear she smiled. This only caused me to cry more.

I looked over to Michael who was now back on the bed with us. "She knows I'm her mom."

Michael kissed my head, and we both stared at her in awe. It looked like she had blue eyes, but at this age, it was hard to tell. She definitely had mine and Mia's hair color. Sepia, Michael liked to call it. We both took turns saying how beautiful and perfect she was. And Michael kept saying, "Just like her mother." Like I said, I didn't know what would become of us, but I was so glad he was there to share this moment, and even happier that he seemed to really love her. I had been so worried he wouldn't.

It didn't take her too long to begin to fuss. Libby encouraged me to try and nurse her. For being so small, she took to it like a champ. She had no issues latching on and sucking. I was relieved as I looked down at her in amazement. She was simply perfection, and I was completely smitten. While

I nursed her, Michael called his parents and talked to our kids. We told them they could come as soon as I was moved to a regular room, but first I had to do fun things like prove I could walk and use the restroom on my own. Gratefully, as she was such an easy delivery, those proved easy and we got the go ahead to be moved to a private room on the floor one up from where we were.

As soon as we were left alone, I let Michael get acquainted with our now-sleeping angel while I showered and changed into my own clothing. I was so done with the barely there blue gown that left nothing to the imagination. Michael told me to leave the door open just in case I needed him. He had always worried after I delivered. He didn't realize how great it felt not to be pregnant, but I was cautious; I learned the hard way not to overdo it after Ashton was born.

I came back out to find Michael laying on the sofa with Dani on his chest. They looked very comfortable together. It almost made my heart break because, just for a second, all seemed right in the world, but I knew it wasn't. I sat down on the bed and watched them.

He looked over to me. "Did my mom know you were going to name her Dani?"

"No. I wanted to surprise her. Your parents have been my life savers these past months. And your dad had told me she was hurt when we named Mia after my mom."

Michael carefully sat up without disturbing Dani. He held on to her like the precious vessel she was. I wanted to hold her myself, but he seemed to need it more than me.

"I'm happy you and my mom get along now."

"It was one of the good things to come out of all of this," I responded.

He looked down at our sleeping baby. "I'm so sorry, Carly. I can't believe I almost missed this." He kissed her head. She looked so tiny against her daddy. "I suppose you want to hold her."

I sat back on the bed and eagerly held out my arms. Michael gently placed her in my arms and kissed my forehead. He sat next to us and kept his hand on my leg. We stayed still like that for a time.

It wasn't too long before our older babies showed up with their grandparents. They were bursting with energy and anxious to meet their sister. Michael jumped up and scooped them both up before they pounced on me.

"You need to be gentle around your mommy and your sister," he kindly said to our overly excited children. He placed them on the bed next to me.

I held out the baby for everyone to see. She was still sound asleep. Danielle and Jack congratulated us both while the kids looked on.

Mia wanted to immediately hold her, and Ashton was as cautious as ever. "You can touch her," I told him. He did so, ever so lightly. Mia would have manhandled her if we would have let her, but Michael set her in the chair, took the baby from me, and helped Mia hold her briefly. Danielle was chomping at the bit to get her hands on her namesake.

During the commotion, Jack came and kissed my forehead. "You did good, my dear," he said.

"Thanks, Dad."

"You know," Danielle said as she gazed on her granddaughter. "Now that we have two Danielle's in the family, I think you should call me Mom."

I looked to her across the room, but I was speechless. Several months ago she could barely look at me without disdain. Michael and Jack were both looking back and forth between the two of us.

I smiled through some tears. "Mom. I like the sound of that."

"Me, too," she replied. Then she went right on cooing at Dani like nothing momentous had just happened. That was her way, and I loved her.

Everyone had their turn holding the baby and by that time, she was awake and crying. She definitely had no issues letting us know she was unhappy. Mia and Ashton were unhappy, too. They didn't want to leave, so we had three crying children, and the fun began. It really made me worry about being a single parent. Three against one weren't good odds. Thankfully, tonight it was three against four, but even that proved difficult as all three seemed to want my attention. It took several minutes of coaxing and explaining, but we got Ashton and Mia to settle down and leave with Mimi and Papa. We got Dani changed, and I started nursing her again.

"I'm sure you're tired. You should probably head back to your apartment," I said to Michael.

He looked stunned at the suggestion. "I'm staying here with you like I always have."

"Oh." *I hadn't thought of that as a possibility.*

"And don't worry about me. You have to be exhausted. As soon as you're done feeding Dani, I'll take her so you can rest."

Now I *was* stunned. "Okay. Thanks."

He shook his head. "You don't have to thank me. I'm the dad and the husband. Remember?"

"Vaguely."

He sat next to me and put his arm around me as I nursed our little one. Without thinking about it, I leaned into him.

"I love you, Carly, and I love our children. It is I who should be thanking you."

I didn't say anything. I closed my eyes and tried to remember what is was like to have a husband around. I liked having one around a lot, but I wasn't sure I should keep this one. Sure, he was here now and acting the part beautifully, but for how long? I wasn't sure if I could get over the pain he caused me and the distrust that I felt. And how would it look to my children? Would they grow up and think I was weak for letting their dad treat me like he had and then just let him walk right back into our lives? All I knew at the moment was I was tired, physically and emotionally. I gratefully handed Dani over to Michael when she was done nursing.

She was still awake, which didn't surprise me. This was her time of day. She wasn't fussy, so that was a plus, but I had a feeling I would be up a lot the next several nights of my life, and I would be alone. It wasn't a pleasant thought to drift off to sleep with, but it was my reality and I was exhausted. Michael left me alone on the bed and turned down the lights. He took the couch with Dani. He looked enamored with her. I quickly drifted off to sleep, watching them together.

I'm not sure how long I slept, but it wasn't nearly long enough. I woke up to Michael pacing the floor with our baby. She wasn't crying, but she was making little grunting noises. And she wasn't the only one making noise. Michael was softly talking to her. I decided to lay still and listen before I got up to use the restroom. He was telling her how we met. I almost said, "She's heard all of those stories from me," but I wanted to hear his perspective.

"The first time I met your mother it was in the middle of night just like now. She kept me up, just like you are now, too. It was the best night I had ever had at that point in my life. But your dad was an idiot then, just like he is now. I almost missed it, Dani. I almost missed you, too. What's wrong with me?" he choked out. "What am I going to do, Dani? I don't want to lose your mom, but I've really screwed up. Do you have any advice for your dad?" he asked her.

"Nothing, kid?

"I know. It's pretty hopeless, but I promise you, I'm going to try and fix it. Maybe you could put in a good word with your mom for me."

I couldn't help it. I laughed. Not at particularly what he said, but that this poor child was like our therapist. How many nights had I spent talking to her about our problems and about her idiot dad?

He turned toward me. "How much did you hear?"

"Enough."

I sat up carefully and moved toward the edge of the bed. I could use some more pain meds. He sat next to me with our baby. I reached out and touched her sweet head.

"Carly, do you still love me?"

I sighed. "Not to quote Tina Turner, but what's love got to do with it?"

"Aren't you the one that said love is the most powerful force on earth?"

"I did, but for months, Michael, I told you and tried to show you how much I loved you and you acted as if that meant nothing to you. In fact, it seemed to push you further away. So what if I still love you? I mean, how long is this going to last? How long are you even going to be around?"

"Carly, my behavior was completely inexcusable, but don't think for a second your love was lost on me. I know it didn't seem like it, but you don't know how hard it was to stay away from you. I'm done fighting it. I don't want to fight it. I emailed Joe tonight and told him I'm not coming back even if that means I lose the opportunity."

"No. You can't do that. You'll only resent me and the kids for coming between you and your dream."

He gently handed me Dani before he took my face in his hands and stared hard into my eyes. Even in the dark I could see his eyes smoldering. "Carly Bishop, what is a dream when you have nothing lasting and genuine to wake up to in the morning? I love being a writer, but it means nothing to me without you, and quite frankly without you by my side, I'm terrible at it. I would give it all up without a second thought and never look back if it means I get to keep you. And the only person to resent in this situation is me."

I closed my eyes and took a deep breath and held my baby close. I was more confused than ever.

Chapter Twenty-Two

WELL, MICHAEL WAS IN EARNEST. HE DIDN'T GO BACK ON THE ROAD WITH Joseph Xavier and he didn't lose his opportunity. Now he was using the technology he had stayed away from for so long. Skyping and FaceTiming became a daily routine for him as he interviewed those in Joseph's world. On several occasions, when he communicated with Joseph that way, I had the opportunity to speak to him and to show off Dani.

We all had to adjust to adding Michael back into our routine. I didn't let him move back home, even though he really wanted to; I was far from being sold on this new and improved Michael. In some regards, he as good as lived with us: he was there from the crack of dawn helping the get kids ready for school, which allowed me to shower without a baby in the bathroom with me, and he didn't leave until Ashton and Mia were put to bed. He even worked there. His excuse was the internet was much faster and more reliable at the house, but I knew it was because he was hopped up on baby love like the rest of us.

Dani was addictive, and we were all hooked. Even though she frequently kept me up and I was emotional from hormones and my husband, I was completely in love with her. There were even some moments in the quiet of the night when I was nursing her that I just would stare at her in amazement. She was perfection wrapped in a pink blanket.

Her daddy was behaving like perfection, as well. He had never been so attentive to my every need. In a way, it was annoying. I didn't know what to do, and suddenly he was so sure about us. He did tread lightly with me, but he was looking for any cue that I was ready to take him back. Dani and

I had lots of talks about him in the wee morning hours. Sometimes she would even smile. One thing was for sure, she loved her daddy. As soon as he appeared every morning, he would take her and she would promptly fall asleep in his arms. That was really annoying, especially when I had been rocking her for over an hour trying to accomplish the same thing.

Ashton also seemed confused. He was happy his dad was around more, but he, like me, was uneasy and reluctant to get comfortable. He still turned to his Papa frequently. It was interesting to watch; Ashton still wanted Papa to take him to soccer practice, but Michael wanted to be the one, so it ended up with Jack driving and Michael tagging along. I knew it pained Michael, but he understood and knew it was going to take some time and patience to undo the mess he created with his son.

Mia, on the other hand, was ready to welcome him home with open arms at any time. She loved having Daddy at her disposal for tea parties with Jilly or to snuggle. Several times I would catch her on his lap up in the loft while he typed away. Not a day went by that she didn't ask me if Daddy could come home for real. It broke my heart when I told her no and to see her face drop. Sometimes there were tears. But what could I do?

I decided I needed to talk to someone, so while Jack and Michael took the kids Trick-or-Treating, I had some one-on-one time with Danielle. While she loved on our Dani, I told her all of my concerns, from plain not trusting him to setting a bad example for my children if I took him back. And embarrassedly, I told her I was afraid to open myself up to him physically because I knew it would cloud my judgment. I obviously wasn't talking about sex, since that couldn't even be on the table until I had my six-week well visit in four weeks, but Michael definitely wanted to be physically affectionate, more than a kiss hello and goodbye.

I knew I was making my mother-in-law uncomfortable, but who else could I talk to about it? Dani was a great listener, as was God, but neither were answering at the time.

Danielle listened and took it all in. She thought about it while I got up and handed out candy.

When I returned, she was still looking adoringly at her granddaughter. "Trust will not come overnight, Carly, but you will have to take a leap of faith if you decide it's worth it, and only you can determine that." She averted her gaze momentarily from the tiny bundle of joy in her arms to look up at me. "I will say it again, you are the best wife and mother I've ever known and you have been an example of dignity and strength through all of this. If you decide to take Michael back, you will show your children what it means to forgive and they will never see that as weak." She looked back down at Dani. "As far as your sex life goes, you're on your own there. I still pretend Michael's a virgin."

We both laughed. And boy, did I need a good laugh.

That night I contemplated what she said while I nursed Dani. I was in that stage where I felt like I would be living in the rocking chair in my room for the rest of my life. I tried to remind myself to enjoy it as this was the last time I would ever do this, but when the clock reads one a.m., it's a little difficult to be rational. I thought about taking leaps of faith and what that would require. I thought even more about forgiveness. I knew, regardless of my decision, I would have to forgive Michael, but that was easier said than done.

Dani went right back to sleep, but I was thirsty, so I headed toward the kitchen after I laid her back down in her cradle next to my bed. On my way there, I noticed there was a faint glow of light coming from the loft. I thought that was odd, so I went upstairs to investigate. There I found Michael asleep on the couch with his laptop resting on his legs. I shook my head and approached him. I removed his laptop and sat on the edge of the couch. He looked so peaceful. I hesitantly reached out and brushed his hair with my hand.

He immediately woke up and grabbed my hand. "Hi, gorgeous." He smiled.

"I thought you went home."

He grinned. "I am home."

"You know what I mean."

"I honestly didn't mean to fall asleep here. I was working on organizing my notes and… well anyway."

"It's okay. You might as well stay now." I smiled.

He sat up, he reached out for me, pulled me onto his lap, and wrapped me up.

"What are you doing?"

"Why do you keep asking me that?" He quietly laughed against my ear. "But if you must know, I'm holding my wife. If memory serves me correctly, you used to like this."

I didn't answer. I was conflicted again because I did like it, a lot. I liked it even more when he began kissing my neck.

"Michael..."

"Do you want to know what I'm doing?"

"Believe me, I know... Maybe you should stop."

"Why would I want to do that?" he asked between kisses.

"I should probably get back down to the baby," I responded.

He groaned. "If you must, but before you go, I want to ask you something."

I yawned. "Okay."

"How would you like to go to the beach this weekend?"

I shook my head in confusion. "Um... I just had a baby and it's a little cold outside."

"Unfortunately for me, this beach trip will not require you to be in a swimsuit," he whispered against me.

I shook my head again. No one wanted to see me in a swimsuit right now.

"Joe wants us all to come to his Myrtle Beach compound to stay with him and his family through election night."

"Michael, I just had a baby and the kids are in school and we... and we... well I don't know what we are."

He kissed the top of my head and rubbed my arms. "Honey, I know, but how often do you get invited to be a part of history? We could very well be sitting in the same room with the newly-elected President of United States on election night."

That did sound inviting. As I mulled it over, Michael reminded me it was only a six hour drive and there would be other kids Ashton and Mia's age there. "We'll have our own room and I'll even sleep on the floor," he promised.

"I'll think about it," was all I could promise

He turned me toward him and kissed me tenderly. "I'll make this as easy on you as possible, but if you don't go, I'm not going either."

Way to make me feel guilty. I knew he wasn't trying to. I knew he was trying to prove his loyalty and dedication to us, but I knew how important it was for him to be there. Win or lose the election, having an up-close and personal view of it would be important to that biography. I also worried that if we did end up staying together, this could be a sticky point later on. I had always wanted to support him in pursuit of his dreams, but I didn't ever want to be the second act again.

I texted Emma first thing in the morning and got her take on me traveling three weeks after delivering a baby.

"You wouldn't be the first, and as long as your bleeding is under control and you feel up to it, I don't see it being an issue," she texted back almost immediately.

After Michael took the kids to school, we both sat on the living room couch, he on his laptop and me on mine, with the baby lying between us sleeping.

"You know I wouldn't be upset if you went without us. I know you have to work and I realize how important this is." I casually threw it out there.

He took off his reading glasses and looked over to me smiling. "Nice try, Carly."

"What does that mean?"

"It means I'm not going without you. Period."

"That's nice and all, but are you going to only take assignments now where the kids and I can come?"

"Carly, you realize after this book comes out I can pretty much do what I want, and I want to be with my wife and children. Plus, I was thinking you could support us now with your business."

I threw a pillow at him, careful not to hit my little bundle of joy, and glowered at him.

He laughed quietly. "Seriously though, honey, I don't want to go without you and when this is all over, I plan on finishing my novel. And maybe, for fun, I'll teach some classes at the university."

"Really? I thought that was too tame for you?"

He reached over, picked up my hand, and kissed it. "Life with you will never be boring."

"Hmm..." I rolled my eyes, turned back to my monitor, and half-smiled. "Okay, let's go to Myrtle Beach."

Not only did that make Michael happy, but Joseph Xavier was also thrilled. He took time out of his very hectic campaign schedule, to personally call and tell me that he and his family looked forward to having us. It really did seem surreal to be going to the home of what could be the most powerful man in the world someday. I had to say I was also intrigued by him. He wouldn't be campaigning that weekend or the day before Election Day because he wanted to spend it with his family; he figured if he hadn't already sold the American people, he wasn't going to change their mind in a weekend. His opponent was having a heyday with it, as was the press, but Joseph didn't care. He said he was a family man and he meant it. It might also have to do with the fact he was about ten points ahead in the polls. In politics there were no guarantees, but I admired him for taking a weekend with his family just in case he won and his life was no longer his to do with as he pleased.

Michael was true to his word. He did most of the planning and packing. I hoped Ashton and Mia's clothes matched. I took care of getting myself and Dani ready. I was nervous about the trip, but I reminded myself that women with babies crossed the plains, and not in nice new 4Runners with climate control and entertainment systems. I worried about things like my breasts leaking and reeking of spit-up, you know all the fun things new moms have to deal with, and then there was the lack of sleep and the unknown status of my marriage. I didn't want to have to pretend we were some happy couple when we were tentative. okay, I was tentative, Michael was gung-ho.

We weren't fighting. In fact we got along well, but I was still reserved and guarded around him. I was still praying for answers, for direction, and for help to forgive him. The only thing I could say was the hate I had felt for him had subsided, and I no longer felt like I wanted to smack him, so that was a positive.

We loaded up bright and early Friday morning. Meaning Michael loaded up and I watched. It was raining like crazy. We didn't get snow in November in Georgia, we got rain. I hated driving in the pouring rain, but Michael assured me it would be okay, and it was only supposed to rain for the first part of our trip. I made him check the weather at least ten times before we buckled in all of the kids. Going from two to three kids seemed like a much bigger leap than one to two.

Michael really was happy. He kept expressing how this was the best of both worlds for him and how much he had missed being able to travel on assignment with me. I guess I had never realized how much that had meant to him and the loss he felt when that was no longer an option. For me, I wanted to separate home and work as much as possible, but I was learning for him, intertwining the two created equilibrium.

As happy as he was, it wasn't an easy trip there. Mix in torrential rains, a carsick Mia, a baby that demanded to be nursed and held, unending traffic, and a sleep deprived mommy, and you basically have a recipe for disaster. Oddly, though, it was Michael that kept his cool and kept trying to keep everyone positive. He was desperate to prove that we could do this, and not only do it, but do it well. I, on the other hand, kept saying this was a big mistake and what were we thinking, but Michael insisted we trudge forward because it was going to be great. His eyes pleaded with me to believe him and to please try, so we trudged forward. What should have been a six hour trip turned into a nine hour arduous trek. We spent the last hour listening to our baby cry and Mia and Ashton begging us to make her stop. I don't think you have ever seen people get out of a car so quickly once we made it past the tight security that was guarding Joseph's luxurious home on the beach.

"Well, that was fun," Michael said as he unbuckled Mia and I retrieved my very unhappy baby. Thankfully, as soon as I picked her up, she calmed down. She loved being held and wasn't used to being in a car seat for long periods of time.

Ashton climbed out from the back. "You should have had a boy, Mom," he announced loudly.

Michael and I both laughed and told him that her being a girl made no difference. He looked between Mia and Dani as if he was begging us to disagree with him. The laughter and just being out of the car hit the reset button on my mood. I took a deep breath and snuggled Dani close. I told myself it was okay to enjoy this. After taking a moment to look around at the scenery, I realized I would be silly not to. I was definitely breaking out my camera.

Joseph came out and joined us. I noticed how his armed detail followed his every move; that would be hard to get used to. It was also a little disconcerting that we were staying with a man that needed around the clock protection.

"You get used to it," Michael whispered.

Joseph was jovial and welcoming as he greeted us. He acted very grandfatherly toward Mia and Ashton. Mia took right to him, but Ashton was a little wary. Dani began to cry again as we were ushered in, so I asked for our room so I could change and feed her and give her the attention she deserved. Joseph had his people bring up our luggage. I didn't have much of a chance to look at his home as we walked upstairs, but the brief glances were eye candy. I heard the noise of children playing and adults in conversation, so I assumed his family had already arrived. Joseph showed us to a large room with a private bath. The room boasted a four-poster king size bed, a sitting area with fine furniture, a large screen T.V., and all the comforts you would find in a fine hotel. It was decorated in warm and inviting tones; it almost made the drive worth it.

Joseph left us alone so we could settle in. Before he left, he reminded us the kids could sleep with his grandchildren in the children's quarters that had lots of bunk beds and a large play area. I told him we would see how Mia and Ashton took to it all and let them decide whether to stay with us or with his grandchildren. I was kind of hoping they wanted to stay with us. I didn't know if Michael and I were ready for sleepovers yet, even though he said he would take the floor.

As soon as he left, I began to take care of Dani while Ashton and Mia explored the room and Michael unpacked.

"Feel free to take the kids down. I'm going to be a while." I wanted to freshen up before I made an appearance.

Michael reluctantly agreed. He walked over to the chair I now occupied to kiss both me and the baby before they went down. "Thanks for being a good sport," he said.

I wasn't sure my behavior would constitute good sportsmanship—I had been pretty cranky the whole day, but I smiled anyway. "I'll be down as soon as I can."

"I can't wait," he responded.

I wondered if this Michael would last.

Dani greedily ate. She acted as if she was starving, poor thing. She was having no issues gaining weight; her little cheeks and thighs were already filling out. She really was the most adorable baby. I took my time feeding her and snuggling her until she fell asleep. I laid her in the portable crib we brought and freshened up by changing my clothes. I was in the weird stage where my regular clothes didn't quite fit yet, but maternity clothes were way too big. I broke down and bought a few outfits for the interim and specifically for this trip. I threw on some jeans and a soft, charcoal gray, turtleneck sweater, fixed my makeup, and called it good.

I carefully picked up my sleeping baby, and we proceeded to find the rest of our family. It didn't take much, I followed the noise downstairs. There was a large gathering in what looked like the family room that was open to the spacious kitchen.

Michael was immediately drawn to us and joined our side. He excitedly introduced me to the group. All of Joseph's daughters were there with their husbands. I think the couples were as follows—Hope and Greg, Michelle and Cody, Natalie and Mark, and Kristine and Dan. The children, including mine, were all in the play room. Everyone was cordial and, of course, interested in Dani. Who wouldn't be?

Michael took our daughter from me. He hadn't been able to really hold her all day and, like I said, we were both addicted. There's something about a man holding a baby that is very attractive, especially when you could see in his eyes how much he loved her as he looked at her. I was only allowed a second to look at Michael before I was bombarded with requests to take photos while I was there for the next five to six days.

"Please don't feel obligated," Joseph said, but he added in, "I would love to have this weekend captured in pictures, especially through your lens. You have a gift."

How could I say no to that? "I would be happy to take some photos."

Joseph was delighted.

"I can do some posed shots, but I would love to do some candid shots if that's okay with everyone." I loved capturing people living life, and what a life this family had. They all readily agreed. Michael's facial expressions emitted pride.

"You are an excellent team," Joseph said. His overt attempt to express his opinion on our status as a couple was not lost on me or Michael.

I grinned, but Michael verbalized his agreement. "There has never been a better team."

There were a couple of aahs from Joseph's daughters. This was going to be a long weekend, I thought.

Dinner preparation was a family affair in the Xavier family. It was fun to watch them interact with each other. His daughters were all close in age. His oldest, Hope, was thirty-six and his youngest, Kristine, was twenty-eight. They all seemed to get along so well together, and it made me a little jealous. I don't think Melanie and I had ever been so easy and comfortable around each other. Even now, as adults, we had to try really hard to be around each other for long periods of time. These sisters seemed to know everything that went on in each other's lives. It was fun to watch and take pictures of them. Joseph and his wife, Marilyn, had done a good job as parents. I hoped someday in the future my three little ones would be so close.

Michael used this as an opportunity to casually interview "Joseph's girls," as they were called in the media. He asked them about their mother and about their favorite memories growing up. It was fun to hear them reminisce about holidays and dates gone badly, but it was touching to hear them talk about their mother and what an example she had been to them. She sounded like the strong, silent type that you didn't want to get on the wrong side of, but from the sounds of it, she was the best friend and fiercest protector you could ever have.

While Michael was in his element, I took several shots of him when he wasn't paying attention to me. I hadn't seen him work in a long time, and realized how much I had missed that. He had a way of making people feel comfortable enough to open up. Watching him through my lens made me see him in a way I hadn't in a long time, probably in a way I should have been more aware of these last several years. He finally caught me taking his picture and looked up and smiled. I lowered my camera and smiled back.

Since I had been caught, I took that as my opportunity to head up to the play room, with Dani swaddled against me, to take some pictures of Joseph's grandchildren. I also wanted to check on mine, even though I knew a nanny was present upstairs. There were three levels to this monstrously beautiful home, and a good portion of the third level was a children's wonderland. I feared Ashton and Mia may never want to go home. The room contained slides, a bouncy ball pen, a drawing and painting station, a theater area, and a mini stage. It was like kid paradise. Heck, even I wanted to stay. I was happy to find Mia and Ashton playing well with the other kids. There were five grandkids in total. Hope and Greg had two boys ages eight and nine, Michelle and Cody also had a seven-year-old girl and a four-year-old boy; that left a three-year-old boy that belonged to Natalie and Mark.

The nanny, Addison, remarked to me how Mia had no issues bossing the boys around and getting her own way. That sounded like Mia. She did say that my kids were well-behaved; that also sounded like them. I had been so grateful for that fact this past year. I don't think I would have survived had I not been blessed with the children I was given.

I tried to carefully remain in the background so I could take some natural shots, but kids love to pose (at least some), so I ended up rearranging them and giving them direction. The boys weren't really into it, except the three-year-old, who was darling with the curliest red hair. I could have eaten him up. Mia and Clarissa were more than happy to pose for the camera, but they had their own ideas about what would be best. I was happy to let them direct me. After all, all I had to do was focus and click, but even that didn't last long. I had apparently interrupted a game of house, so I made my way back downstairs.

On my way down, I ran into Joseph.

"Carly, I was hoping to run into you."

"Well, here I am." I smiled.

He smiled in return. "I would like to show you something in my office."

"As a politician, that sounds nefarious."

He laughed heartily. "Maybe I should hire you as my public relations consultant. You would certainly keep me out of trouble."

It was my turn to laugh, but I agreed to follow him to his office down the hall. I wasn't sure an office near the playroom was a good place, but he probably enjoyed being close to his grandchildren. I knew I would. He led the way and opened the double doors to a masculine office with lots of wood, leather, and bookshelves. I also recognized several foreign art pieces I'm sure he collected during his travels. His office reminded me of several of my father's offices throughout my growing-up years.

At first he let me walk around and admire the art and the pictures of his family over the years. He followed me as I walked around. It was as if he was waiting for me to discover on my own what he asked me in for. It didn't take me long to come across a picture of him and my father together in India, both sitting atop elephants, no less. I touched the picture almost reverently. I looked down at my sleeping baby that was wrapped against me. So many times I had wished my parents were alive to enjoy my children, especially during this last year. I had desperately wanted my mother.

My father and Joseph looked like men that were on top of the world in the picture. It was so weird to think that this man next to me was a friend of my father.

"That picture was taken only a month before..." He didn't finish.

I knew what he was talking about. I still remembered that day, how I frantically watched the news and tried desperately to reach my parents. I remembered Michael not leaving my side for a minute and how he held me without saying a word when my worst fears were confirmed. He knew there was nothing he could say, but his actions spoke volumes.

A small tear found its way down my cheek. "Thank you for showing me this." I figured our little pow-wow was over, so I made a motion toward the door.

"Carly, can I talk to you?"

I turned back toward him. "Sure."

He motioned for me to sit on his leather couch where he sat next to me. For a guy that usually looked unfazed, he was acting awfully nervous.

"I wanted to apologize for our last meeting. I probably sounded insensitive, but I had no idea."

I rested my hand against his for a moment. "Please, no apology is necessary. How could you have known?"

He smiled sweetly at the gesture. "I hope you don't mind me saying, but I noticed you're not wearing your wedding ring. Are you…?"

I rubbed my finger. "Confused?"

He gave me a knowing grin.

"You know, several times I caught Michael holding your ring and staring at it. At first, I didn't realize what it was, and when I found out, I was quite surprised."

I looked at my empty finger. "Believe me, no one has been more surprised by all of this than me."

He gently patted my hand. "But you're working things out?"

I shrugged my shoulders. "I don't know. I guess. He wants to, but… but I don't know. I wanted to for so long, but he crossed a line and I don't know what to do."

He looked at me for a moment without saying a word. He reminded me so much of my dad. I could see why they were friends. "Can I tell you something in confidence, Carly?"

"As long as it isn't some secret inner working of the government."

He laughed. "You really are delightful. But no, this is much more important."

I gave him my full attention.

"To look at these pictures that surround us, you would probably think we look like the perfect family, but as you know, no family or relationship is perfect. Moments of perfection, yes."

I smiled down at Dani. She was one of those moments for me.

"But most relationships have moments of great imperfection, and sometimes those are insurmountable, or so they may seem. Marilyn and I had that moment about twenty years ago. At the time, my business was booming, our daughters were healthy and beautiful, and we were making more money than I ever imagined." He looked around. "It was the year we began building this house," when he looked back my way, he looked saddened, "but success costs."

I wasn't sure I wanted him to go on. His look was too pained, but I didn't stop him.

"For me, I was on top of the world. I was traveling the world and providing for my family in a way I never dreamt was possible, but my long absences were beginning to become problematic, as you can imagine."

Yeah, I know a thing or two about long absences.

"So much so that when I was home, all we did was argue about it. It wasn't that I wanted to be away from my family, but I didn't see any way to get around it at the time. She felt burdened and abandoned, and no amount of money could fix that for her. This all went on for some time, that is until I came home early from a trip one day and found that Marilyn... let's say she found a way to deal with her loneliness."

I think my eyes may have popped out of my head. I wasn't expecting that, and I really didn't want to hear it. It made me feel ill inside. I thought about getting up and running out of the room or plugging my ears and saying *lalalala*, but that seemed juvenile, and his look for understanding prevented me from moving.

"So... what did you do?"

"Well, I won't say what I did in the moment, it was not her or my finest moment, but after the initial dust settled, I did what most would do, and rightly so, I suppose. I tried to end the marriage."

"But obviously that didn't happen. How did you overcome such a betrayal?"

He took my hands. "One day at a time, but I also began to realize how much I had taken advantage of her."

"But... still, she..."

"I'm not trying to excuse her behavior, and she never tried to, either. I'm just saying I realized if I wanted to make our marriage work, I needed to make some changes."

"How did you ever trust her again?"

"It was difficult. It took some doing, and a lot of time."

"Were you afraid she would do it again?"

He nodded.

"Did you ever really get over it?"

"It was anything but easy, but we did, and we came out better and stronger for it."

"So are you trying to give me advice?" I smiled.

He laughed again. "You are enchanting, and I think your husband is completely undeserving of you."

We both stood up. "Thank you. I won't share what you told me."

"I appreciate that. Not even my daughters know."

I gave him a surprised look.

"Marilyn deserves to have her spotless reputation with our girls. She's the reason they're the women they are today," he responded.

I could respect that.

Chapter Twenty-Three

WE WALKED OUT AS THE NANNY WAS BRINGING THE KIDS DOWN FOR DINNER. I could smell the heavenly scent all the way up where I was. We walked down in a flurry of hungry kiddos. Their excitement woke up Dani, and she wasn't thrilled at all. Her cries reverberated through the house, so much so that Michael met us on the second floor stairs.

He extracted Dani as everyone else left us and followed their stomachs downstairs. She quieted immediately in his arms.

"What have you been up to?" he asked as he looked adoringly at our daughter.

"Joseph was just interviewing me for the position of first lady," I teased.

He looked up immediately and for some reason, he didn't think that was funny at all. He pulled me to him and Dani. "Then he's asking for the biggest fight of his life."

"Is that so?"

His eyes burned in response as he bent down to kiss me softly on my lips. It was the first time I had really responded since he came back. He smiled, pulled me a little closer, and kissed me deeper.

I pulled back and took a deep breath. "We should probably go downstairs."

"Okay, *Mrs.* Bishop."

I rolled my eyes. I didn't need to be reminded I was married to him. But I think saying it gave him comfort. What was I going to do with him? When he kissed me like that, I knew what I wanted to do. It's one of the reasons I had been very careful about engaging physically with him. My body would easily betray me if I wasn't careful.

My conversation with Joseph had not been lost on me as Michael and I walked down to dinner together, hand in hand. But how many times does it actually work out? I wanted a guarantee that wasn't available. I knew there were no guarantees in life. Even though Michael had promised me when we got married that we were the bona fide real deal and that we would be honest with each other no matter what, he betrayed all of that. Sure, he didn't cheat on me, per se, but it felt like he had. And yes, I recognize now some things I could have done better, things maybe I should have recognized, but I didn't do anything out of malice or neglect. I just didn't realize that our ideals were misaligned. I would have been willing to change and compromise, but he didn't ever give me the opportunity. Was this our opportunity? Our opportunity, like Joseph said, to be better and stronger?

I didn't have much time to think about it because dinner was a boisterous affair with so many people. I wasn't used to this many people. Michael and I both came from small families, but I found I liked the large family scene. I was happy we added one more to our small brood. I was pretty sure I could get used to a big family.

After dinner, it was games and then dessert. One of Joseph's daughters made the most amazing pumpkin cake. I thoroughly enjoyed the conversation that went along with it. I think I could easily be friends with all of them, and hoped I would be. They all seemed down-to-earth and centered. Joseph was right, his wife had done a beautiful job as a mother.

As the evening wore on, it was more than apparent that the children needed to be in bed. Mia was whiny and Ashton was nodding off near my side. Dani was raring to go. She was still having a hard time with her days and nights. Before Michael and I even asked, Mia said she wanted to sleep in the children's room. I was hoping when we got Ashton awake enough to ask him, he would disagree, but he surprised me and said he wanted to, as well. I could tell my husband was pleased with the turn of events. I wanted to override them, I was the mom, after all, but I could tell the kids were looking forward to it, and having all of our kids in the same room was probably not the best idea. Dani could wake the dead when she really got going.

We all went to our room first. Ashton and Mia changed into their pajamas and brushed their teeth. Michael offered to take them up and tuck them in. I agreed and quickly used the time while he was gone to change myself without him present. I threw on my flannel pajama pants and a matching form-fitted t-shirt, brushed my teeth and washed my face, and brought my baby to bed to feed her.

Michael returned a half-hour later. He shut the door and stood there for a moment staring at us. "I'm not sure there is anything more beautiful than watching you nurse our babies."

He was laying it on thick, but I smiled at him. "How did Ashton and Mia do?"

"Mia decided maybe this wasn't such a good idea, so she's in Ashton's bed."

That was my girl.

He propelled himself off the door and headed toward his suitcase. He had no qualms changing in front of me. I tried to focus on Dani, but my eyes kept wandering toward my now bare-chested husband. Oh…he looked good. I knew he worried about getting older, but so far he had done it very well. He threw on some pajama pants and told me he would be right back. He was staying shirtless on purpose. As my heart rate increased, I told myself he was still sleeping on the floor.

He didn't take long joining me. He sat near me on the edge of the bed smiling like a fool and looking like he couldn't have been happier. I wasn't sure how to feel, so I looked down at my baby who was just finishing up eating. I held her up to burp her, but Michael took her from me. I had missed him doing that at night for me. He stood up with her and talked to her as he patted her back. She looked so itty-bitty next to him. I couldn't say it enough; he looked good. Really good, especially as he held our baby against his bare chest.

I watched him pace back and forth with her. He kept looking my way, too. The tension in the room was palpable. I almost felt like I needed a cold shower. Instead I sank into the plush bed and pulled the covers up.

Michael magically got her to burp and fall asleep quickly. That was so wrong. Did she not realize who birthed her and carried her for nine months? Oh well. I was grateful she was asleep at a decent time. He laid her gently in her crib and then looked at me like, now what? That was a very good question. I thought for a minute. *Do I invite him to bed?* I knew what that meant. It meant I was willing to try and work this out, and there was no going back. My heart was pounding out of my chest. I didn't know what to do, so I threw the pillows next to me at him. I instantly felt horrible. His face dropped. He slowly walked over with pillows in hand to turn off the lights.

I lay down on my side to face where the baby lay a few feet away from me. I heard Michael open the closet to retrieve the extra blankets. I felt like I couldn't think straight. I had so many conflicting emotions. Then I felt Michael near. He placed himself on the floor between the bed and the baby.

"What are you doing?" I whispered.

He reached up from the ground and held my hand. "I just want to be near you," he responded.

We lay there for several minutes, holding hands in the dark, not saying a word. It must have been kind of uncomfortable for him to hold his arm up, but he never made a move to let go. It was really sweet, and it made me feel guiltier.

"Carly?"

"Yeah?"

"I loved seeing you in action today."

"I felt the same way watching you." Silence. "Michael?"

"Yeah?"

I took a very deep breath and tried to calm the butterflies in my stomach. It was so weird to feel this way about my own husband. "Do you want to... not sleep on the floor?"

He jumped up like a spring and practically vaulted himself over me. Before I knew it, his arm was around me and I could feel his warm breath against my head. That's when the emotion came. I felt so dumb crying, but this was a big deal for me.

"Baby, are you crying?"

I nodded my head yes.

He turned me toward him, so now I was facing his bare chest. I continued to cry into it.

"What's wrong?"

"I missed this... and I'm scared."

He held me tighter. "What are you afraid of?"

"In a matter of speaking, you."

He let go just enough to look at me and stroke my tear-stained cheeks. "Why are you afraid of me?"

"Because I miss you and I want you, but I don't know if I should after what you did. How do I know that you won't wake up tomorrow or another ten years from now and decide that you don't want me again? Do you even know the power you have to hurt me? How can I trust you with that power?"

He stroked my hair and kissed the top of my head. "Carly, I know nothing I say will ever make up for what I did to you. I know that I have a long road ahead to earn your trust, but I will do everything I can, because I do know the power I have, and I'm so sorry I abused it." He kissed my forehead. "Baby, remember the night you gave me back your ring and told me not to come back?"

How could I forget? I nodded my head yes.

"I felt real, physical pain. I know I didn't do what I should have then, but you leaving me hurt like hell, and then having you slip further away from me was unbearable. You don't know how sorry I am if I caused you even a small amount of the pain I felt when you left me. I know my promises are hollow right now, and I'm asking you to take a shot in the dark, but I love you and I don't ever want to be without you again."

"I love you, too," I whispered.

Even in the dark I could see him smile before his lips found mine. It was almost like the first time he kissed me, but better because we knew each other and all of our nuances. It was amazing. The tears that fell now were the kind that only joy can bring. I knew we had a long way to go, but there was something in his kiss that told me he meant what he said. It wasn't a hungry kiss, but a slow, I have all of the time in the world, kiss. It was the sweetest kiss I had ever had and I wished it could have gone on all night, but as parents with a newborn, that wasn't in the cards. As he held me to him, I laid my head on his chest and felt as if I had come home. I fell asleep quickly and soundly.

When Dani did wake us up at around three a.m., Michael kissed me once, got up and changed her, then handed her to me to nurse. As much as I missed my sleep, there was something about gazing down on her sweet little face in the quiet of the night that I loved. Tonight it was made sweeter as I rested against Michael, while Dani ate to her heart's content. I had missed sharing these moments with him. And he seriously had the touch where she was concerned. Within half-an-hour, she was back in her crib sleeping soundly, and I found myself back in her daddy's arms, more at peace than I had felt in over a year.

I naturally woke up a little after six a.m. It was the most sleep I had had since Dani was born. As I stirred, Michael opened his eyes.

"Good morning, gorgeous," he whispered.

"Good morning, Bishop."

He hugged me tight and kissed the top of my head. "I've missed that name."

"I've missed that guy."

"I've missed him, too," he replied.

My hands found their way down his chest to another name I missed. It was the only tattoo either one of us had. I still couldn't believe when he got it, but you do weird things in foreign countries when you are punch-drunk in love on your honeymoon. I brushed my fingers over his heart and 24B.

"I'm thinking of tattooing Carly on my butt."

I started laughing quietly. "Please don't."

"You could get a matching one on yours that says Michael or Bishop."

"How about you give me my wedding ring back and we'll call it good."

"Oh."

"What? Did you lose it?"

"Of course not, but I don't have it with me."

"That's fine, but I think poor Joseph may get his hopes up now."

He growled and rolled over so he hovered over me sexily. "I don't care that he's guarded by the Secret Service, he would be on the losing end of that battle."

I rolled my eyes at his macho machinations.

He stroked the length of my cheek. "I love you, Carly."

Before I could respond, he kissed me, but hungrily this time. We got all sorts of tangled up. It was a great way to start the day, but alas, our baby decided it was time to get up, too. Michael kissed me hard one more time before Dani hit a fever-pitched scream; he walked over to pick her up and changed her diaper. I loved hearing him coo at her.

While I took care of her, he showered and got ready for the day. As soon as he was ready he went up to check on our older babies. Co-parenting really was the best. Michael brought back down my pajama-clad kiddos who jumped on the bed along with Michael. Happy didn't even begin to describe how I felt at this moment looking at my whole family together. It was like Joseph said, perfect moments.

We all stayed on the bed and took turns holding Dani. For Mia, Dani was a doll replacement. In fact, ever since Michael had come back and we brought Dani home, her doll, Jilly, was hardly brought out. Ashton was very gentle and loving toward Dani. He was going to be a terrific big brother to both of his sisters. Maybe he would even forgive me for not giving him a brother. Michael and I kept smiling at each other as we watched our children. It made me wish I could freeze time, but I did the next best thing: I got my camera out and took several pictures.

As I looked through my lens, I hoped and prayed I was making the right decision. Being a family felt right. I knew it wasn't going to be easy, and I knew the road before us would have some bumps and probably some major potholes, but I couldn't think of anyone else I wanted to take that road with more than Michael.

We spent the rest of that weekend taking chilly walks on the beach and going to church together with the Xavier family. Michael hadn't been to church in years. That was my kind of thing, not his, but as we sat in the beautiful cathedral hand-in-hand on Sunday, Michael whispered that he wanted to make this a family thing when we returned to Pine Apple. I couldn't have been happier about that, and I knew his parents would be thrilled to have us all together every Sunday.

Monday came and Michael and Joseph were gone most of the day. Joseph wasn't campaigning, but he was at his campaign headquarters thanking everyone who had worked so tirelessly on his campaign. He also had to do some interviews for the national and cable stations. I used the day to take pictures of each of his daughters' families and to get more acquainted with them. I couldn't tell if they wanted their dad to win or lose the next night. Of course they wanted him to win. They felt like he could do a lot of good for our country, but they knew how hard it was going to be on their family. It had already been rough. I couldn't imagine having to live under such a microscope, and we all know how we are when someone belittles or defames those we love; that was something they would have to deal with daily. It would be quite the sacrifice. I knew I would never look at any president the same way ever again.

Monday night everyone seemed on edge. I tried to keep my brood up in our room and away from the fray. Michael, needed to be in the middle of it, but I wanted to give their family the alone time they deserved with their dad.

I knew tomorrow morning there would be news crews and people galore crawling everywhere. I almost wished the kids and I had gone home, but when Michael came to bed late that night, he held me in such way that said he needed me to be there with him, and more importantly, he wanted me there with him.

Tuesday dawned early for Michael and for Dani, too. We tried to enjoy just a few moments of quiet time together before Michael left to be with Joseph. I tried to stay out of the way. I spent most of my day in the playroom with the nanny; frequently we would have adult visitors, including Michael who sneaked up a couple of times. Michael asked me to join him, along with Joseph and his family, in the large theater room that night after the kids had gone to bed. That's where they were watching all the election results come in. He offered to hold Dani if that would help. It probably would; she, like her mother, loved to sleep in his arms. I agreed to, even though I felt a little self-conscious. I knew that room would have a camera crew in it, but I couldn't miss out on the experience.

I came down at nine p.m., and numbers and projections were already starting to come in from the east coast where polls had been closed for a couple of hours. Michael and I had voted by mail, but Michael had gone with Joseph that morning as he cast his vote. Michael and I sat in the back and watched as the family cheered or cried as he won or lost states. Two hundred and seventy electoral votes was the magic number. I noticed Michael had tried to remain emotionless as a good journalist should do, but after a while I think he remembered he was this man's biographer and it was okay to root for him. I knew I was.

Dani handled the noise tolerably well. I kept her swaddled against me for the most part, but Michael couldn't resist holding her for part of the time. As the night wore on, and the energy increased in the room, the calmest one was Joseph. He laughed and joked easily. It was one of the reasons I liked him so much and felt like he would be a great leader. My favorite, though, was his daughter Hope; she threw popcorn at the large screen T.V. when snarky commentators put down her dad. I imagined she was like her mother in her fierce defense of her family.

The night dragged on, and I eventually leaned against Michael and tried to close my eyes. As a mom with a newborn, I didn't do late nights well.

"Why don't you go to bed," Michael whispered.

"Not a chance, Bishop," I whispered back.

He kissed my head in response. I wanted him to know that I supported him. One late night wasn't going to kill me. At least I hoped not, but I was so thankful that by one a.m. it was clear Joseph had this in the bag. The elation in the room caused our little Dani to go into hysterics; it was then I took my leave. I'm sure I would hear the concession speech from his opponent many times over the next several days on the news, so I didn't need to stay up to see it. I was thrilled for the Xavier family. They would be an excellent First Family.

I'm not sure what time Michael came to bed, but he wrapped me up and kissed my neck as soon as he hit the sheets. I had missed sharing a bed with him. I sank right against him.

"I love you, Carly," he whispered in my ear.

I sighed and fell right back asleep.

We decided that even though we were pretty beat the next morning, it was time to go home. The flurry of activity at the Xavier compound was more than any of us, especially our baby, wanted to deal with, and Michael was anxious to really be home. When I told him he could move back in; he couldn't have been happier, but I warned him that I couldn't and wouldn't go through the misery he had put us through this past year.

"I know my promises don't carry the weight they once had, but I've seen life without you and I can't bear that," he said in response to my warning.

I hoped with all my heart he meant it.

We came home and the busyness of our trip followed us. Michael had deadlines to meet and the holidays were approaching. But as busy and as tired as I was, I was happy, like really happy. I was approaching Thanksgiving this year with a renewed sense of all I had to be thankful for and with a determination not to take it for granted. Michael was determined, too. Though he had to work long hours, he made sure every day that we had family dinners together and that between dinner and bedtime, he didn't work. It meant there were nights when I would look over in bed and he would be up, quietly typing away. When that happened, though, he always traded his laptop for me.

His parents couldn't have been happier. As we gathered around their dining room table for Thanksgiving, both of their eyes shined as they looked around the table at all of us. They both gave me knowing smiles. My relationship with them was one of the best and brightest spots out of this whole mess. The holidays would now lack the awkwardness that had always existed between us. For that, I was truly grateful.

The only thing off was that my finger still lacked a ring, and Michael was behaving mysteriously about it. It started to become annoying, so I quit asking about it. "If you want me to look single, so be it," I said in resignation.

His eyes burned. "I'll follow you around twenty-four-seven if I have to."

Finally, on my birthday, November twenty-eighth, the mystery was solved.

I came home late in the afternoon from my six-week postpartum check to find my house eerily quiet. I assumed at least the baby would be fussy and ready to eat, but I didn't hear a peep as I walked into the kitchen while looking through the mail.

"I'm home," I called, thinking I would be greeted by my children it was my birthday, after all, and I thought we had plans to go to dinner, but no one responded. Then I heard the soft melodic sounds of Journey playing, so I followed the sound to the living room. There I found my husband sitting in front of the lit fireplace on a blanket full of food, looking more handsome than ever, and holding what looked like flutes of sparkling cider.

I smiled. "What's this?"

He motioned for me to come closer. I slipped off my shoes and eagerly approached him.

He raised his hand and helped me sit down next to him. "Happy birthday, baby."

I kissed him. "Thank you, but where are our children?"

He smiled seductively and raised his eyebrow. "Ashton and Mia will be conveniently spending the night at my parents' house." Then he held up the baby monitor. "Dani is asleep upstairs."

I looked at him worriedly at that news. I wasn't ready for her to be in her crib yet.

He smiled again. "She'll be okay. I think we deserve a little alone time."

I liked the sound of that. We hadn't had any alone time since he had been back.

"So," he asked, "how did your appointment go?"

I knew what he was getting at, so I smiled. "I was cleared for all physical activity."

He pulled me closer and kissed me deeply. "Perfect. It looks like we'll both get our favorite birthday present tonight, then."

He reached over, and from behind the nearby ottoman, he pulled out a tiny bag. "First this, though," he said as he handed it to me.

I took the little red bag and removed the tissue paper to find a black jewelry box. Michael reached into the bag and removed the box and held it up in between the both of us. He stared at it for a moment as the firelight danced in those beautiful blue eyes of his. After a moment, he carefully opened the lid to reveal my wedding ring, but it looked quite a bit different than I remembered. "Carly, that secret account as you called it, I opened that account right after we got married."

My eyes widened and he grinned. "Not for what you think," he said. "I opened it because I felt bad that I couldn't buy you the ring you deserved."

"But I loved that ring."

He placed his finger on my lip. "I know you did, baby, and that's one of the many reasons I fell in love with you, but I wanted you to have the best, so I thought if I saved a little whenever I could, I could eventually get you the ring you deserve."

He took the new ring out of the box, reached over and picked up my hand, and gently slid the huge sparkler on my finger that had been begging to be occupied. I looked at the ring and it looked like my old band, but he way upgraded the diamond. He took back my hand and kissed it before he reached over and handed me a sheet of paper. I took it and looked it over. It was a statement of a closed out account. I don't know why, but tears started running down my cheeks. He smiled and took the stupid piece of paper and tossed it in the fire.

He turned back to me and began kissing every inch of my face. "I love you, Carly," he said between kisses. "Thank you for marrying me in the first place and then staying with me even though I don't even come close to deserving you."

I reached up and held his face in my hands, the face I loved so much. I smiled. "You better never forget it, Bishop."

Epilogue

I SHOULD BE SLEEPING, BUT I FIND IT HARD TO TURN AWAY MY GAZE FROM two of the most beautiful creatures on this planet. On one side, I have my infant daughter that, thankfully, has taken after her mother in both beauty and charm. Lying next to me is the reason I even began this blog in the first place, my reason for living, the mother of my children, the woman that completes me and makes me better in every way, the woman that occupied seat 24B twelve years ago to the day.

Twelve years ago I was the most self-centered, egocentric man in existence, but all it took was one flight in the middle of the night and this enchanting woman had me thinking of nothing else but her. That night I learned what true happiness was. I only felt that happiness grow as I pursued her and eventually made the best decision of my life when I asked her to be my wife. For so long I realized that true happiness for me was allowing her to occupy my thoughts and to put her every need and want above my own.

Unfortunately, this past year I forgot where the source of true happiness was for me, and to my family's and my detriment, I became that man I was before she entered my life. I turned my gaze inward, and in doing so, I almost lost it all. My selfishness took my family to the brink of destruction. And for what? Only caring about myself made me more miserable than I had ever been before.

But this woman who sleeps so peacefully next to me, who could have so easily let me go, and should have, showed me greater love than I ever imagined possible and more than I deserved. She has always said that love is the most powerful force on this earth; not only does she say it, but she lives it. She embodies love, and because of that, she is a force to be reckoned with. I was beyond foolish to even attempt to dismiss that.

So, here in the dead of the night, I try to convey with words a small inkling of how I feel about this woman who has stuck by my side from the very beginning, and I find myself failing at the task. Or maybe not. Maybe such thoughts and feelings can only be understood within the heart, and the only way they can be known is through our own actions. Because truly, what are professions of love worth with no action to back them up? I guess my only hope is that I can spend the rest of my life showing this woman that bears my last name now how much she has, and does, and will, mean to me always. Because she has, and will, always be it.

The Girl in Seat 24B.

The End

Jennifer Peel

IS A FIFTH GENERATION COLORADO native who currently calls Alabama home. She is the mother of three amazing children who have grown up way too fast. She enjoys the mountains, vacations at the beach, date night with her wonderful husband, late night talks with her kiddos, touring model homes, pink bubblegum ice cream…and writing.

To learn more about Jennifer and her books, visit her website at:
www.jenniferpeel.com

You can also connect with her on
Facebook and Twitter (@jpeel_author)

Other books by Jennifer Peel:

Other Side of the Wall
Professional Boundaries
House Divided
Trouble in Loveland
Jessie Belle
His Personal Relationship Manager

If you enjoyed this book, please rate and review it on Amazon.com & Goodreads

To learn more about Snowy Peaks Media, visit their website at: www.snowypeaksmedia.com

CPSIA information can be obtained
at www.ICGtesting.com
Printed in the USA
LVOW13s1743151116
513060LV00009B/856/P

9 781942 298267